The Arcadia Project

THE PERPLEXING DISAPPEARANCE OF JILLIENNE LANDON

Juliana Andrew

ISBN
978-1-959365-73-0 (Paperback)
978-1-959365-74-7 (eBook)

For

My Husband Roy

"Forever"

TABLE OF CONTENTS

Chapter 1   The Beginning 1

Chapter 2   Remembering Jillienne 18

Chapter 3   Unravelling... 52

Chapter 4   Stalemate.. 77

Chapter 5   Trouble With Women... 99

Chapter 6   There's Always Another Song 126

Chapter 7   The Arcadia Project.. 135

Chapter 8   Confessions and Forgiveness.............................. 162

Chapter 9   All the Other Women.. 192

Chapter 10 For the Love of Jillienne..................................... 214

Chapter 11 The Final Chapter 228

CHAPTER 1

The Beginning

February 13, 2008
The Office of Virginia Teal

The receptionist called my name and opened the door into the therapist's office. I was met by a woman in her mid-forties with an outstretched hand. She was petite with shoulder-length blonde hair. She was not at all what I thought a psychoanalyst should look like.

"Hello Mr. Landon, I'm Virginia Teal. Please take a seat, anywhere you like."

I chose an armchair near the window. With some official-looking papers in hand she took the seat opposite me and asked how I would like to me addressed. I told her that "Dan" was fine.

She looked puzzled for a second then smiled. "I see, Dan it is. I just need some basic information from you before we get started. For the record, Jordan Ford Landon is your birth name, but you prefer to be called Dan, am I right?"

I nodded in agreement. "I chose to be called Dan over Jordan two years ago." A few minutes later after a few basic questions she asked how she could be of assistance to me.

"I'm only here to placate my eldest daughter. She thinks that my talking to a complete stranger, especially one with credentials, will help me move on. She's wrong though because I will talk to anyone who will listen…you know, the homeless man on the park bench, the cab driver, the neighbor's dog…you get the picture."

She smiled. "I do. What is it exactly that she thinks you need to move on from?"

"Oh, just a little thing like my wife leaving me." I said blankly.

"I see; how long ago was that Dan?"

"Two years and one day ago; that's the day my life as Jordan ceased to exist."

"Do you remember the exact date?"

"It's not something that one would forget, especially when it was only one day before we would have celebrated our thirty- first anniversary which falls on February the fourteenth which incidentally, is also her birthday."

"So you were married on Valentine's Day, and this time of year is difficult for you?"

I laughed half-heartedly "Yeah sure, I only miss her at this time of the year. Actually, we were married on July the 10th 1977. February the 14th is the day I started loving her for real."

"Can you elaborate a little more Dan?"

"That was the day she turned seventeen. She called me from the downtown bus station during a torrential rain storm. She had taken a bus from Shelton, our home town, and asked me if I could come and get her."

"And you obviously did. Is there some significance to her turning seventeen?"

"You might say. You know from my questionnaire that I am a high school principal, but back in 1973, the year I met Jillienne, I was working towards completing my doctorate in education. She was only fifteen. It wasn't fitting that I should have a relationship with someone who was a minor and nine years younger than me. She came to me on that day in February because according to her, she was legal."

Virginia pondered for a few seconds before she spoke.

"I am most interested in your story Mr. Landon and look forward to our next session as this one is mostly just a greet and meet…that is, if there is to be another session?"

"Hell, "I said. "I've got money to burn and it will keep Hope from nagging, so sure I'll give it another try." I answered getting up to leave.

"Just one question before you go; has your wife been in contact with you or your daughter?"

"No Ma'am, not me or any of our four children, not her brother or her sister or our parents."

"What about friends?"

"She had no close friends, just as I have none. All we ever needed was each other…or so I thought."

"So, two years ago your wife left you, and you haven't heard from her since, is that right? What were her reasons for leaving?"

"She walked out the door telling no one where or why she was leaving. She left a short cold note stating that I should not try and find her. Her departure is very disturbing as we were very happy. In fact, day by day, our love grew for each other, and she told me how much she loved me every day; and then poof, she was gone. The reason or reasons she chose to leave were a mystery, and remain a mystery today. Every day I search for an answer, and every day I come up cold. You know the old saying, "Beware the Ides of March"…believe me; the Ides of February are a lot more menacing."

"You will have to refresh my memory regarding the Ides Mr. Landon, and how you think they have some sort of connection to your wife's leaving."

"It's just conjecture that the thirteenth of February had anything to do with it. Thirteen is supposedly an unlucky number, and it was that exact date that Julius Caesar thrice denied the crown offered to him by Marc Antony. We all know how that turned out. All months have Ides, just as they have Kalends which always fall on the fifteenth of the month, and Nones, which fall on the fifth except some months on the seventh. The Ides fall eight days after the Nones, which is the thirteenth, and thus the Ides of February. I could go into great detail regarding 16th century lore, but I am sure that it really has nothing to do with Jillienne's reasons for leaving. It is just my little idiosyncrasy linking the two dates, so sorry for that."

Her smile was one of empathy. "There is no need to apologise. I am interested in everything you say and do as it will only aid me in helping you. We will try and assemble all the pieces of this dilemma together. I will schedule you for an hour next visit. My secretary will be in touch; and Mr. Landon…Dan, please try and keep busy over the next few days. Get out and try something new. Brooding is not good for the soul."

She walked with me to the door. I did not comment. How the hell would she know what was good for me? I wasn't brooding; I was reflecting. How often had I gone there…back to 1973?

It wasn't the time of year anyone would want to set foot in Shelton, and yet there I was accompanying Clayton Connors home to help him chaperone his sister's fifteenth birthday party. Like Clay, I was born and raised in Shelton. I knew of his family as they owned and operated a retail hardware and lumber business. I had accompanied my father there many times to pick up materials for his construction company. Clay was two years younger than me so we hadn't hung out together. I knew that he had a sister, but always thought she was older. Clay and I were on opposing rugby teams at college and that's how we became reacquainted. We hit it off and became good friends. When he had asked me if I would like to help him out with his little sister's party I had thought, what the hell, I'd surprise my parents and I had nothing better planned. I think my exact words to him were: "Why not, Shelton is such a dismal muddy mess in February and I'm a little tired of all this greenery and blossoming down here."

Clay's parents had expectantly been called out of town for a family emergency which meant that no one was there to supervise Jillienne's planned party. Clay could not disappoint his little sister so he had volunteered to chaperone. On the three hour car ride there I had mentioned to Clay that I thought his sister was older, like maybe eighteen. He had laughed.

"You must mean Audrey, our step-sister."

I had asked him which of his parents had been married before and he had chuckled again.

"Neither, its Jillienne's little rant. I'll let her explain. I will warn you ahead of time though that my sister is not like any other teenager you have ever met before."

I asked him which sister and he said, "Jillienne, of course. She is going to be a femme fatale one day. I'm sure she has already broken a few hearts."

"It's been a while since I was a teenager, but I can recall having my heart broke a time or two."

"Yeah, a few hot and heavy kisses and we thought we were in love especially if the girl happened to look like Natalie Wood. God, I wouldn't want to go back there again!"

"I'm with you on that brother. So, who would you compare Jillienne to?"

"I can't narrow it down to just one. Imagine a girl who has Marilyn Monroe's pout, Raquel Welch's wild auburn hair, Audrey Hepburn's big dark eyes. Put that inside a body like any one of them and then mix it all up with a quart of Barbara Eden's "Jeannie's" playfulness, a pint of Wonder Woman's strength, a bushel of stubbornness like Scarlett O'Hara, add in a pinch of Mrs. Robinson's audaciousness and a dash of teenage innocence, and viola, my little sister.

It was my turn to laugh. "I can hardly wait to meet her."

"Don't say I didn't warn you in advance."

"Warn me about what?"

"I'm pretty sure she is going to try and talk you into doing something utterly outrageous so just remember what I said when she tries to con you."

"And, just what do you think a fifteen year old teenage girl is going to con me into doing?"

Clay shook his head. "If only I knew Buddy, if only I knew."

We arrived in the township of Shelton just before two in the afternoon. Clay dropped me off at my parents for a visit with them before the party. It was already in full swing when I arrived five hours later. There were six or seven vehicles in the driveway with a few kids sitting in them…drinking and necking, no doubt. I rang the doorbell; no one answered so I let myself in. There wasn't anyone upstairs so I followed the music downstairs. Clay caught sight of me at the bottom of the stairs and beckoned me over.

"I am so aging myself." I shouted. "I don't remember ever playing music this loud!"

"You'll get used to it. Let me see if I can find the lady of the hour."

"No, let me see if I can locate her based on your brotherly description."

"Go ahead Bro, be my guest. Mind the punch for me will you? I need to get everyone down here, take away their keys and lock the doors."

Yeah, that was going to go over like a lead balloon. I scanned the room but found no one matching Clay's description of his sister and concluded that he had been putting me on. The kids were all gyrating to some song I actually recognised. I watched this girl materialize out of the crowd, throw her arms in the air, crouch down and pop up just a few feet from me. Two guys lifted her unto a little table. She motioned someone to turn the music off, shrugged her shoulders and grimaced.

"For all of you whom haven't heard the house rules yet, I am obliged to enlighten you. No smoking in the house, no booze," she giggled, "**the** punch has been "punched" by my big brother and he will also escort you to the porch if you must smoke. Have fun and oh, absolutely no tripping upstairs to the bedrooms!" She smiled and her eyes wandered until making contact with mine. I gestured to her with two fingers in the air. I did not look away from her; I couldn't. She made her way directly towards me. This was no fifteen- year old; it must be the older sister. I was immediately set straight on that. She stopped two inches in front of me and looked up at me with her big brown eyes and smiled provocatively.

She put a finger up to her lips, blew on it and then shook it like she was cooling it off. "You can be no other than Jordan Landon because there was no other tall, dark and handsome gentleman invited to my party. I am most pleased with my brother's surprise birthday present."

I was a little surprised at her innuendo but managed to laugh. "And you must be the belle of the ball, Jillienne Connors." I took her hand and was tempted to kiss it but shook it instead.

"I am most delighted to meet you Miss Connors."

She giggled. "Time will tell. Oh, there you are Clay! Your friend and I have introduced ourselves. Thank-you so much for my surprise present." She stood on her tiptoes and kissed Clay who replied that he hadn't given her her present yet.

"What, you mean Jordan's not it?" She pretended to act disappointed.

Clay looked at me as Jillienne dragged him unto the dance floor. "Do you see what I was talking about now?"

I laughed and nodded. Jillienne asked him what lies he had told me about her. She yelled something to me. I couldn't be sure if I had heard her right over the ear-splitting music but it sounded like, "Don't you go anywhere; I'm not through with you yet."

And indeed, she wasn't. For two years I let her flirt with me. I became more and more captivated by her frivolity and audacity every time I was in her company. She was unlike any other girl I had ever known. She constantly told me that she was going to marry me someday and that I had better wait for her. I couldn't act on my feelings towards her as I was nine years older than her and really, she was still a kid. For two years everyone thought I regarded her as my little sister and I tried to do so, but it didn't work. I was pretty sure that she was the most popular girl in town as she had many suitors. She always had time to flirt with me though. Our conversations would go something like this:

"Are you married yet Jordan?" She'd ask playfully.

"Nope, are you?" I'd reply.

"Nope, I'm still waiting for you. Am I old enough for you yet?"

"Nope."

"Dang! Well I'll be a day older tomorrow, how about if I ask you then?"

"Sure, why not."

One day, while I was waiting for Clay, she plunked herself down on the sofa beside me and showed me a picture of a wedding dress in a magazine. "Do you like it Jordy?"

It was the first time she called me Jordy.

"It's pretty, don't you think? Do you think I would look good in it or would you prefer something plainer?"

I played along as usual. "Oh, is this for our imaginary wedding?"

"How long do you think you can keep putting the inevitable off for Jordy?"

The doorbell rang. "Damn it," She cursed, "it must be that octopus, Billy Wilder! I told him not to come until seven."

She got up to answer the door but I pulled her back down. "Just a minute young lady, what do you mean by octopus?"

"Oh, surely you know, you're a man…you know, Russian hands and Roman fingers!"

She got up again. I told her to tell Billy to amuse himself for a bit because she wasn't ready yet. She said she was so, and I said *I* wasn't finished talking to her yet. She sighed and said she had already had "the talk" with her mother. I told her she was going to hear it from a guys' point of view so she had better listen carefully.

She saluted me. "Yes Sir!"

Lucky for me that Clay arrived. The two of us gave her a lesson on the unsavoury attributes of teenage boys, unwanted pregnancies, and sexually transmitted diseases. She sat with an amused smile on her face and pretended to be flabbergasted at some of the images we painted for her. Ten minutes later she asked if we were through. We nodded that we were.

"Okay, just because you two lost your virginity in the backseats of your father's cars because your hormones were in overdrive doesn't mean to say that I am going to tonight or any night. I can promise you it will only happen when I am damn good and ready and it will be with the right man." She looked directly at me. "Thanks for the chat boys, but I already knew all that." She winked at both of us and said she hoped we were looking out for ourselves because it was a jungle out there and she didn't want to see us in the clutches of some desperate horny housewife. Clay shook his head as his little sister skipped her way out the door.

"I wish I wasn't privy to what goes on out there Jordan."

I patted him on the shoulder. "She's smart Clay; she's not going to do anything foolish."

"Are you trying to convince me or yourself?" He laughed. "You could put an end to this you know…you could tell her that you are going to wait for her to grow up, but only on the condition that she quit running around with every Tom, Dick, and Harry. That just might settle her down."

"All in due time Buddy, all in due time. Now let's say we hustle our butts out of here and get to our own hot dates?"

He looked at me quizzically. "I know she has one hell of a crush on you, but surely you are not taking her flirting seriously?"

"You mean with that little auburn tease that just flounced out of here…not a chance."

He asked me if I was sure about that. I told him that I was but smiled slyly to myself.

Clay worked at the family business during the summers and I worked for my dad in his construction company, building and refurbishing bridges. The summer of 1974 I was working out of town five days a week so I only came home on weekends. One Saturday evening in early August Jillienne phoned me and asked me to take her to the movies. I was a little startled and excused myself saying I was pretty exhausted and asked her where all her friends were. Maybe Clay and his girlfriend Sandie would go with her.

"They've all seen it. I had to babysit every evening last week so couldn't go. I really, really want to see it Jordy…please say you will come. I really don't want to go alone; I'll even pay your way and buy you popcorn…"

I laughed. "Is that all you have in your bargaining bag?"

"You know there could be more…"

I had gone too far. "What's the name of the movie?"

"The Exorcist."

"I don't think so young lady! It is not a movie I want to see, and it certainly isn't one that I would recommend for you."

"I don't want to be the only one in town who hasn't seen it. I **am** going and if you don't want to come with me then I will just have to go alone; thanks anyway. Good-bye Jordan."

I knew she was baiting me. I pictured her pouting like a five year old. "Hold on Jillienne…I don't want you going to a horror show all alone so I will take you. What time does it start?"

Why had I said that I would take her instead of just "go with you"?

I paid for the tickets while she got the popcorn. I suggested we find seats at the back on the second tier. She informed me that was where all the "would be lovers" sat and it wouldn't be fitting for a man of my statue to sit there with a teeny bopper.

"In fact," she said, "perhaps you shouldn't even walk in with me; someone might see you and report you to the school board or governing agent of teachers, or, whoever."

I told her that it was pretty dark in the theatre so she needn't worry about my reputation.

The movie was pretty graphic and a little too gory for my tastes. First Jillienne just looped her arm through mine and held my hand, but as soon as the exorcism scenes started, she would bury her head in my chest and then ask if it was safe for her to look. I swear the movie was three hours long and couldn't end soon enough for me. While the credits were still streaming she grabbed by hand and rushed me out before the lights came on. Once outside I asked her if she would like to go for a coke. She said no, but we could go park somewhere and "neck." I took her straight home. She thanked me for escorting her and kissed me on the cheek saying that it wasn't always going to be like this and that our time was coming. I left her at the door thinking that if she was older, or I was younger…

It was the last week in August, Friday the thirtieth, my last day of work. I pulled into the driveway and saw a red convertible parked at the curb. I hoped I was wrong about the owner of the car, but I wasn't. I walked in and found Dell Lyon sitting at the kitchen table having ice tea with my mother.

"What are you doing here Dell?" I asked. "I thought you were in Europe for another week?"

"I've seen all I want to and I wanted to see you, so here I am; surprise!"

"You should have called first Dell. I would have told you not to come. Truth of the matter is that today is my last day of work and I am off on a little holiday before classes resume."

My mother looked at me questionably, got up and said she would give us some privacy. She stopped at the door and said that she had signed for an official looking document for me. I excused myself and followed her into the living room.

"What's this about you going on a holiday? This is the first I am hearing about it."

"It's the first I am hearing about it too Mom. I had to think of something fast and that is what popped into my head."

"I take it that you are not pleased that she is here then?"

"No, I am not. Where is the letter?"

"What letter?" She smiled coyly.

I kissed her and said "Thanks."

I no sooner sat back down at the table when Clay and Sandie walked in the back door. They were lifesavers. Clay knew Dell as we had double dated several times last spring. I introduced her to Sandie and asked Clay to entertain them while I showered. It was already 6 P.M. so it was too late to send Dell packing, so what was I going to do? By the time I was cleaned up and dressed I decided that I would take her out to dinner and check her into a motel room. My best friend foiled me.

"What's this about you taking off on a holiday Buddy?" Clay asked puzzled.

"Have you forgotten that we were taking Jillienne to the water park in Kingston?" Of course he had no idea what I was talking about.

"Who is Jillienne?" Dell asked.

Sandie turned away trying not to laugh. It took Clay a little longer to catch on; he mumbled something unintelligible.

Good God, I had involved three people in my lie already and all because I didn't have the nerve to tell Dell that I didn't want anything to do with her. I thought I had made it clear to her last May that there wasn't any future for her and me, but apparently she hadn't taken me seriously. She was the progeny of a wealthy businessman and his socialite wife. She was only going to college for something to do and I don't think she had any intention of ever putting her law degree into use, that is, if she ever succeeded in getting it. I had no idea how she had made it to her last year as she wasn't the brightest bulb in the pack. I regretted the short affair we had and it now looked like I was going to pay for that indiscretion. I hoped she'd be long gone before Jillienne found out about the stupid cock-and-bull story I had involved her in.

"Is anyone going to tell me who this Jillienne is?" Dell asked again.

"She's Clay's kid sister." I confessed.

She seemed satisfied with that and said that it sounded like fun and could she tag along and help babysit and where was Kingston. Now what was I supposed to do? Thank God for Sandie.

"We booked really late and the Inn is full so there would be no place for you to stay, but we can all do something tonight, okay?"

Dell was about to say something but I interjected before she had a chance. "I don't know about you guys but I am starving so let's get a move on. What does everyone fancy?"

"I don't know, let's decide on the way." Clay suggested.

Dell insisted that we take her car as she wanted to get a good look at the town. She passed the keys to Clay and said that she and I would sit in the back. Great, just what I needed, a ride through town in an open convertible with a woman I couldn't stand and didn't want to be seen with. Sandie's intuition kicked in and she looped her arm through Dell's and walked ahead giving Clay and me a chance to talk. He grabbed my arm and asked me what the hell that little charade was all about.

"Thanks for playing along. Sorry, but that's what I came up with. I'm not very good at lying and obviously, I'm worse at telling the truth."

"And, what's the truth?"

"I don't want anything to do with her."

"Then why on earth did you invite her here?"

"I didn't; she was here when I got home, having tea with my mother. I'm pretty sure she expects to spend the night with me, but that's not going to happen. Drive by the Country Inn and I'll rent her a room."

"Oh yeah, that will work. What's up with you Buddy, I thought you two hit it off last spring?"

"She's a piranha!"

"Say no more, we've got you covered."

Just before we reached the car I asked Clay where Jillienne was. I hoped she was at home.

"Do I look like her keeper? Out on a date I guess or getting ready to go on one. Why do you want to know where she is anyhow?"

I didn't answer him. I climbed in the back seat. Dell was all over me immediately. I held on to her hands and told her that I was going to book her into a motel.

"I thought I could stay at the house with you but a motel is probably better." She looked at me knowingly. I wanted to crawl into a hole.

I was a grown man of twenty five and I had had a few so called love affairs over the years, one that I definitely wanted to forget. Some had ended fairly cordially and I was still friends with a couple of them. The difference here was that I had absolutely no feelings or respect for Dell. She wanted everything her way and paraded me around to her parents and friends as if she was showing off her future husband. I was disappointed in her in every aspect of a relationship and so I broke it off with her after a few months. She told me that she was going to remain faithful to me while she was on her European holiday and that perhaps I would miss her so much that I would see the light and realise that we belonged together. That did not happen.

We were parked on Main Street in front of several restaurants trying to make up our minds where to eat when Dell whispered to me that she wasn't hungry except for me. She grabbed me, pushed me down on the seat and locked her lips on mine. I wrestled her away from me asking her what the hell she thought she was doing. She laughed vulgarly. I heard a little gasp behind me, turned and looked into the dejected eyes of Jillienne. The look she shot at me was pure revulsion. I wish there was a hole I could crawl into. Tears streaming down her face, she turned and ran down the street like the devil was chasing her.

"Christ!" I swore at Dell. "See what you have done!"

I climbed out over the door yelling "Jillienne"! She had already rounded the corner and was out of sight. I ordered Clay to take me back to the house so I could get my car. Dell was saying something obnoxious about Jillienne and me. She flatly accused me of seducing my best friend's little sister and that he was all right with it. Sandie turned around and told her to shut her foul mouth. Clay followed me into the house to get my keys.

"Is she right Jordan? Have you been fooling around with Jillienne?"

"I haven't got time for this right now Clay; I have to find her and explain what just happened. And no, I have not touched your sister, but you know she thinks she's in love with me…I have to set her straight once and for all. Can you give me that?"

He stepped out of my way and nodded. Dell was standing beside her car. She asked me haughtily what she was supposed to do now. I just looked at her and laughed and told her to figure it out. She told me to go screw myself. I said it would be a hell of a lot more rewarding then screwing her. I did not here her retort, but am pretty sure it was uglier than sin.

I found Jillienne on the path that skirted the river half a mile before her house. I drove ahead of her, parked, and walked down to meet her, and said, "Hi."

"Go away, I don't want to see you or talk to you." She tried to get passed me.

"Well, I want to see you and I really need to talk to you. Will you come and sit with me?" I gestured towards the bench that sat overlooking the river. She sat down, crossed her arms and looked straight ahead.

I sighed. "I'm sorry that you had to see that irresponsible public display, but in my own defense it was none of my doing. I was just as surprised as you were, believe me."

"It's none of my business what you do and with whom you do it with in the back seat of a car, but **that** was in broad daylight and in the middle of town! What happened to your self- respect? I had no right to reacted so vehemently; I don't know why I did." She was close to tears again.

"I know why. You see me as this upright supporter of moral values, and in your eyes I just crossed the line. You want there to be something between us, but that can never be Jillienne. You have to quit believing that we were meant for each other. I am so far ahead of you in life that you can never catch up. I have a life that doesn't and can't include you the way you want it to. I am oh, so very fond of you, but that is as far as it goes or ever will. Do you understand me Sweetie?" Hell, why had I called her sweetie?

She carried on as if she hadn't heard a word I said. "Who is she and are you in love with her?"

"Hell no!" I exclaimed. "She arrived here this afternoon out of the blue. I did not invite her and she means nothing to me."

"She is just someone you screw then?"

"I wish you wouldn't talk like that Jillienne."

She looked me straight in the eye. "Why, that's the way you "adults" talk right? It's not making love, it's screwing. Well, it's not for me and I'm glad I saw you in a whole other light before it was too late." She attempted to get up but I held on to her arm.

"What do you mean before it's too late? Nothing is going to happen between you and me; how can I ever get that into that thick noggin of yours? Have you not been listening to me? I'm leaving tomorrow and I want you to be perfectly clear that there is no future for us. Hell, I might be married before I get back next year…" I wondered who I was kidding.

"And, I may not be your virginal little sister next year neither."

"Don't talk like that Jillienne."

"Why?"

"Because I don't like it. I don't want you to think of sex as a rite of passage. I want you to fall in love with someone who is worthy of you. It will all come in time; you just have to be patient. You are only sixteen and you have your whole life ahead of you."

"Well, I have already fallen in love and I thought he was worthy of me, but apparently not, so done and undone! I'm going home now. You only think of me as your little sister so I guess I have to be content with having another brother… can I give you a sisterly kiss?"

She kissed me full on the mouth. I should have pushed her away but I didn't, I couldn't. It was probably the sweetest, and yet the most passionate kiss I had ever had the pleasure of enjoying. She stood up and put her fingers to her lips and placed them on mine and whispered that she still loved me and she'd see me in six months. I watched her walk away. What the hell did that mean?

"Damn it Jillienne, does a brick have to fall on your head?" I yelled after her.

CHAPTER 2

Remembering Jillienne

February 21st, 2008
The Office of Virginia Teal

"Good afternoon Mr. Landon, I trust you had a pleasant weekend." Virginia said cheerily.

"As a matter of fact I did." I lied.

"So you took my advice and did something interesting?"

"Yes, Miss Teal I did. I'm sorry, is it Miss, Ms. or Mrs.?"

"Virginia will do just fine." She replied assertively. "Now, about your weekend…"

"Let's see, Friday night I went to the Legion and joined in on the line dancing. You see I don't have a partner anymore so all other forms of dancing are out of the question. Saturday I wandered down to the corner bar and had a few beers with strangers and watched some sport event on the television. Sunday, as usual, I made brunch for my family and that is about it. And you; how was your weekend?"

"I had tea with the Queen. I thought that line dancing was a thing of the past?"

I told her she might be right. "To be perfectly honest, I made brunch, but tea with the Queen beats beer with strangers every time." I may have winked at her.

She smiled, but seemed a bit uncomfortable and readjusted herself in her chair. I hoped she didn't think that I was flirting with her. You can't flirt with someone when your wife is still front and center in your head. She asked me if I wanted to talk about Jillienne's seventeenth birthday. It was nice to know that she had been paying attention last week. I told her that I revisited that night practically every day since she had been gone so sure, I could talk about it. She told me that wasn't healthy. I told her to tell my mind and heart that. She sat back. I assumed she was expecting me to give her the details. I would make it brief and not relate the whole intimate story to her like I had to myself as I was driving to her office today. No, what actually took place that February 14th 1975 I could not share with anyone.

I was never late for anything, and yet here I was running almost half an hour late for my date with Eleanor. My mother had called to tell me that her youngest sister was very ill. She needed someone to commiserate with besides my father, and I, being the only child was it. I could not cut the conversation short just because I had a date, and so I listened and sympathised and promised to call her tomorrow. I had no sooner hung up the phone when it rang again. I was sure that it was Eleanor and I was all set to apologise. I picked up the phone and was surprised to hear a cacophony of horns blasting in the background. I wondered where she was calling from. I said "Hello." Before I could get another word out a little voice spoke my name and it sure as hell wasn't Eleanor's.

"Jordy, can you come and get me?"

Only one person ever called me Jordy. "Jillienne, is that you?"

"Yes, it's me. Will you come and get me?"

"Where are you?" I asked alarmingly.

"I'm at the bus station." She answered solemnly.

"Are you here; are you in Vancouver?"

"Yes."

"Why, why are you here Jillienne?" I was afraid of her answer.

"To see you Jordy."

"Don't move; I'm on my way." Where did I expect her to go? I cursed as I grabbed my keys and headed out into the rain. It took me fifteen minutes to get to the depot. I must have covered a dozen scenarios as to why she was here. The only one that made any sense was that she had run away from home, and yet that made no sense at all. It was six thirty three when I pulled into the fifteen minute parking zone. My lights shone on a little waif of a girl standing on the curb in the pouring rain. She looked very much like my Jilly. I slammed the gear shift into park and jumped out and ran towards her.

"What the hell are you doing out here Jillienne? Why didn't you wait inside for me?"

"There were too many people in there."

That made sense to no one but her. I picked up her suitcase and took her arm and led her to the car. I opened the passenger door for her and tossed her saturated case into the back seat. I cranked up the heater fan. I wanted to get her back to my apartment and into dry clothes as fast as I could. I didn't ask her why she was here again until we came to a halt at the first traffic light.

"I came to see you Jordy. It's my birthday today. I'm seventeen and I can be with you legally now." She was shivering, but she managed to get the words out.

This was my guiltiest fantasy. I glanced at her and couldn't tell whether she was crying or if it was only droplets of rain cascading down her face from her wet hair. I told her we would talk about that when she had showered and changed into dry clothes. I suppose I sounded angry as she asked me if I was mad at her. Against my good sense I reached out and found her hand and squeezed it and told her that I wasn't angry with her.

"I couldn't stand it if you were upset with me Jordy. I just wanted to see you so badly."

"I probably would have come home at Easter you know?"

"I told you in August that I would see you in six months…don't you remember?"

I did, but I wasn't going to acknowledge it. Instead I asked her what she would have done if I hadn't been home when she phoned. I told her Clay was on the island with Sandie so that left her sister Audrey. I asked her if she would have called her.

"I knew you would be home." She said affirmatively.

"You knew no such thing! You didn't think any of this through did you Jillienne? Do your parents even know where you are?"

"I told them I was going to be spending the weekend with Sarah."

"So you lied to them?"

"Sort of."

"Sort of? It's an out and out lie. This isn't who you are Jillienne."

She sniffled and tried to wipe the condensation off the window with her hand. "I think you know perfectly well who I am Jordy."

"I thought I did, but apparently I was wrong. You say you came to be with me…what does that mean exactly Jillienne?" I demanded.

"You know damn well what it means!" She cried.

I swore. I guess she thought I was swearing at her as she wrapped her arms around herself and didn't say another word.

"I wasn't swearing at you…it's this damn unrelenting rain." I apologized.

I pulled into what passed for a parking garage at my apartment and told her to wait in the car until I came around for her. By the time I got to her she was already out and standing under the leaky roof. She was going to be trouble; there was no doubt about it. I was pretty sure I was going to see a side of her that I had never seen before. I was the grown-up here and she was the child so it was up to me to set the boundaries. I hoped to God I could.

I took her arm and led her up the stairs to my apartment on the second floor. I helped her remove her wet coat while she kicked her shoes off. I directed her to the bathroom, turned the shower on and told her to get undressed and get warm while I retrieved her suitcase. Thinking that her clothes would be damp I grabbed one of my oversized jerseys and a pair of joggers and tossed them into the bathroom door telling her to put them on. I heard her say over the running water that I was bossy. After I had collected her bag and placed it in the bedroom I realized that I was rather wet myself so changed into a flannel shirt and dry pants. I met her coming out of the bathroom sans the pants I had given her. The jersey came down to her knees. She had a towel wrapped around her head. I led her into the living room and sat her down on the hassock. I wrapped my mother's newly knitted afghan around her and removed the towel from her head. I rubbed her wet hair vigorously at first and then gently. I wasn't too sure who was enjoying it more…her, or me.

"What am I ever going to do about you Jillienne?" I said wistfully.

"What do you mean "about me"?" She asked turning around scrutinizing me.

"I knew you were going to be a problem for me the day I met you." Hell, I hadn't wanted to admit that. She started to say something but was interrupted by the shrill ringing of the phone.

"You had better get that; it's your girlfriend Eleanor. I heard her on the answering machine when you went out to get my luggage. She's worried about you. I'll give you some privacy." She tossed the afghan onto the sofa and threw the towel at me and stomped off in the direction of the bedroom.

Damn it! I picked up the phone while Eleanor was still talking. "I'm here, no need to worry. I should have called you, sorry. Truth of the matter is I have been on the phone for half an hour with my mother. Her sister is quite ill and I needed to try and comfort her. I am just not in the mood to go out so I am going to have to cancel."

"But I called you twice and you didn't answer."

"I must have been getting something out of the car. I didn't check the phone for messages."

"Well, there is nothing you can do about your aunt tonight and getting out will take your mind off of her. Besides, these are very expensive tickets…"

I interrupted her. "I'm sure you can find someone else to go with you Eleanor."

"But I want to see you. If you don't feel like going out then I will come over there, okay?"

"I have something else happening right now so we'll talk another day. Good night Eleanor." I hung up while she was still talking.

I was pretty sure that Jilly had heard the whole conversation and I wasn't wrong. I walked in on her pulling her jeans on up over a pair of black panties. Her back was to me.

"So you used the "sick aunt" card did you?"

"It's true, my aunt is really quite sick."

"I hope it is not your Auntie Rita; I really like her."

"No, it's my Aunt Trudy."

"Still, I am sorry. I won't contribute to your problems Jordan. Just as soon as I get dressed I will be out of your hair."

I stood at the door and watched her struggling to do her bra strap up. I asked if I could help. She shot me a dirty look over her shoulder. She gave up and threw the bra into her open suitcase, took out a tee shirt and a long sleeved oversized sweater and pulled them on over her head. She searched for socks, sat on the floor and put them on and said she was ready to go. I asked her where she thought she was going. She said that it was a sure thing that she couldn't stay here and she had enough money for a cab and a cheap motel room so would I please call her a taxi.

"Do you really think I am going to let you go to some flea ridden motel? You don't know me very well do you? You're staying here, and you know it!" I walked past her and pulled the drapes over the blinds. I have no idea why I did that. She was still sitting on the floor.

"You're right Jordan, I don't know you. The man I see in my dreams doesn't exist; do you want to know why? It's because I never see him with anyone but me. Sometimes my dreams turn into nightmares though and I see that girl from last summer and a dozen other faceless women with you and then I just wake myself up. Now look at what I have done. I've come and intruded on you and your girlfriend…I am so stupid and I am so sorry thinking that you would welcome me with open arms. I really need to go Jordan."

I turned around and reached out to help her up but she disregarded my gesture and rolled away and got up on her own. "You're not stupid Jilly and she's not my girlfriend. She's just someone I see now and then."

"You called me Jilly." She said looking at me with puppy dog eyes.

If she wanted to melt my tough façade she was doing a damn good job.

"I always call you Jilly." I admitted uneasily.

"You've never called me that before." She asserted.

"Maybe not to your face, but when I talk about you or think about you, I do."

"You think about me?" She asked in her little girl's voice.

"Yes, damn it, I think about you!"

"Why are you so angry? Does it make you angry to think about me?"

"Yes."

"That's not much of an answer; why?"

"I shouldn't have to explain it to you **again**. I'm too old for you and that is never going to change. You made a mistake coming here. You can spend the night, but then you have to go back to Shelton. I'll sleep on the couch." I grabbed a pillow off the bed and headed for the door.

"It's not even eight o'clock…do you expect me to go to sleep especially after what you just told me? You really think of me as a child don't you? When I am thirty, you will be thirty nine; when I am seventy, you will be seventy nine. Older men have always had relationships with younger women, and vice-versa. It's been going on since the dawn of time. Do you think of me as a Lolita?"

"Thanks for the math and history lesson and no, I don't think of you as Lolita and I am certainly no Hubert Humbert or whatever his name was. How do you even know about Lolita?"

"I do know how to read you know!" She said adamantly. "You think becoming involved with me is improper and that your morals will be compromised don't you? Someday you may have girls in your classroom who are my age and it would be grounds for dismissal if you had a relationship with any of them, and you see me as one of those girls…am I right?"

"Yes and no. You are my best friend's little sister and I look on you as…"

"Oh," she stopped me with her hand, "say no more. I've already embarrassed myself enough for one day. I guess I read something in your eyes that wasn't there. If you want me to be your little sister then I will be. Please forget that I said that I wanted to be with you as that was not the real reason I came here. I have had a lesson in humility and I will not make the same mistake again." She yanked a blanket off the bed and held it out to me. "Perhaps I am tired after all. I will be all right here alone so you should continue on with your plans with Eleanor. Good night Jordan and please forgive my foolhardiness."

I took hold of the blanket and pulled it propelling her towards me. "Do you really think I'm going to let you get away with this?"

"With what…what do you think I am trying to get away with?" She said innocently.

"Why are you here Jillienne? What exactly did you come all this way for on your seventeenth birthday?"

"I just wanted to get away from home. I thought maybe you would help me celebrate, that's all. I'm sorry; I didn't think the whole thing through." She lied.

"I think not. You came here with every intention of seducing me didn't you?"

"No, I don't even know how to do that."

"Well, you are doing a damn good job of it."

"I'm not doing anything." She said without conviction.

"Oh well, excuse me! What do you think "I came to be with you." means? "I'm seventeen now Jordy, we can be together." Together for what Jillienne, to go to a movie, have dinner, what?"

She dropped the end of the blanket and backed away from me. "Stop interrogating me Jordan."

"I just want an honest answer. You came with the intention of having sex with me, right? You want to have sex, right?"

Her eyes were watering. I was badgering her and I wasn't very proud of it, but she had changed her story once too often and I needed to find out her true intentions once and for all.

"Why do you have to make it sound so dirty? Is that what you are used to with your lady friends…just sex, there is no love involved?"

I smiled maliciously. "That's right Honey, there is no love involved. It's just pretty much, wham, bam, thank-you ma'am. Now let's get down to the reason you came here…" I reached out to grab her and she slapped me across my face. She slapped me hard. I rubbed my face.

"Stay away from me Jordan! I don't like this side of you."

"Come here Jilly."

"No, I'm afraid of you."

"You know I would never hurt you. Come here, I want to kiss you."

She kept backing up until she ran into the edge of the dresser. "Well, I don't want to kiss you!"

"Are you sure about that?"

"Yes, I'm sure." Her bottom lip was trembling.

"You don't want to kiss me like you did last summer?"

"No, I loved you then; I don't love you anymore."

"Well, I still love you."

The words hung there in the room for what seemed like an eternity. She just stared at me. It was like she couldn't digest what I had just admitted. Frankly, I couldn't myself. I had finally said that I loved her out loud. I felt like a millstone had been lifted from off my shoulders.

I took a deep breath. "It's true Jilly. I've pretty much been in love with you since I first laid eyes on you. The day our eyes locked across the room on your fifteenth birthday; the same day that you told me you were going to marry me. Do you remember that day?"

She came at me and beat on my chest. "All this time, all this time and you never told me. You knew how I felt about you…why, oh why?"

"You know why."

"If I have to hear that worn out excuse about age again I'm going to scream so loud that the neighbours will come running!" She promised.

I took her hands in mine. "It wasn't the right time for us Sweetie. I had to bide my time and hope you didn't get tangled up or fall in love with one of your many suitors. There were times I thought you were serious when you would say you loved me, and other times I thought you were just amusing yourself. I had to laugh and pretend that it was all harmless fun, but my heart told me something else. I knew I loved you and I tried convincing myself that it was only the kind of love between a brother and his kid sister. That was all right because I couldn't possibly love you the way a man loves a woman. I knew I had to stay away from you and that's when I decided I wasn't going to come back to Shelton for a year. Then there was that debacle on Main Street which led to you kissing me. It took all my will power not to kiss you back. Now you are here and I really need to kiss you."

She stepped towards me and lifted her head and our lips met for a very long time.

"You taste just like you did last summer," I said taking in a deep breath, "like sunshine and moonbeams and innocence with a hint of naughtiness…wait a second, there is something more there…do I taste butterscotch?"

"Maybe; I hate a whole bag of butterscotch mints on the bus because I was so nervous."

I laughed. "How were candies supposed to relax you and why were you nervous?"

"I thought you might reject me and you did. Dad always has a drink of Scotch when he's uptight so I thought the Scotch mints might do the same for me."

"Oh Jilly, my sweet, sweet Jilly; that's just about the craziest thing I have ever heard." I took her in my arms. "You have taken me completely by surprise and though I am happy that our feelings are out in the open, I am not prepared for anything further to happen between us tonight. We need to take things slow and get to know each other, okay?"

"I pretty much know everything about you that I need to Jordan. I know you like mystery novels and cowboy movies, and full moons and walking on the beach in the fog. Your favorite singer is Neil Diamond and your favorite actor is Charlton Heston. You could live on hamburgers and French fries and chocolate milkshakes. You love working with your father in construction, but your true calling is in education. You are courteous and trustworthy and you have a pretty good sense of humor. You respect your parents and women. You believe everyone deserves a second chance and I'm pretty sure that you have a huge capacity for love. You have a really big heart which I hope you will entrust to me. On the other hand, I know you dislike loud, boisterous people. You hate clam chowder and turnips. You don't care for people who talk incessantly without really saying anything. You don't like the color orange, yet you love oranges. You don't care for snow and you don't like to dance. I know that you have very strict principles and that you are going to struggle with your feelings for me because part of you believes that a physical relationship with me is morally wrong. But, it isn't. I love you and you say you love me so please don't put me on a shelf waiting for me to be twenty one. I may just have an expiry date."

I had to smile at that. "I hope you don't have an expiry date Jilly. Perhaps the reason I don't like to dance is because I've never found anyone that I want to hold in my arms for that long. Would you care to see if you are the one?"

I took her in my arms and danced her over to the radio and tuned to a station that played slow mellow music. She put her arms around my neck.

"I doubt very much that you haven't held a woman for the duration of a song. We will dance and you are going to like it because

I know something about you that you have been afraid to admit, and that is, that **I am the one**."

"I think that I have pretty much confessed that already and I sure as hell hope you are because frankly, I am getting tired of looking. I know a few things about you too." I paused next to the night table and told her to open the drawer. She did.

"Is that the book of eighteenth century poetry that I gave you for your twenty fourth birthday?"

"It is, and I read a verse or two at night and jot down little lines that remind me of you." I opened a page that I had tagged. "This one, "She Walks in Beauty" by Lord Byron; every stanza reminds me of you and I read it often."

Big tears rolled down her face. If I was looking into the face of love it suited me just fine.

"Are you still planning on keeping me at bay Jordan?"

"I don't want to…oh, believe me I don't want to, but when I said I wasn't prepared for you, I meant it. I can't protect you Jilly."

"Do you mean that you don't have any contraceptives? What were you planning on using when you visited Eleanor then?"

"I was going to stop at a pharmacy on the way over."

The hurt I saw in her eyes was devastating. "I didn't mean that Jillienne, honest I didn't. I don't have a physical relationship with her. I'm sorry; that was very insensitive of me."

"I try not to picture you with other girls but I know that is unreasonable. You are a full blooded, virile man and I am not that naïve as to think that you don't have half a dozen girls in your harem, so I am not offended."

"My harem…well, that's a good one. I might as well have taken a vow of celibacy as I haven't had a physical relationship with a woman in a very long time."

"How long?"

"Since sometime last spring."

"Not even with that harlot from last summer?"

I had to laugh at her description of Nell. I decided to be honest. "No; we had a fling once, but it was meaningless and she wasn't worth the dime I spent on her."

"Well, I'm here and she's not and neither is Eleanor or anyone else. I still want to be with you and you don't have to worry that I might get pregnant because I am not ovulating. Or are you worried that you have some disease that you might pass on to me? Has this bed been well used?"

Again I smiled. "No Jillienne, I am not worried about any disease and only I have slept in this bed. The mattress was still wrapped in plastic, tags intact when I moved in last week."

"Well good then."

In one quick move she pulled her shirts up and over her head. She wiggled her jeans and panties to the floor. She stepped out of them and stood their looking smugly up at me.

"God, you're beautiful." I murmured.

"He made this body just for you." She said softly.

"Oh, He did, did He, and what about these sultry, pouty lips? Are they just for me too?"

"I don't pout."

"Yeah, you do, but it is oh, so sensual. And what about the hunger in these deep brown eyes…is it for me too?"

"Yes."

I was finding it a little difficult to breathe as I reached behind her head and took hold of a generous clump of her magnificent, long auburn hair. "And, what about this chestnut mass of hair…" I pulled on it gently. She arched her neck and moaned.

I picked her up and carried her to the bed. I pulled the covers back and laid her down. Her arms were wrapped tightly around my neck. I told her she was going to have to let me go. She said she was never letting me go because if I did she was pretty sure I was going to walk away and come up with yet another reason why we couldn't be together.

"I'm not going anywhere Sweetie." I promised. "I'm going to lie with you and we are going to talk."

"Talk; you want to talk? I just bared my soul and my body to you and you want to talk? Are you freaking kidding me Jordan?"

She relinquished her hold on me.

I was mesmerized by the fire in her eyes, but I was determined to say my peace. "Jilly, you have no idea how much I want to love you, but I am worried about the consequences and there has to be some ground rules, okay?"

"What consequences? I told you I won't get pregnant and this isn't a game so why does there have to be rules?"

"You may be disappointed and..."

"Stop right there. I've waited for this moment for two years Jordan. I've waited for you to hold me and kiss me and I hoped beyond hope that you might love me and you say you do...nothing is going to go wrong. If after tonight you decide you don't want a relationship with me, if everything you said to me is bull and you don't really love me, or if I disappoint you, or if it is more than your ethics can take, then I will walk away. We will never have to see each other again. Is that enough of an affirmation for you?"

"It's not me I am worried about Jillienne, and those are not the rules I was talking about."

"What then, what?" Tears were forming in the corner of her eyes. I wiped them away.

"Everything I said to you is true and I can guarantee you that I will never be dissatisfied with you. It is not me or my scruples I am worried about. I love you and I truly want you to be mine, but you need to be sure."

"I want never-ever to be over with."

I asked her what she meant by that.

"You told me that we could **never** be together, not **ever**, not in a million years."

I laughed heartily. "I'm pretty sure I didn't say "in a million years", but yes, "never ever" has pretty much come and gone. Are you sure about this Jilly? Do you really want to be my girl? You won't be able to go back to Shelton and carry on with your boyfriends anymore. You are going to belong to me, do you understand? This isn't going to be just a one- time thing…"

"Oh for God's sake Jordan, will you please shut up? I'll agree to anything if you will just quit talking"

She pulled the covers back and and I surrendered to the sweetest passion I had ever known.

I woke up with my arm still around her. I lifted it gently and rolled over to see what time it was. I was surprised to see that it was only four a.m. and wondered if I'd been asleep at all. I turned back and watched Jillienne sleeping. She had a contented smile on her face and I hoped I was the reason why. My stomach was growling and I realized that I hadn't eaten since a late breakfast yesterday. I inched my way out of bed but was stopped.

"Where do you think you're going Sailor?" She said in a deep sultry voice.

"I didn't mean to wake you Sweetie. Truth of the matter is that I'm starving; how about you?"

She smiled. "Not so much anymore thanks. I think I could eat a nice juicy hamburger though if that's what you had in mind."

I bent down and kissed her. "Maybe later, but right now you are going to have to settle for eggs. Give me ten minutes okay."

I hadn't done a big grocery shop since I had moved in and had pretty much been eating on the run. It wasn't my favorite thing to do anyhow, but being a bachelor pretty much made shopping a mandatory chore. I had no sooner cracked a dozen eggs into the hot frying pan when I heard footsteps behind me. She put her arms around me and leaned her head on my bare back.

"By the looks of those egg shells I would say that you invited the whole apartment complex."

"I told you I was hungry and you need a lot of eggs to make an omelette."

"Oh, are we having one of your famous omelettes?"

"Who says they are famous."

"My brother."

"All I have to put in it is cheese and so it is going to be very plain. Will you pour me a cup of coffee and pop the bread into the toaster please?" I kissed her as she handed me the cup.

She opened the fridge door and said we had better go shopping and thank goodness there was ketchup and peanut butter. She sat down at the table and watched me.

I folded the cheese into the delicately cooked egg mass and gave it a couple of minutes before I dished it up. I sat hers in front of her and ran my hand through her bedraggled hair. I said cheekily that if I didn't know better I'd think that she'd been on a bender or something else a lot more rapturous.

She smiled sensually at me as she poured a generous amount of ketchup all over her eggs and spread peanut butter on her toast.

"That's quite a combination there." I commented.

"A good one too; just as good as Jilly and Jordy I would say. Are you happy with me Jordy?" She asked coyly.

I put my hand over hers and told her that I was the happiest I had ever been. She smiled and said that she was too. We ate in silence until she caught me staring at her. She put the fork down and asked me if she had spinach in her teeth. I reminded her that there was no spinach in the omelette. She said she knew that so why had I been watching her sleep earlier and was now watching her eat. I told her that I just wanted to get my fill of her while I could. She looked at me strangely and asked what I meant.

I didn't answer her, but instead asked her if she still wanted to marry me.

"Do you think last night changed my mind? Of course I still want to marry you!"

"Then I think we had better go shopping for a ring when the mall opens."

"A ring," she stammered, "a ring… what kind of a ring?"

"An engagement ring of course! I can't take you home to your parents and tell them that we spent the night together if my intentions towards you aren't serious."

She was trembling. "Did you just ask me to marry you Jordan Ford Landon?"

I nodded that I did. She was out of her chair and into my lap before I had a chance to brace myself. The chair cracked and we went tumbling to the floor. After we quit laughing and she quit smothering me with kisses I asked her if I should take her answer to be a yes.

"You big boob, did you honestly think I would say no?"

"It crossed my mind. Maybe you didn't have a good time with me last night?" I answered in the form of a question.

"Well if that is as good as it gets then I'm pretty sure I will be ecstatic for the rest of my life! I will be the best wife ever I promise! I will never ask for anything except that you love me for the rest of your life."

"Yeah, well we will see about that. Now, what say we get your butt off the cold floor and back into bed where it belongs? We have a few things to talk about."

"Talk, you want to talk again?"

"Dan, did I lose you?"

Virginia's voice brought me back to the present. Damn, had I gone there again?

"Sorry, my mind has a tendency to wander. No, I have no problem relating my first night with Jillienne. As I said before, she phoned me from the bus depot and asked me if I would come and get her and I did. I mean, what was I supposed to do? I couldn't let my best friend's little sister spend the night alone in the big city and besides, I was curious as to why she had come. Did I mention that I had a date that night? Well I did, and I didn't bother cancelling it. I found Jillienne standing outside in the pouring rain soaked from head to toe. I got her to my apartment and put her in the shower while I went back to the car to retrieve her suitcase. The woman I was supposed to go out with called while I was outside and Jillienne heard her on the answering machine. She told me that my girlfriend had phoned and that I had better call her back as she was worried about me. I guess I made my excuses to whatever her name was and went into the bedroom to find Jillienne dressing. She apologised for intruding on me and my girlfriend and asked me to get her a taxi to take her to a motel. There was no way I was going to do that and told her so. Then we got into the reason she had come to see me on her seventeenth birthday which was because she was now old enough to be with me. She said she had made a mistake thinking that I had feelings for her and that I wanted to be with her too. I guess I preached to her about the cold hard facts of life and in doing so I scared her into thinking I wasn't interested in anything but sex. I tried to kiss her and she slapped me. She backed off saying I was frightening her and she didn't like that side of me. It was then I told her I loved her and had always loved her. The next morning I asked her to marry me and the rest, as they say, is history."

"After just one night together you proposed marriage? Did you feel obligated to do so?"

"Hell no! For two years I had watched a steady stream of young suitors try to win her heart while I denied my own feelings for her. I finally came to terms with myself that night, and that was that I had loved her from the first minute I laid eyes on her. I wasn't about to let her go home without a commitment from me for she was the one I wanted to spend the rest of my life with. She said she was prepared to live with me in sin, but the virtuous side of me had kicked in and the solution for us to be together was to get married."

"She obviously said yes, and you were married a few months later. I take it that her parents did not object?"

"They were surprised to say the least, but they already knew me and considered me as part of their extended family so it wasn't like she had run away with a stranger. Her mother did ask her if she was was pregnant and Jilly said that maybe she was, but seeing that last night was the first time we had been together she doubted it."

"So you had been a friend of the family for some time?"

"Actually, no. I had known Jillienne's brother Clayton through school but we didn't become good friends until we met up at college. He invited me to help him supervise his sister's fifteenth birthday party. Their parents had been called out of town for a family emergency and if he didn't go then the party would be cancelled. I had said "Sure, why not?" On the trip back to Shelton he told me all about Jillienne. He said that she was somewhat of a flirt so not to be too surprised if she came on to me and that I shouldn't be too shocked at anything she might suggest. I had laughed telling him that I didn't think a fifteen year old teenager could shock or tempt me. I changed my tune the minute our eyes met."

"I see, and so that was when your relationship began?"

"I guess you might say it did. She informed me that day that she was going to marry me and for two years our relationship consisted of light hearted teasing and promises that weren't realistic. Never in my wildest dreams did I ever think that things would turn out the way they did."

"Yet you admit that you were in love with her all that time… would you not have confessed your feelings for her at some point in time if she had not come to you?"

"We will never know will we?"

She smiled. "I suppose not. You say that her parents were surprised when you announced your engagement; did you tell them in person or on the telephone, and what about your family?"

"I took Jillienne back to Shelton the next day after we had picked out an engagement ring, so face to face. She had wanted to stay with me and had an answer for every reason why she couldn't. Believe me, I did not want her to go but it wasn't practical that she stay. My apartment was in Burnaby and my teaching position was out in the valley. Some nights I didn't get home until seven and I didn't want her staying alone that long and she needed to go home and finish her grade eleven. I told her I would come home on spring break and long weekends and that we could get married in early July. She conceded, though reluctantly. We stayed at my parent's house whenever I went home. They had turned the whole basement over to be when I was in high school so that I had a place to entertain my friends, and now it became a haven for Jillienne and me. My parents already loved her, a fact I had not been aware of. They insisted that we stay with them. Her mom and mine were well acquainted because of their involvement with the Anglican Church. Jilly would accompany her mom over to our house just for the fun of it. She spent most of the time hanging out with my dad in his shop when he was home. In fact he taught her how to drive and how to change a tire and all the basics of car maintenance. She doesn't care to drive and there is no way in hell she would get her hands dirty doing a man's work, like changing a tire." I laughed saying my dad didn't know that though. "She confessed to me that her visits were really an attempt to learn more about me. Believe me; my mother had no trouble singing my praises. I didn't have any siblings to compete with for my parent's affection but I always envied all my friends who had sisters and brothers. Jilly blessed me with four children and if she had of been able to we would have had more."

"Let's talk about your children. How did they react when Jillienne left, and what do they think were her reasons for leaving the way she did?"

"All right, I will start with Hope. She is our eldest; she is thirty, a substitute teacher and married to an emergency room doctor. They have twin girls, Hannah and Lannah who are nine. Jillienne cherished them and they her. They were only seven when she went away and they cried for days. They still ask me when their grandmother is coming home." I got up and walked to the window and stared down at the rush hour traffic. Without turning around I told Virginia that it was Hope who suggested that I seek a professional's help. She was devastated that her mother left the way she did and blamed herself for not seeing that her mother was troubled. I turned back to face Virginia. "Jillienne's destiny was to be a mother. She doted on Hope from the minute she was born and all through her life. She treated all our children equally, let me clear on that, but Hope was always her baby. Sometimes I think she misses Jillienne more than I do. She was positive that something sinister happened to her mother because it didn't make any sense that she would go somewhere without me as we were always together. Jillienne didn't like to drive and she was afraid of flying, and she got woozy on boats, so she must have been abducted. When the evidence pointed that Jillienne left of her own free will, Hope still refused to accept it. She puts on a good front for me, but she is still pretty broken up. I fear her marriage is in trouble because she spends so much time worrying about me. She thinks it is her job to look after me until her mother comes home. She believes with all her heart that Jillienne is coming back. It's been two years without a word so that isn't very realistic, but I haven't the heart to tell her that I do not think that her mother will ever be returning. Perhaps she is the one who should be seeing you."

I sat back down in a chair facing Virginia. "So that is daughter number one. Next are our sons, Connor is twenty seven, and Rusty is twenty five. Connor is married and he and his wife Beatrice have a twelve month old son. His name is Joshua. He was born on Jillienne's birthday last year. Rusty is unattached at the moment. Both boys adored their mother and they blame me for her abrupt departure. They say I didn't give her the freedom to do what she wanted. They said that I put her on a pedestal and that she got tired of hovering on it. They have also accused me of having an affair with another woman. I have no idea where they got that cockamamie idea from." I pulled my wallet out of my inside pocket and extracted two pictures of Jillienne. I passed her one. "This photograph was taken the Christmas before she went away. Now tell me, what man in his right mind would ever even look at another woman when he has this beauty to come home to every night?"

"She is beautiful Dan."

"Yes, she is, and not just on the outside, but on the inside also." I passed her the other photo.

"This one is Jillienne on our wedding day."

"Really…she doesn't look any different." Virginia said somewhat doubtfully.

"No, she hasn't changed except like the rest of us, put on a few pounds, but believe me, they look good on her. Hope and she are taken for sisters more often than not." I took the pictures from her and returned them to my wallet.

"It's true though, I did worship her, but I never stopped her from doing anything. Truth of the matter is that she only wanted to be my wife and mother to our children. Now in retrospect, maybe I was wrong. Maybe I missed something, but I don't think so. Anyhow, both boys live on the island so we don't see much of each other anymore. They still phone once a month to see how I am doing. It is all a charade though as they only really want to know if anything is new with regard to their mother's whereabouts. Our youngest child is Faith. She will be twenty in July and she is the last one to see Jillienne alive." I sat back in my chair and waited for Virginia's next question. It was immediate.

"So you think Jillienne is dead?"

"Sometimes I do. Faith believes that her mother went away to die because there is no other explanation as to why she would leave the way she did."

"Is that possible; was she ill?"

"Not that I know of. She hardly ever got sick. She had been getting what she called "silly little electric headaches" to her right temple a month or so before. Our family doctor, Donald Quayle, dismissed them as nothing to worry about. He said they were blood vessels compressing the nerves in the temple. I believe he called it trigeminal neuralgia. I don't recall her complaining about them very much. I honestly don't believe she was ill. I quit trying to convince Faith of that even though we had a thorough discussion with Dr. Quayle immediately after her disappearance. He gave her a clean bill of health. I think that because Faith was the last one to see her mother weighs heavy on her. She thinks she should have noticed that something was off with Jillienne that morning."

"What did she say was different?" Virginia leaned forward and asked inquisitively.

"I don't think it was much. It was a little past eight and Faith was hurrying to get out the door. Jillienne got up from the kitchen table where she always sat having a second cup of coffee while seeing Faith off to school. She took Faith in her arms and told her that she loved her and that she was hers and daddy's little girl, and to be a good girl for us. Faith said she had laughed and said. "Oh Mom, I'm always good. Can I take your car?" Jillienne had told her that she had no need for it, and so of course she could have the car. Faith has played that last conversation over and over again in her mind feeling that she missed something in her mother's voice that should have set off an alarm. And then she says to me, "Daddy, I didn't even tell her that I loved her back." She used to cry a lot, but she has hardened herself now and chides me whenever I do my nightly ritual of talking to

Jillienne's picture before I go to bed. We have no closure and I don't know if we ever will."

Virginia was about to say something but was interrupted by a knock on the door. Her secretary poked her head in the door, apologised and said she had the conference call waiting. I looked at the clock. My session was ten minutes over scheduled time.

Virginia swore. "Damn it, I forgot!"

"Not to worry, we were out of time anyhow."

"Sorry Dan; will I see you next week?"

"I have teacher-student- parent conferences all week so I will have to skip." I walked to the door and turned back just as Virginia was picking up the telephone. "You know, I really did have it all. For thirty one years I had the perfect wife and the perfect marriage, and then it was all gone… gone in the blink of an eye. I guess it wasn't as picture-perfect for Jillienne as it was for me. See you in two weeks."

March 13th

I met Virginia in the lobby of the Carmichael building where her office was situated. She was carrying her briefcase, her jacket, and a small paper bag, and was definitely flustered. I relieved her of her valise and we rode up in the elevator together. She explained to me that she was running late because she'd had to make a house call. I remarked that I didn't know therapists did that. She said that this was a most unusual case and that it involved a fifteen year old girl whom she had just admitted to the hospital for further assessment. It had consumed her whole afternoon and had resulted in her cancelling all her afternoon appointments. I told her I was sorry but I hadn't received the memo. She said that she had not cancelled mine. I asked her why as she was entering the code into her office's key- lock.

"I didn't like the way we ended our session last time Dan, and seeing you were unable to have an appointment last week, I felt it imperative to keep this one."

"So, it ended abruptly because you had an important call, no big deal."

"You were despondent when you left, and I didn't like you leaving in that state of mind. You had just come to the conclusion that your perfect marriage wasn't so perfect after all, and that you were the reason your wife had left you…am I correct?"

"You think that was the first time in two years that I thought I was the reason Jilly left? Hell no, I make that assumption at least half a dozen times every day. No need to be concerned Doc; I am not going off the deep end. I've been on a collision course with hell for a very long time, but in my darkest hours there is always a ray of hopefulness and that is my daughter Hope's optimism that her mother is coming home to us as soon as she has dealt with whatever it was that took her away from us. For her sake, I have to keep the dream alive."

Virginia smiled as she hung her jacket up and I deposited her briefcase on her desk. She asked me if I would mind if she checked her messages, just in case there was any update on Carole. I presumed that was the young girl she had been talking about. She passed me the paper bag and asked if I would join her as she put an ear bud in her ear and listened to her messages. I extracted two oversize cups of steaming coffee from the bag and nodded my thanks. Two minutes later she took her seat opposite me. She sighed and said that she would be glad when the day was over.

"How about we just sit here and enjoy our coffee and put our session off for another day?" I suggested. "I think you're in need of some down time and nothing is going to change with me in a week…nothing, except if Jillienne comes home, then that will change everything."

"Thank-you Dan for being so considerate, but believe me, sitting here and talking to you is all the break I need." She leaned forward. "I'd like to play detective with you regarding Jillienne's disappearance, is that all right?"

I laughed. "Be my guest, but I can assure you that we have exhausted every possibility."

"One never knows; shall we just see where this goes? Tell me about the days prior to her leaving. Was she despondent or unusually agitated? Was she quieter or more talkative; did she appear nervous at all? Was there anything different about her persona?"

"I wish I could say that there was, but I have wracked my brain over and over again for two years and never once come up with anything outstanding about her behavior. I have to take you back again, back to the eve of our wedding so you can get a better understanding of the strong, loving, and yet zany person she was. She had written me a note. As I told you before we were staying at my parents' house, but she insisted that we not spend the night together as it was bad luck before the wedding. I didn't believe in such things, but she was adamant and so I walked her back to her parents' house. She didn't even invite me in and sent me away with the note which I was supposed to read at home and then call her. She said she would be waiting upstairs in her bedroom for my answer. I waited until I was out of sight and then opened the envelope. I laughed when I read it, turned around and went back. I stood at the bottom of her room and threw pebbles at the window until she came to see what was going on. She opened the window and asked me what I thought I was doing. I told her I wasn't ready to say goodnight and that I was coming up. She told me to stay there as she would come down.

"Well," she had said, "are you going to accept my conditions or not?"

I said that I was and anything else that she might come up with because I was her love slave.

She said "Good, now it's my turn to walk you home."

That wasn't going to happen, but I let her take me down to the river where we sat with our feet in the water and made out a little. She was always spontaneous like that, and except for the nights she spent in the hospital after giving birth, we have not spent one night apart…until…" I did not finish my sentence. "Sorry, guess I got off the track there. What was it you asked?"

"That is quite all right. I am very interested in every aspect of your life with Jillienne. Can you tell me what was in the note?"

"Sure, why don't you read it for yourself?" I pulled out my wallet and handed her the tattered piece of paper.

"You carry it with you?"

"Yup, it and the last one she wrote." I tapped my chest pocket. "That one is right here."

She handed it back to me. "This is too personal. How about you just tell me what's in it?"

"Read it; that way you will get to know her. You will see how funny she was and that what she wrote was still the way she was thirty one years later."

I watched her carefully unfold my treasured paper. She looked at me and I told her to go ahead. I knew every word of it by heart and in my mind I was reading along with her.

My Dearest Jordan,

Before you consent to marry me, there are a few conditions I would like you to agree to. First, I am not going back to school in the fall. Second, I will not be getting a job after we are married. I will continue to work waitressing until we move to Fort St. John, but that is it. I do not wish to work outside our home as the only career I want is to be your wife and mother to our children. Lastly, you can never look at another woman. I mean it! If I even hear about you ogling some other dame…well, I strongly advise against it as it could very well be grounds for divorce.

That's all. I won't ask for anything of you but to love me unconditionally until the end of time. If you agree then I will be yours tomorrow and I will stand by you and the decisions that you make for us. I love you more than you can ever imagine, and I always will. By the way, I am pregnant and so you are going to have to marry me anyhow!!!

I AM the love of your life…Jilly

Virginia stood up and walked over to her desk where she picked up a small plastic clear envelope. She inserted Jilly's letter into it and handed it back to me. I thanked her and wondered why I hadn't thought of preserving it that way. She then asked if she was right that Jillienne was only seventeen when she had written it.

"She was, but seventeen, twenty nine, thirty six, there was no difference; she was always the same right up until the day before her forty eighth birthday, and then…" I shrugged my shoulders. "She was/ is the love of my life and I did know how much she loved me, and that is why I can't understand how she could leave me…I suppose I will never know what happened."

"Wait a minute now, let's not get ahead of ourselves. We are not through analysing her last few days. I'd like to say though that I'm pretty sure I would like your Jillienne."

I laughed a little. "Oh, you would like her all right, but I can guarantee you that the feelings would not be mutual."

"Why?"

"Because you are an attractive, unattached, childless woman with a career, that's why."

"Did I tell you that I was unattached and had no children?"

"Sorry Doc, I shouldn't assume things without knowing the facts."

"Well Dan, you're assumptions are right. I have no children and they are the reason that my husband and I divorced. He married me fully aware of the fact that I did not want children. The problem was that he already had two children by a previous marriage. They were seven and nine at the time. They hated me from the get-go. I was not one bit fond of them either. Leon had shared custody of them so they were with us on weekends and holidays, or I should say they were with him. I resented the time he spent with them and three years later we divorced. He eventually went back to his first wife. I left Ontario where I had been employed by the province as a councillor for troubled youths. I moved out here and went into private practice as a clinical therapist six years ago. I prefer to work with adults. So yes, I am exactly the kind of woman your wife would have no use for."

"Sorry about that Virginia; please forgive me for my suppositions."

"Think nothing of it. I am the one who broached the subject when I asked why Jillienne wouldn't like me. For a minute there I thought I was the client and you were the shrink."

"You call yourselves "that"?" I said grinning.

"Sure we do and lots of other names too. Surely you have counselled many students in your role as principal?"

"Initially I did, but am more than happy now that we now have professionals on hand that deal with all the problems that come with today's youth. Maybe I am wrong, Jillienne may very well have liked you, but the odds that you two would have even met are astronomical because I would have no need to be receiving council if she was still here would I?"

"No, I don't think you would have the need as her disappearance is the only reason you are here in the first place. Do you realize that sometimes you talk about her in the present tense and then you suddenly switch to speaking of her in the past tense?"

"I'm not sure that I do."

"It's not uncommon to do so as you are living in two different realms. One, you believe and so want to that Jillienne is "just away", and that she will be returning home any day, and this is the world you want to live in as it is the most comforting. Yet, on the other hand, you know that is not realistic as she has been gone too long, and that is when you revert to speaking of her in the past tense. This is not at all appeasing to you and so you switch back to the present. Does that make sense to you Dan?"

"Yes, I suppose it does."

"All right then; let's go back to the beginning. I think you are seeking some kind or assurance that you were not the cause of your wife's sudden departure, and we are going to examine every aspect of the days leading up to that fateful day so that you can find some peace. But first, I need you to tell me about her friends. You said she didn't have any female friends…is that because she was a jealous woman? Did she not trust other women to be around you or was it **you** she didn't trust? I kind of gathered that from the letter she wrote the night before your marriage."

I wanted to laugh, but just chuckled slightly instead. "Well, I never gave her any reason to mistrust me and vice versa. We were locked in our own little world and we had no need for friendships outside of our families. Jilly's brother Clay and his wife Sandie are the only couple we spend any quality time with. There is always some social event happening at the school and Jilly is always by my side. She is cordial to all the female staff and faculty wives, but has never befriended any as she has no need to. She doesn't believe in "coffee klatches", ladies luncheons and gossiping with the girls or girls' night out. She has always been home when the kids get out of school and ninety percent of the time when I got home. The only times she wasn't waiting for me was when she was driving one of the kids to a sporting event or appointment. She was always waiting for me… right up until the day that she wasn't."

"It does sound like you had a pretty perfect marriage Dan. Not many people can say that, but something went wrong, horribly wrong and I hope we will come up with a plausible explanation that you and your family have somehow overlooked. So, Jillienne did not care for the female gender, but what about males? Did she have any men friends that you knew about and if so, how did you feel about that?"

I chuckled again. "Oh yeah, she had male friends. Well, let's just say they were friends to her, but if you were to ask them or their wives, they would all say that they were in love with her."

Virginia looked a little perplexed.

"It's not what you think, let me explain. Hank lives across the street from us with his wife Elaine who works days at a grocery store a few blocks away. Hank is a paraplegic and suffers from anxiety attacks when he is left alone for too long. He was left wounded, alone and presumed dead for five days in Afghanistan three years ago. Jilly is his life-line during the day. She visits him at regular times throughout. She has pinpointed when he is most vulnerable and makes sure that she or someone else is with him at these times. She was instrumental in obtaining a service dog for him and it has made a world of difference in his life. He even ventures outside with his faithful companion by his side now. Then there is Jock. He is a ninety year old man who lives with his eighty six year old wife Judi at the end of our block. Jilly checks in with them every day and plays cards with Jock for a couple of hours once a week when his daughter takes Judi shopping. Jock is still mobile and he and Jilly had started accompanying Hank on short walks up until…well, you know. There is always a casserole or sweet treat in the works too. Then there is Timmy who lives next door. Now this is the one I am most leery of. He is thirteen and looks upon my wife as if she is a Goddess. He always seems to think that she requires help, like carrying things in from the car, taking the garbage can to the back yard or pulling weeds. He just magically appears. I have found the two of them enjoying a glass of milk and a piece of chocolate cake at the kitchen table many a time. She also helps him with his studies. His family has only recently emigrated from Poland and both work so I guess she became his surrogate. I never cared much for him and now I can't get rid of the little bugger. He is constantly badgering me about

Jillienne. Where did she go, why did she go, when is she coming home, etcetera, etcetera. Hank has me on speed dial. He keeps an eye on our house for any sign that looks suspicious. We will get into that later as I relay the few facts regarding her disappearance. Jock calls every day. They all miss her. I've become more involved with their lives now, but I am no substitute for the woman they idolized. They are not the only ones who miss her; the house plants all died, and Lionel the cat ran away from home."

Virginia smiled. "I think on that note we will leave it there for today. You keep looking at your watch so I am thinking you have somewhere to be?"

"Sorry; I'm picking Faith's fiancée up at the airport at six thirty as she's having an interview at precisely that time so is unable to. I've still got a few minutes."

"Is Faith interviewing for a job?"

"In a way, I guess she is. Cree, her fiancée is a palaeontologist, and Faith wants to join him in the field in Peru after they are married. She has no such credentials yet, but has high hopes of being accepted as a volunteer under his sponsorship. She has switched courses several times over the last few years going from dreams of becoming a teacher to a children's advocate lawyer, but now it is palaeontology or nothing. She has been enrolled in classes since last spring; three months after she met Cree. She figures meeting with the head of the palaeontology department can't hurt and will enhance her chances of being chosen. Myself, I hope it won't hinder her, but do they really want newlyweds working together?"

"Why not; it sounds like to me that she has the willpower and will succeed at whatever she wants to. I wish her good luck. Now, getting completely off the subject, I have an invitation I would like you to consider. Do you like music?"

"Are you asking me out Doc? Isn't that against some moral ethics or something?"

She seemed very amused. "No, I am not asking you out, but if I had the inclination to then I would have to lose you as a client, and I don't want to do that. That is not the case however as I have sworn off men, so don't get your hopes up. And, I certainly would never become involved with any man, client or not, who was head over heels in love with his wife even though he didn't know whether she was alive or not."

I tried not to laugh, but it didn't work. "Aah, so you have switched sides have you?"

"Perhaps I would if I could find a girl like your Jillienne..."

Still chuckling I answered her. "Then, you would really be barking up the wrong tree."

"Who's to say?" She said smiling. "I am hosting a small musical event at my house next Saturday and would like to extend an invitation to you. It is to benefit todays' underprivileged youth who show great promise in the music field but do not have the funds or opportunity to pursue such a career. Three former recipients will be performing; a flutist, a pianist and a harpist. It is very casual so no need for a tux or even suit and tie. Several of my more affluent, yet level-headed…sorry, don't know how else to describe them, clients are charter members and the rest of the guests are just friends and colleagues. It usually lasts an hour or so and then it is just chit-chat, and refreshments. Is it something you might be interested in?"

"That depends; do you consider me as one of you level-headed clients even though I am still holding on to the dream that my wife who has been missing for two years is going to come back to me?"

"Yes, you are probably the most well-adjusted person I know, client or not."

"I wouldn't be too sure about that, but yes, I accept the invitation. May I bring a date?"

"Certainly you may. You hadn't mentioned that you had started dating again. I guess I should say, "Good for you.""

"That's probably never going to happen Doc. The date I am referring to is my daughter."

"I will be delighted to meet Hope, or is it Faith?"

"Maybe both, and I suppose my check-book?"

"That's entirely up to you, but it is not a requisite."

She saw me to the door and I took the steps instead of the elevator. I climbed into my car and was about to start the engine when a voice caught me completely by surprise.

"Jordan Ford Landon, what the hell do you think you are doing?"

I looked around; there was no one in the car or outside of it.

"Do you hear me Jordan? Look at me, you promised me you would never flirt with another woman and yet, there you were blatantly flirting with that woman! What has come over you?"

I turned around again. I shook my head, but she was gone. She had scolded me and now she was gone…again. I took a deep breath and got out of the car. Virginia had just stepped out of the elevator and was walking towards her car. I yelled at her.

"She's alive Virginia!"

"What?" She yelled back.

"Jillienne… she's alive."

"What's happened?" Virginia asked walking towards me. "Did she call, has someone seen her…what Dan?"

"I heard her, plain as day. She chastised me for what she thought was flirting. It was like she was sitting right next to me. Now what do you say, am I still one of your more rational clients?"

She shook her head and told me to get a move on or else I was going to be late.

I waved and pulled out of the underground parking lot with a smile and a joyful heart.

CHAPTER 3

Unravelling

February 13, 2006

Another week had passed. I would be off for Shelton to visit Jillienne's and my parents for a few days during Spring Break. They were all living in the same retirement home having given up their houses two years ago. I was now reduced to staying in a motel, and without Jillienne it was boring and lonely. Our parents were all still remarkably healthy so I could spend the better part of the days visiting and taking them on outings. Jillienne's mother's mental well- being had deteriorated noticeably since her daughter's disappearance. On my last visit she had continually asked me how Jillienne was and why hadn't she come with me, and then she would remember why and start crying. I guess I couldn't expect her to come to terms with her loss as I hadn't myself. I really wasn't looking forward to the trip, but duty calls.

The week had gone by remarkably quick in part to Faith and Cree keeping me busy. Jillienne would have liked Cree. He was funny and smart, and dedicated to his profession. More than that, he loved our youngest daughter passionately. He said he had fallen in love with her at first sight, so we had that in common. He never failed to ask to speak with me when he would call Faith…he treated me better than my own two sons. He was finishing up his projects at the Royal Tyrrell Museum in Drumheller, Alberta before the wedding. He was able to stay with us for three days before he had to return to work. I was going to miss him just as much as Faith would. She had laughed when I told her and had said she doubted it very much.

It was March 20th; one month had passed since my first session with Virginia. After our usual polite greetings she got right down to business settling in the armchair across from me.

"I think it is time that we went back to day one and the first few days before and after Jillienne's strange departure. Try not to leave anything out, no matter how inconsequential you might think it is, okay? I'm assuming that you saw her before you went off to work…am I right? Okay, was anything different about her persona or routine?"

"We both got up at the same time, six-thirtyish, as usual. I kissed her and told her I loved her, as usual and she responded in kind. I went off to shower and she went into the kitchen to make the coffee. I'm not accustomed to eating in the morning except maybe a piece of toast with jam or peanut butter, but she was already poaching eggs and frying bacon when I got out of the shower. I asked her what the occasion was and she said that she was feeling guilty about always sending me and Faith off to school on empty stomachs. "Besides," she had said, "I'm hungry myself." So, that was different, but I didn't think anything of it. She straightened my tie at the door as I was leaving and handed me an apple and my lunch money. She kissed me and told me she loved me." I shrugged my shoulders. "Maybe she hung on to me a little longer than usual, but I can't be sure. I kissed her forehead and told her to behave, just like I always do. I waved to her from the car and watched as she closed the kitchen curtain. That was the last time I saw her."

Virginia put her hand over her mouth. "God, you make me want to cry."

"I'm sorry, but you wanted me to tell you everything."

"And, you must. Now what is this with the lunch money?"

"I never carry cash so Jilly always sends me off with twenty dollars in hopes that I will find the time to have a decent lunch. I usually spend half of it and the rest goes into the kitty to help feed some of our less fortunate students."

"I see. What time did you get home that day? Did you talk to her at all during the day?"

"I usually call her at twelve thirty or so just to say hello. It is not always possible, but I did that day. She did not answer, and so I guess she was already gone. I shouldn't say "I guess" because I know that a taxi picked her up at half past ten."

"How do you know that Dan?"

"I told you that Hank, from across the street, was always observant. He happened to be looking out his window at that particular time and he saw Jillienne get into a cab."

"Was she accustomed to taking a cab? You said she didn't care to drive so this really wasn't out of the ordinary was it?"

"She rarely called for a taxi; she really didn't care for the way they drove. She would drive to the market that was four blocks away if she needed something, but usually we would do the shopping together on the weekend."

"Okay, so as far as you know she had no plans for the day?"

"She never mentioned anything to me. She was tired from the busy weekend, and I thought she was just going to stay home and rest."

"Why was the weekend so busy?" Virginia queried.

"We always had a date night on Saturdays, but because the boys were coming home for her birthday celebration for that night, we went out on Friday instead. She didn't beg off or say it was too much. She seemed perfectly happy that we would still be having our accustomed date. I took her to The Rendezvous, one of her favorite restaurants as it has a live band and a dance floor. She loved to dance and she made me love it too. While we were having cocktails… Jilly only drank when we went out and she would sip on her drink of choice all night. I gave her one of her birthday presents. It was a bracelet with fifty black pearls and one diamond centered in the middle. I don't mind telling you that it cost me a pretty penny, but she was worth every one of them. As it turns out, it was the only piece of jewelry that she took with her when she left."

"She must have really loved it then. How did she react?"

"She got all misty eyed and asked if we could dance. We usually waited until after dinner, but I couldn't refuse her. We didn't so much as dance, just swayed a little to the music…I even remember the song; it was "Bridge Over troubled Waters." Pretty ironic wouldn't you say? She cried openly then, soaking my shirt a little. We laughed, sat down and had a delicious meal and were home by nine. She was still overemotional but I didn't think much of it because she gets like that now and then. She did ask me why there were fifty pearls on the bracelet because she was only going to be forty eight. I told her that the thirty three pearls were for how long I had loved her, and there were seventeen more because she was seventeen when our love became real. The solitary diamond was for my everlasting love for her. That only reduced her to tears again and she asked if I knew how much she loved me and I told her I did. When we were getting into bed she asked me the same question. She said it was very important that I knew that she would love me forever. I said I did."

"She wanted you to know that Dan. For some reason she couldn't tell you she was leaving or why, but she wanted you to know that she would always love you. I wish there were more men like you; men who weren't afraid to admit their feelings and loved their women with such passion. Damn it, I'm all teary-eyed again! I'm sorry; this isn't very professional of me."

"I assure you Virginia that I am not one of a kind."

Virginia wiped her eyes. "Well, I disagree with you. I don't have any clients, men or women who can relay their feelings with such passion and sincerity as you do. Sometimes I feel like a failure as a therapist because most of my clients are too up-tight to let me see their true emotions."

"Take it from me, you are no failure."

"Am I any different than the man on the park bench or the dogs you confide in?"

I laughed. "Yeah, you talk back."

She smiled a little and suggested I get back to the day I came home and found Jillienne gone.

"Sometimes the kitchen door is locked and sometimes it isn't. I've told her and Faith a thousand times that they should keep all the doors locked at all times for their own safety, but they don't. It was unlocked that day. I walked in calling out her name. She didn't answer. Her car was home so I figured that she was probably across the road at Hank's. I called out for her again. Faith came down the stairs and sat half way down and said, "She's not home." I asked her where her mother was. She shrugged her shoulders, got up and told me that there was a note for me on the kitchen table. I found it; the envelope had been opened. Faith had followed me into the kitchen. I asked her why she had opened it as it was clearly marked "Jordan." She didn't say anything. I read it, and here it is, in stark black and white, a little dog-eared, and just as unemotional as it was two years ago." I passed the note to Virginia. She took it from me hesitantly. She read it out loud; it sounded just as it ominous as it did every time.

Dearest Jordan,

> *I have to go away. I cannot tell you why; it's just something I need to do. Please do not try and find me as it will be futile.*

> *Please take care of our babies and yourself.*

Sorry J

Virginia passed it back to me. "Except for the "Dearest" part, it is cold and very uncharacteristic of the Jillienne I have come to know through our sessions. She didn't even sign her full name…did you think someone else wrote it, did you think she had been kidnapped?"

I got up and walked over to the window and fiddled with the drapery cord, a diversionary habit I had become all too familiar with. "I asked Faith what the note meant. This is how our conversation went."

"How in hell do I know; I didn't write it!"

"Don't use that tone or language with me young lady! Now tell me, **where** is your mother?"

"Read my lips Daddy, **I do not know!** She wasn't here when I got home…just the note."

"And you opened it even though you could see it was addressed to me? Why"?

"I honestly don't know. I just felt compelled to do so. I wish I hadn't."

"Did you call your sister?"

"She's not picking up, I think she was subbing today."

"Well it is past five so she can't still be at school. Did you leave her a message?"

"Of course I did, I'm not stupid!"

"No one said you were Faith. We'll just have to wait for her to call. Meanwhile, let's see what's missing."

She followed me into the bedroom. "Nothing is missing. Her jewelry box is still in tack. She didn't even take her wedding rings."

"Sure enough the rings were sitting right where she always left them at night. Before going to bed, and when she made bread were the only times she ever took them off that I knew of. I opened a drawer on my dresser and retrieved the key to the safe. Faith informed me that as far as she could tell, nothing was amiss, but she wasn't sure how much cash we kept on hand. I wasn't even sure myself because Jillienne handled all the money, but I was pretty sure there should be at least two thousand dollars. I went to the safe that was located in the back of our closet and discovered that, among other things, it contained five thousand dollars. According to the time lock, the safe had been assessed at four p.m. that day. Faith confessed that she had opened it. Nothing was recorded before that since December last. I asked Faith how she knew about the safe. She said Jillienne had told her about it years ago, just in case something happened to us. She had told her that all our assets would be tied up if we both died at the same time and she wanted Faith to have a nest egg. I had not been privy to this morbid, but sensible plan. I sat down on the bed; the note was still in my hand. I told my daughter that her mother did not write it.

"It's her handwriting Daddy."

"She must have been coerced into writing it. She would never write something so unfeeling…she would never leave us, never. She left the door unlocked; she's been kidnapped."

"So yes Virginia, I believed that she had been abducted. I told Faith that I was going to call the police. She asked me to wait and talk to Craig. I asked what she thought that would accomplish and she reminded me that he had a friend who was a police detective and he would know what to do. I told her that she was behind the times as Marty Reagen had retired and was no longer with the department. I was about to pick up the phone when it rang. It was Hope."

"Excuse me Dan, who is Craig?"

"Sorry, he is Hope's husband."

"Oh yes the doctor; go on please."

"I'm afraid that I took my frustrations out on my girls that day. I lashed into Hope asking her why she hadn't returned her sister's calls. She said that she was calling to inform us that her cell phone had been stolen that day and so had not received any messages, and was something wrong. I told her there was most assuredly something wrong and she had better have some answers for me. She said. "Why are you yelling at me Daddy?" I apologised and told her I was half out of mind worrying about her mother and did she know where Jillienne was. She said she did not and asked me why I was so worried. I told her about the note and to get over to the house as fast as she could and not to bring the twins. She said that I was scaring her and I told her to just hurry. I poured myself a stiff drink, placed it on the kitchen island and went outside. Faith followed me and asked me where I was going. I told her that I was going to check out the car and garage for any clues. She told me that she had the car all day as Jillienne said she would not be in need of it. I told her to go back in and stay glued to the phone. I crossed the street hoping that Hank had seen her. He had; he had seen her get into a taxi cab at precisely ten thirty that morning. She did not appear to have any luggage and he had assumed that she was just going shopping. He could not tell whether she had a purse. The taxi company was Black Cab. I thanked him. I did not tell him the contents of the note, but of course I had inadvertently added him to the worried list.

Hope and Craig arrived and I went through everything with them again. I told them I was going to call the police. Craig was the voice of reason. He said they would probably take note but wouldn't do anything for forty eight hours as she was an adult and then there was the note. I wondered if we had to tell them about the note. Faith suggested calling Marty again because maybe he could give us some advice even if he was retired. Craig said that he could call him but perhaps we should wait until tomorrow because we might hear something from Jill tonight. Jill is what he called Jillienne; they are very close. It always seemed as if they shared some secret that the rest of us weren't privy to. I thought that it was odd that he wasn't overly concerned about her note and consequent mysterious departure. I questioned him asking if he knew something that the rest of us didn't. He didn't actually answer me but instead said that on second thought it might be best if he put a call through to Marty right away. It was then that I learned that Marty was still on the job as a consultant with the police department, but that he also worked on his own as a private investigator. I'll make this short and tell you what he discovered with what Hank had told me. The Black Cab Company affirmed that Jillienne had indeed been a pick-up at ten thirty on the day in question, and that she had been dropped off at the Tsawwassen Ferry Terminal at eleven ten the same day. Marty had obtained the cabbie's name and had questioned him at length regarding Jillienne's appearance, her state of mind and their conversation. His name was Filo. He said that Mrs. Landon had been his fare several times before and he saw no difference in her behavior. She had not appeared to be anxious or in a hurry, and was polite as always, acquiring about his family. He was pretty sure that she was wearing a light brown raincoat, nothing on her head and he remembered her paying him from a little gold pocketbook. He had asked her if she was just visiting the island for a day or if it was an extended stay and she had replied that it was going to be very brief. A security camera aboard The Queen of Victoria validated that she was on board and wearing the brown raincoat, and that she was hatless. It showed her sitting with two other women. One was a regular passenger and was tracked down and also questioned. She remembered Jillienne because as she said; "No one could forget that mass of long auburn hair." So, Jillienne wore her hair down that day which is a little strange as she usually always wears her hair in a French roll when she goes out as she can't stand it flying around and smacking her in the face, especially if it is raining."

Virginia interrupted saying that maybe it was a deliberate signal that she was sending. She knew that you would track her down and would see that she was alone and there of her own free will, didn't I think.

"The question is; was she alone? You may be right Virginia because I was given access to the tapes and it does appear as if she looks right into the camera and smiles the way I like to think is for me and me alone. But, here's the thing…the other woman is not clearly visible, but she and Jillienne get up and leave their seats at the same time. They board the bus together, but don't sit together.

However, they are seen disembarking at the same stop in Victoria which incidentally is in front of a new department store opening. They disembark and into a swarm of people all waiting for the doors to open. Jillienne and this other woman disappear into the crowd and are never seen again. Never seen again, never heard from…nothing. It's final, she's gone and she is never coming back to me."

I picked up my jacket from where I had laid it on the couch and headed for the door.

"Don't leave like this Dan. Please stay and we can talk some more."

I turned around and forced a little smile. "I'm done Virginia, I'm done; see you around."

I walked out; her pleas to come back followed me down the hallway. I caught sight of her calling after me as the elevator doors closed. I had no intention of ever returning.

It was late afternoon when I saw Faith for the first time on Saturday. She came in the back door and placed a few bags on the kitchen island. I asked her where she had been.

"I didn't want to wake you this morning Daddy as I knew you hadn't been sleeping much in the last few nights so I snuck out and took the twins shopping and to lunch. I see you are cooking so you must be feeling better."

"It doesn't get any better Faith. I'm making your mother's spaghetti sauce; are you home for dinner tonight?"

"I thought we weren't going to have a big meal before we went to your shrink's shindig tonight. Have you forgotten?"

"First of all, she is not my shrink and no, I haven't forgotten. I guess I just forgot to tell you and Hope that I was bowing out."

"Why?"

"I had a rough session on Thursday, and I have chosen not to continue with "therapy." It is not doing me any good. It is not going to give me any answers, and so I will just deal with my guilt on my own just as I have been doing all along."

I went back to stirring the sauce. Faith came over and took the spoon out of my hand and told me to sit down. For some unknown reason I did what she asked.

"Maybe you can't see it Daddy, but ever since you started your sessions with Virginia your step has been a little lighter, you joke more and I am pretty sure you are talking less to Mom's picture and usually sleeping better. You have absolutely nothing to feel guilty about; we have told you that a million times. You two had the perfect marriage and relationship; you couldn't have possibly loved each other more. She had to be fighting some sort of demon and we will probably never know what it was, but life goes on and so must you. You know that old saying that it takes a village, well, we are your village and you must let Virginia be a part of that also. Hope and Craig will tell you the same thing. Now, I think you should reconsider about tonight…what do you say?"

"Does this mean you are changing your career again? Are you giving up paleethnology to become a therapist?"

"God, no! I see you every day Daddy so I see the change in you and it is all for the better."

"You think so? Nothing has changed inside of me Faith, and no amount of counselling will ever change that. I will never stop talking to your mother; maybe I just don't let you see me dancing with her picture as often, but believe me, she is still with me twenty four hours a day."

Faith hugged me teary-eyed. "I know Daddy, I know, but I think a change of venue will be good for both of us. I am missing Cree and Hope never gets to go out because Craig is always on call so don't make us go unescorted please."

"You have your mother's way of persuasion you know?"

"She never had to persuade you to do anything! You would have given her the moon if she had asked for it."

"I wish she would have asked for more, I wish she had of…"

"Don't get all maudlin again. Come on, let's finish that sauce."

We stood at the door of Virginia's mansion with an armload of gifts that included a bouquet of gladiolas, a very expensive bottle of wine and a first edition of "Alice Through the Looking Glass." Faith had chosen all of these offerings on her own recalling that I had mentioned Virginia's love of gladiola; the wine was a given. When I asked her why the book, she said that it covered so many personalities that it must amuse psychiatrists all over the world. She had obviously seen way more in the storybook than I ever had. I asked her how much I owed her for the gifts. She said that I had already paid for them so I supposed she had been into the safe or else had pilfered one of my credit cards. It was inconsequential.

Virginia smiled knowingly at the bouquet and hugged the hardcopy of Alice to her breast. I would make sure to tell her that it was Faith's idea and not mine. I commented on her humble abode; she laughed and said that divorce was sometimes very rewarding. All in all we had a very pleasant evening. Virginia was a charming hostess, the venue was entertaining, and I didn't even mind the mingling too much. I did find myself analysing the other guests trying to figure out which of them were also clients of Virginia's. I didn't come to any conclusion as everyone appeared to be perfectly normal; {whatever the hell that was,} and didn't appear to be hiding any hostilities. Perhaps I was the odd man out.

As we were leaving Virginia put her arm through mine and told the girls that I was one of her most favorite people and she was very sorry that she had never got to meet their mother. She hugged them and told them to keep the dream alive that Jillienne would come home one day.

We hadn't even fastened our seat belts when Faith started asking me what my actual relationship was with Virginia. I asked her what she meant.

"Well, it's quite obvious that there is a more going on between the two of you than there should be between a therapist and client."

I make eye contact with her through the rear view mirror. "We have become friends Faith, but I assure you that is all and that's all it will ever be. She understands my pain and helps me feel better about myself. I'm almost at the point where I don't feel totally responsible for your mother's leaving. Didn't you tell me earlier that you thought my sessions with her were helping me?" I started the car.

Hope reached out and touched my hand. "I know you weren't the reason Mom left Dad. We will probably never know what drove her to leave, but we are all coming to terms with it. I will never give up on her though. I do think that Faith is right though; Virginia has a crush on you."

"Thanks for thinking that a woman like Virginia might be attracted to your old dad, but we are just friends, and it will remain that way. I never so much as looked at another woman in the thirty one years your mother and I were together and nothing has changed there. She is still my wife, and I have no need for that kind of female company. Two years has not diminished my love for her; it is front and center every day and I can guarantee you that I will feel the same way until the day I die. Are you both clear on that?"

"I know that Daddy, after all I am the one who hears you talk to Mom every night so I know you are lonesome. I don't think that it is so far- fetched that other women are attracted to you. You are a middle aged cultured, strikingly handsome man, so I'm pretty sure someone is going to come along and turn your head…don't you agree with me Hope?"

"Sort of, but I don't like to think that someone could ever take Mom's place."

"And, no one could." I patted Hope's hand. "And, for you, my back-seat driver," I eyed Faith in the mirror again, "I am fifty nine years old and that's not exactly middle-aged. Your mother was my soul mate and I ain't lookin to replace her."

"What would your students think if they heard their revered principal tossing the word "ain't" around?" Faith laughed. "And you know that sixty is the new forty don't you? Anyhow, as I was saying…"

"Conversation over girls; you two will be the first to know if I ever decide to cheat on your mother." I hadn't intended to raise my voice, but it appeared I had to.

"Very funny Dad, as if you would tell us! And, it wouldn't be cheating because Mom is gone." Faith stated.

"It would be cheating to me, and you would know just as I did when you and Cree started doing the 'dance'."

"Dance, is that the new word for making out? How did you know?"

Hope chimed in. "We all knew; it was written all over your face. You were so funny, talking excessively, avoiding eye contact, and feigning illness so you could avoid brunch."

"And you, Hope…do you think you had pulled one over on me and your Mom?"

"Did Mom never tell you? She confronted me in my bedroom and asked me outright if Craig and I were sleeping together. I did not lie to her. I was very embarrassed until she told me the story of how she conned you into making love the night of her seventeenth birthday."

I was amused. "She actually said that she conned me?"

"She said she practically had to beg you because you were so worried about how young she was. She said you came up with every excuse in the book. Is that the way it was Dad? Suppose if you had chosen to deny her…Faith and I wouldn't even be here."

"Well, that was never going to happen. So we didn't go into great details with you kids about our first night together, but we always talked openly about our love for each other. Our one wish was for you girls and your brothers to find everlasting love as special as ours was… still is. Think we lucked out with you two, but the word is still out on Rusty and Connor."

Faith asked how come she didn't know about her mother seducing me.

I shook my head as I stopped for a red light. "This is certainly not a conversation that I ever expected to have with my daughters. How did we get on this subject anyhow?"

"Come on Dad, the jig is up; tell us all. Were you a stuffed shirt and champion of respectability even back then? Oh, my God, were you a virgin?"

Before I could respond Hope turned in her seat and laughed at her sister. "Come on Faith, Dad was twenty six; do you really think his virtue was still intact?"

"I'm glad you two are enjoying yourselves at my expense. If your mother was here…" I suddenly felt very sad and stopped talking.

Faith patted me on the shoulder. "Sorry Dad, I didn't mean to upset you."

"It's okay honey. I never thought I would ever have to be a dual parent to two cheeky girls. I'm very thankful that Jillienne was here during your adolescence. I didn't enjoy my 'talk' with the boys, but you girls would have been a whole new nightmare. I'm pretty sure that you have already read my comments in the book of poems your mom gave me?"

Hope said she hadn't and didn't even know one existed.

"Faith?" I asked trying to see her in the mirror.

"I caught Mom reading it one day and I asked her what it was and she told me it was a book of poetry that she had given you. I asked her if I could read it and she said that you had wrote comments in it that weren't for anyone but her, so no."

"You are both free to read it. I started making comments in it even before we declared our love for each other. I have something else I want you to see…it's the letter your mother wrote to me on the eve of our wedding."

"Did you move the book Dad because it isn't in the drawer by your bed anymore?"

"You're right, it isn't there. I just remembered that your mother locked it in the safe."

"It isn't there neither Daddy; we've been in the safe half a dozen times and we would have noticed it, don't you think?"

"It has to be somewhere Faith…we'll look again when we get home."

Hope said that if it wasn't there then it was because her mother had taken it with her.

April 10th

Janice, Virginia's receptionist greeted me warmly. "Good afternoon Mr. Landon; we missed you last week. I trust you had a pleasant visit with your parents over the spring break."

I laughed and said that I missed myself sometimes too, but yes, the visit was enjoyable. She said Virginia was waiting for me. I found her sitting on the floor in a yoga position. I asked her if she was comfortable. She replied that I could join her. I flung my jacket on the couch and sat down in her chair and asked what I could do for her. She smiled and got up and shooed me out of her seat and asked me what happened to me last week. She thought I was only skipping the March 27th appointment. I told her that I had taken a sabbatical.

"May I ask why?"

"You may."

"But, you're not going to tell me?"

I shrugged my shoulders. "It's just something I do now and then. I call a cab and have the driver let me off at the ferry terminal. I find a seat that is about where I think Jillienne sat on her final voyage and try to imagine what she was feeling and thinking when she left me. I take the bus into Victoria and retrace her steps and I disappear into a crowd at a shopping mall. I accomplish absolutely nothing. I come home feeling rejected and confused all over again. I talk to her picture as I always do, tell her what my day was like, and how much I miss her. I have a couple of stiff drinks, go to bed and feel sorry for myself. The next day I pick myself up, lick my wounds, put an 'x' on the calendar which chronicles her absence, and tell myself that this may be the day she comes home. Now, aren't you glad you asked?"

"Yes and no. Yes, because I am glad that you shared your emotions with me. I am wondering though if something or someone triggers you to go on these little recreations of what you believe to be Jillienne's last voyage, and we will talk more about that in a minute. No, because I see the pain in your eyes and hear it in your voice. I wish that I had the power to release you from your suffering. I worry about you."

"No one can relieve me of my sorrow Doc; only Jillienne and death can. Do you take all your client's miseries to heart? If you do, you are carrying a mighty heavy load, and I will relieve you of some of it right now. It has been two years and fifty one days since my heart and soul decided she had to leave, and I'm still here, alive and kicking though not too vigorously. I'm lonesome as hell for her, but I'll hold on because of Hope and Faith. I would never abandon them as their mother did."

"Hold on Dan…we don't know if Jillienne left of her own free will do we? I'm convinced that there was a reason so let's explore the possibilities okay?"

"Do you not think that we haven't already exhausted every imaginable explanation over and over again? But, if you have another theory, I'm open to suggestions."

"Let's start with you telling me what articles she took with her. I'm sure that you know everything that is missing."

"Funny you should say that because until a few weeks ago I hadn't realized that a book of poetry that she had given me even before we were a couple was missing. I thought it was in the safe as Jilly hadn't wanted the girls to read all the sensual notations I had penned in regarding my feelings for her. I thought once that I might take it out, but rejected that idea right away as it would just cause me more sorrow. It is not in the safe, so it is missing. The pearl bracelet I gave her three days before she left is gone, and Faith thinks a family photograph is missing, and the clothes on her back, that's it."

"That can't be all…what about her passport, driver's license, bank cards…"

I interrupted Virginia. "They are all still in her wallet which is in the purse she was using at the time or in the safe. As far as we can tell she took no form of identity whatsoever."

"So you have ruled out that she went out of country?"

"I haven't ruled anything out Virginia."

"Of course not because she could have obtained a duplicate bank card or purchased false identity…Dan, did you ever consider that she may have witnessed a crime of some sort and was whisked off into a witness protection program?"

"We have checked with the banks and credit card companies; they have assured us that she was never issued duplicate cards or new ones. Apparently, the original ones would have been cancelled if that had happened. We tried using them and they are all still active. No money has ever been drawn out of her personal or our joint bank accounts. She never wanted her own account but I insisted she should have one. The only time she ever used it was for gifts for me. I deposited money into a saving account every payday for her for her personal use, but it mostly just sat there and gathered interest. If she had of witnessed a crime she would not have been able to keep it to herself, so that theory doesn't wash. Craig's detective friend did all the digging for us and came up empty at every round. It appears as though he did everything possible, but he never turned up another piece of evidence as to where she went after she got off the bus. The other woman, whether she was with Jillienne or not remains a mystery all on its own. We did file a missing person report with the Police and the R.C.M.P., but nothing ever came of that. I shouldn't say that because last winter a body was found matching her physical description and I was called in to identify the remains. It shook me up as I had never seen a corpse before and I thanked my lucky stars that the mangled body was not my Jillienne's. We are pretty sure that she wasn't snatched off the streets to be sold into prostitution as those low-lives who make their disgusting living that way want girls younger in age. She may have run off to join some cult though."

"Oh, how horrifying viewing that body must have been for you! I am so sorry you had to be go through that. You don't really believe that she would have joined a cult do you?"

"Nope, but I am plum out of theories. I said it before and I will say it again…the only logical explanation is that she suddenly stopped loving me and didn't have the heart to tell me to my face, and so she decided to disappear off the face of the earth."

"Well that is just you punishing yourself again for thinking you failed her some way. From all accounts she loved you with all her heart, and I am pretty sure that you know that or else you wouldn't have held on so long. And, another thing…she wouldn't have left her children if she had been given a choice. No, Jordan Landon, something else is afoot here!"

"Which brings us right back to a stalemate doesn't it?"

"For now, but we mustn't give up. Someone out there knows something and it is just a matter of time before some new evidence emerges. You are convinced she wasn't involved in some kind of conspiracy, and I'm willing to stake my career on the fact that she hadn't stopped loving you…so, what else is there? I think we have to investigate her state of mind and health a little deeper. Is there a possibility that she was worried about getting older? Do you know if she was experiencing menopausal symptoms because they can play havoc with a woman's emotions?"

I got up to leave as our time was up. "She would joke about how warm she was when no one else was and passed it off as early onset menopause. Nothing had changed in her "monthly womanly thing" as she called it, and her moods never fluctuated. She made sure that I knew exactly what I was in for and said that she would not put me through what our mothers had put our fathers through. Oh, come on…you don't think she left because she was afraid of that? No, that wasn't going to happen as she said she wouldn't waste one minute of her life succumbing to prehistoric attitudes that women just had to live with yet another "curse." She had no qualms about going on hormone replacement therapy if she needed to, so no to that suggestion also."

"Just when I think that I may have stumbled onto something you dispel it once more, but I think her health has to be investigated further. Now before you go I want to return this to you."

Virginia handed me the copy of "Alice Through the Looking Glass."

"I can't accept this Dan. You may not know this, but it is worth a small fortune."

"Really? I didn't buy it, Faith did. She bought it for a song at a flea market. What kind of fortune are we talking about here?"

"Five thousand dollars or possibly a lot more…a flea market? Well obviously whoever was selling it had no idea."

I laughed. "I can guarantee you that Faith did not pay anything outrageous for it as my bank account has not been drained."

"Oh, so you did pay for it?"

"Yup, her job as a housekeeper doesn't pay too well."

"She's your housekeeper? How does she have time with school and all?"

"Her boss is pretty lenient and she knows the combination to his safe, and his heart."

"You're a real comedian Dan Landon. I love the relationship you have with your daughters, but I still think you need to get out and meet more people. Any chance of that happening?"

"Maybe when school's out." I smiled and said that I would see her in two weeks. She asked why two weeks. I told her I didn't need her as much anymore. She said she was hurt and wished she hadn't done her job so well.

"There's always another song on the jukebox so don't pat yourself on the back just yet."

"I have no idea what you mean by that remark."

"Sure you do…tomorrow is another day and there will be something else that reminds me of Jillienne, and I'll find another reason to blame myself for her leaving, and then I'll be back sitting in that chair, and you'll try to convince me that there was another reason why she left, and not because she stopped loving me. So you see, the song never ends, it goes on and on."

I'm pretty sure I saw a tear in her eye just before I closed the door.

Jillienne and I used to take little walks around the neighborhood on Sundays after the family brunch. We would stop and chat with everyone we met and watch whatever was going on in the playgrounds for a while. It had been many years since we had followed our kids around taking in their various sporting events. Hope was the only one who never cared for soccer, softball or hockey. She did play volleyball though as she said as it didn't require getting dirty or working up too much of a sweat. She was like her mother that way. Hannah, one of the Hope's twins felt the same way, but the other one, Lannah, had to try everything.

It was Sunday, April the thirteenth and a brilliant sunny day. My walks had been getting longer and longer on the weekends. March had come and gone, and so had the daffodils. Jillienne's flower garden had once more been overflowing with them and other spring delights. Faith would pick new bouquets every other day and place one on the kitchen table and one on the coffee table in the front room. A month or so after her mother had left I found Faith at the kitchen sink arranging the golden yellow flowers with some green branches from the fruit trees and talking to her mother.

"There now Mommy, I picked these just for you. They are so very beautiful just like you. I promise I will look after your garden until you come back home. I love you Mommy."

She had heard me and turned to ask if I liked them. I told her I did and took her in my arms and whispered that her mother loved her too, and would be home soon. I was not one bit embarrassed to be crying with my daughter. That was two years ago and counting.

The fragrant scent of lilacs greeted me at every corner. I smiled remembering how Jillienne loved them, but she couldn't have them in the house as they made her sneeze. I felt invigorated and kept walking way past my usual turn around. I found myself in an area which was completely new to me. I was on top of a hill looking down on the busy roadway off to the west. I noticed what appeared to be a colorful little community at the bottom of the hill, one I never knew existed. I wasn't too sure I wasn't fantasizing…perhaps I had indeed stumbled on the mythical Brigadoon. I snapped out of my trance, convinced myself that it was real, and trotted down the hill to investigate. From the top of the hill I had seen that there were rows of houses on every street. They all seemed to be of the same framework, but different in color; I estimated there to be hundred or so. It was like every other neighbourhood; children playing, people chatting over fences and working in their gardens. They greeted me warmly as if they already knew me. I tried to assign a country to their tongue, but wasn't sure if I was right. Most of the older folk spoke English, though not perfect in their enunciation. The accent I detected was definitely European, but me being too damn polite for my own good, did not ask any questions. I proceeded on. Half way down the street I came upon The Church of Arcadia. A man was standing on the newly mowed lawn talking with a young lad of about ten or eleven. I took him to be the one who had just completed the mowing. I told him that he had done a good job.

He beamed at me. "Thank-you Senor. I always do my best for Padre De Rosa. Soon I will have enough money to buy a new tire for my bicycle and then I can ride like the wind again."

I felt compelled to pull out my wallet and hand over the money he needed. Luckily, I had left my wallet at home as it wouldn't have been kosher to do so. The Padre patted him on the back and said he'd see him next Sunday after church, and thanked me for my kind words to Jordao.

"Jordao," I asked, "is that a European pronunciation for Jordan?"

"Si, I believe it to be so. The name roughly translates to mean 'a flowing river.'"

I laughed. "I always wondered what my name meant."

"So now you know; would you care to join me in a cool glass of sangria Senor Jordan?"

"I would most definitely like that. I have ventured far beyond my usual Sunday stroll, and a nice refreshing drink would hit the spot."

I followed him into the rectory off the side of the church. I asked him if I should address him as Father or Padre.

"You should call me Emilio. Sometimes I remove my hat of sanctity and replace it with a ball cap or a sombrero. I also like to be hatless, and you my friend, what hat do you wear?"

I took the sangria from him and sat in the chair he directed me to. "I am the principal at Queen Elizabeth High School on weekdays, and weekends I spend as much time as their schedules allow with my two daughters and granddaughters and other family members."

"And, your wife," he asked focusing his eyes on my wedding ring, "she is with you too."

"Oh, she is always with me Padre...I just don't know **where** she is."

"This is not good I fear. Has something happened to her? Is she no longer with us?"

"That is just it; we do not know if she is alive or dead."

He prompted me to elaborate and I did. I unloaded my distress and sorrow and great sense of loss to this stranger, this man of the cloth. I confessed my guilt just as I had with Virginia, but somehow it was different. I believe I was looking for absolution, and he gave it to me. I was near to tears when there was a knock on the door. Emilio excused himself and opened the door to a young girl and boy.

"Come in children, come and meet my new friend Jordan. He is a school teacher so be very careful with your words." He said grinning.

They both offered me their hands and apologised for interrupting them, but their Mama had need of their father's help as the kitchen sink was clogged again.

Emilio sighed. "I suppose it is time to call the plumber. Tell your mother I'm on my way."

I told him that I was somewhat of a handyman and offered to look at the problem. I was welcomed into the house by his wife Elise. I discovered that the problem was a clogged outflow drain and had it unplugged within a few minutes. Elise asked her husband why he couldn't have seen what the problem had been.

"The good Lord entreats me to administer to *His* flock and all those who come seeking my guidance," he looked at me when he said that, "for that is my work. These hands are meant to heal the soul and the heart, not to unstop drains."

She shook her head at him just as any wife would. She invited me to stay for supper, but I declined the offer graciously saying my daughter was expecting me home. Emilio walked me to the road saying that it was just as well that I had other plans as his wife probably had other chores in mind for me to tend to. I replied that I would be pleased to do so another time.

"So, Senor Jordan, you are coming back to see us?"

I replied that I was and would see him next Sunday, and that I may just make it back for the eleven o'clock service.

"I will look for you among the parishioners, and will be pleased to see you. In the meantime, I will pray for God to hear your plight and bring you peace of mind, and to keep your Jillienne safe and well until you are united with her once more. Bless you my Son, and go with God."

I know there were tears in the corners of my eyes. I felt no shame, but I knew in my heart that I had made a friend for life, and I had renewed hope that Jilly would be coming back to me. I climbed the hill and looked down on Little Portugal. This small settlement did appear to be the definition of Arcadia; an abode of the blessed, peaceful, and spiritual. What had led me here…I chalked it up to providence.

There was a message on my phone and a note on the table. I clicked the play button on the answering machine. It was Hope. "Where are you Dad? Faith is already here. Can you make it for an impromptu dinner? Call us."

I thought that Faith told me she was making supper; I must have misunderstood. I was not a fan of notes left on the kitchen table anymore, but I read it anyway. It was from Faith saying she was at her sister's. I glanced at the clock. It was almost five…where had the time gone? I dialed Hope's number and asked if she could hold dinner for an hour, and that I would be right over as soon as I showered.

Of course they wanted to know where I had been all day. I told them where my walk had taken me and how I had made a new friend, that being Padre Emilio. I said that he had inspired me and that I was contemplating attending his service next Sunday.

"Really Dad, that doesn't sound like you." Faith asserted.

I replied that I had attended church recently when we all went to Shelton to visit with her grandparents during Easter.

"Recently…I was seventeen and Mom was with us so that was three years ago. Is that what you are referring to?"

"I can't believe it was that long ago." I said.

"Well, Mom has been gone for more than two years so…"

I wished I had never brought the subject up as now there we were, missing Jillienne again.

CHAPTER 4

Stalemate

I did keep my appointment with Virginia on Thursday. She had been surprised as I had told her that I wouldn't be in need of her counselling so much anymore. She asked me why I had decided to come. I told her that I didn't know what to do with the time slot, and that I had forgotten to cancel it. She smiled and said she was glad. I told her that I thought I was on the threshold of letting go of my guilt and anger and forgiving Jillienne. I was going to make a push to take her advice and try and move on with my life. She said that I had come a long way in such a short time. I had laughed and told her that I didn't think twenty six months was such a short time.

I reiterated the events of my Sunday, and informed her that I had enrolled in a photography class that was starting up the following Tuesday. She was very pleased to hear that I was out experiencing new things and meeting new people. Then she asked me to tell her about Jillienne's and our early years together if it wouldn't upset me. I told her that it wouldn't and that there wasn't a lot to tell, but she insisted, so I started with our non-honeymoon.

"As you know, we were married in early July. We had decided not to spend the money our parents had given us as a wedding present on a trip. Instead we used the funds to fix up an old trailer my uncle had given us. We would have our honeymoon in it on our way to Ft.St. John in August. That was where I had accepted my first full time teaching position. The trailer came in handy as it took some time for us to find a decent place to live. Hope was born there in 1976. We left there in the summer of 1979; Jillienne was seven months pregnant with Connor. The next few years seen us residing in Duncan, Port Alberni and Nanaimo. Rusty was born in 1983 in Nanaimo. He was a breach birth and Jillienne had a difficult labor. I was scared to death and vowed there would be no more pregnancies. The doctor saved me from sterilization by saying that Jillienne would not be able to conceive again. She was not happy, but accepted it as God's will. We had three healthy children and that was more than anyone could ask for. Jillienne started gaining weight early in 1988. She didn't complain and just chalked it up to holiday indulgences. Truth of the matter was that she was pregnant, and she had known it all along. She kept it from me until it was too late to terminate the pregnancy because she was sure I would have asked her to. I would not have as life is sacred, but I had a hard time convincing her of that. I was upset with her for keeping it from me and made her promise never to keep anything from me ever again. Well, we know how that turned out don't we? Anyhow, I worried needlessly for the next six months. She had an easy pregnancy, and Faith was born forty minutes after I got Jillienne to the hospital. I wasn't taking any chances and two weeks before the delivery date I moved the family to a motel in Victoria to await Faith's birth. At my insistence Jillienne turned her care over to a gynecologist there in the city, and we travelled there for check-ups every three weeks. Faith was our miracle baby. When Faith was two I accepted the position of vice principal here, and we bought a house that was under construction, and we made it our own. I became principal of Queen Elizabeth High fifteen years ago. That's pretty much it. Boring as ole hell, but I would give anything to be bored like that again."

"I know you would Dan. I have the feeling that you and Jillienne didn't have too many differences, am I right?"

"Only two come to mind. We disagreed on a wedding present for Hope and Craig, and then there was the great sewing machine disaster."

"Oh, this sounds intriguing…what's the sewing machine disaster all about?"

"Jillienne didn't own a sewing machine. She did little mending jobs like hemming or sewing on buttons. Her mother, or mine, had shown her how to mend socks using a light bulb. Jillienne used the holey socks as dusting cloths instead. Anyhow, quite a few years back, Hope was still at home so I guess it was ten or twelve years ago, we were watching television when this ad came on for a fancy sewing machine. Jilly said that it must be a marvelous contraption because it could do anything, and wouldn't it be handy. I hadn't realized at the time that she had actually been ridiculing the idea that it could do anything, and I ordered one for her. I wanted it to be a surprise. Believe me, it was. I arrived home one day and found it sitting in its cardboard box on the front room floor. She had peeled the crate back just enough to see what was in it. She hadn't answered me when I had called out for her when I came in so I figured she was busy somewhere else or at Hanks'. I called out her name again and Hope came down the stairs and said that her mother was in the bedroom. Hope advised me not to go in there. I asked her why. She told me to go and look in the kitchen and I did asking her what I was supposed to see. She said, "Nothing."

I clued in then. The kitchen was immaculate, nothing was cooking on the stove or in the oven. There was nothing in the refrigerator that even resembled dinner. There was a note on the table though. It said that the kids could order whatever they wanted to eat, and to tell their father that if he ever wanted to see her again he had better return that "thingamajig" that was taking up space in her front room back to hell as that must have been where it came from. I broke out in raucous laughter. Hope told me that I better restrain myself as Mom could probably hear me. I asked her where her sister and brothers were and she said, "Hiding." I told her to order pizza or whatever and that I was going to take her mother out for dinner. She asked me if I was delusional.

"I knew I was taking my life in my hands when I walked into the bedroom and asked Jillienne if I had ordered the wrong machine, but I did it anyhow. She was sitting in her chair by the window reading. She threw the book at me. I caught it and asked her if she would like to go out for dinner as apparently the cook had taken the day off. She got up and flung everything off the dresser at me including a lamp and an antique clock."

"I would have done the same thing! Whatever possessed you to say such a thing?"

"I guess I wanted to see how far she would go…this was so not her, but it was fun seeing a side of her I never knew existed. Anyhow, when there was nothing left to hurl at me, I walked over and took her in my arms. She tried to beat on me, but I held her so tight that she couldn't. Finally she broke down and asked me if everything she already did was not enough for me and did I now want her to start making all our clothes. I didn't get to answer her as all the kids were yelling outside the door asking who was killing who. Jilly yelled back at them to go away as we were having a fight and then we would probably make up and they didn't want to be witness to any of that. We never did go out for dinner."

"What happened to the sewing machine?"

"I took it into the den planning on sending it back on the weekend. When I came home the next day, it was gone. I didn't bother to ask what she had done with it thinking she had donated it to the thrift store. It remained a mystery until Faith was in the seventh grade and was enrolled in sewing class at school. She asked us if we would consider buying her a used sewing machine. I think she had completely forgotten about her mother's tantrum regarding 'said machine' from years ago. Jillienne looked at me in a very particularly odd way and smiled. Then she told Faith that she may as well use the one in the attic. I had been up there many times and never once had I seen a sewing machine. Jilly assured me there was one there and directed me to its location. I had no doubt in my mind that it was the one that I had bought for her, and it was. I brought it down and asked her how she had managed to get it into the attic. She didn't answer me and walked away. Apparently, it was still a sore spot with her. It is still in Faith's room and to my knowledge Jillienne has never had anything to do with it."

"And, that's it? That's the biggest argument you ever had? What about the wedding present?"

"Oh, that was nothing. I wanted to send Hope and Craig on a honeymoon to Costa Rica but Jilly wanted to furnish their apartment instead. We had a few lively discussions until she convinced me that I was wrong and that a weekend at the Empress in Victoria would suffice as a shortened version of a honeymoon. I took it as a partial win."

Virginia rose and said. "I can hardly wait for your next reveal."

"There is one funny story I will share with you. As I have told you before, we were not very sociable. Besides our Saturday night date or playing cards with Clay and Sandie, a night out for us was going to the ice arena to watch the boys play hockey. Summertime took us to the ball or soccer fields. There were certain parents that we conversed with but never accepted any of their invitations to parties; we just weren't interested. However, the day came when we didn't bow out. It was supposed to be a get together to honor our boys' hockey coach as he was retiring after twelve years. We mingled and I had a few drinks and Jilly nursed her diet soda. Then it was as if the Red Sea parted…all of a sudden all the men had deserted me and I was in a throng of women. I didn't know where Jilly had gotten to. These "women" seemed to be competing with each other offering to refresh my drink or get me hors d'oeuvres. They interrupted each other to tell me little anecdotes that they thought would interest me; they didn't. I was more than a little uncomfortable. I finally spotted

Jillienne coming out of what I assumed was the kitchen. A man I hadn't been introduced to was right behind her. She walked very quickly towards me and asked the three vultures surrounding me to excuse us. She took hold of my arm and escorted me to the door. I asked her what was wrong, thinking of course that one of the kids was sick. She asked me to find Jenny, who was the hostess, and get our keys back. I was surprised that they, along with everyone else's were not in the bowl that we had been requested to leave them in… just in case we imbibed a little too much and required a ride home. That was never going to happen, but I dropped my keys in the bowl anyway saying "What the hell." Now, Jilly was telling me I was naïve. I asked her what she meant by that. I did not care for her answer.

"Which one of those so called housewives did you fancy going home or upstairs with tonight?"

I asked her what she was talking about.

"Well my darling, this little celebration is all a ruse to cover up "the wife swapping" charade. So, if you don't plan on going to bed with someone other than this sexy, auburn-haired woman beside you, I would highly suggest you track down our keys!"

I was embarrassed that I had been oblivious to the obvious. I found Jenny; she was not happy that I had demanded my keys, and tried to persuade me to stay and that it was just harmless fun. I asked her if she thought it would be harmless fun if I knocked the block off any man that so much as looked at my wife in a lecherous way. She told me that I was an uptight prude and that my body said one thing but my outdated righteous brain wouldn't let it answer the call. I heard laughing behind me; it was Jilly.

"Oh dearie, so sorry to disappoint you, but the only woman who is privy to this man's torrid lovemaking is me." She winked at Jenny and thanked her for the invite to the shabby side of town." Then my charming wife took my arm and said, "Let's go Darling."

We went out the door kissing and laughing and waving to the astonished sinners.

"So there Virginia, that's it; we are two pretty square people. Our one night of intended debauchery, in someone else's mind that is, turned into a comical learning experience. Jilly told me she thought her drink had been spiked and that she had been offered a weekend on some guys yacht. I wanted to go back in and and accost him, but Jilly insisted that she had already dealt with him. I asked her how. She said she accepted his invitation and told him that her husband and four children would be delighted as they had always wanted to go for a cruise on a fancy yacht. I then asked her about the man who had followed her out of the kitchen, and if he had made advances towards her too. She said, and I quote: "Oh, he only wanted the same thing that you want from me every night!"

Virginia laughed. "I like her spunk. I can hardly wait for the next story."

I told her there were no more tales to tell.

"I doubt that very much Dan Landon, but I am very pleased that you can talk about your life with her now without it depressing you."

I wished that I was just as convinced. I was moving on…sort of.

I went home to an empty house as I so often did those days. Faith was busy with her studies or off with her girlfriends or visiting Cree. He was unable to take any time off from his work at "The Dinosaur Factory" as the twins called it. They also referred to him as "Dino." The Drumheller airport was only a few miles out of town so I would put her on a plane on a Friday evening and pick her up late Monday. Cree had invited her to accompany him on a dig in the vicinity of Edmonton for the weekend which meant that she wouldn't be home until late on Tuesday evening. It was my first photography meeting so Hope was going to pick her up.

I guess anyone who has ever lost a loved one would say that coming home to an empty house day after day was heart wrenching. To me, it was like walking through a graveyard. The first thing I do is turn the stereo on. It is always tuned to a country classics music station that was Jillienne's favorite. She had umpteen favorite singers.

She was particularly happy when Ferlin Husky was singing. She said that I sounded just like him.

I warmed up some leftovers and decided to give my camera a dusting. I knew I would probably be the laughing stock of the club because my camera was indeed a dinosaur. I had pretty much left the still photographing of the family up to Jillienne. My job had been to document each child's progression through the early years with the movie camera. I had carried on the tradition with the twins up until they were five. I had not taken it down from the shelf in four years. I knew there were cameras on the market now that were more compact and efficient than ours, and hopefully I would get some tips on purchasing one tonight.

I had slung my camera case over my shoulder two days ago when I had ventured into "Little Portugal" again. I was hoping to snap a few pictures of the people who lived there. They were most obliging. I had arrived too late for Padre DaRosa's sermon, but spent the afternoon with him as he had chosen to follow me around with my camera and introduce me to his parishioners. I learned that the community was made up of many nationalities not just Portuguese. There was Italian and Greek, just to mention a few. I enjoyed conversing with them and learning the cultures of all the different ethnic groups. I particularly liked how jovial all the women were. Two nights later I met Martina Winfred.

That was on my first meeting with the photography club. The classes were held at Moscrop Institute of Technology, a trade school that I was very familiar with. I had attended many seminars there and had also been a key speaker a few times. Many of my students had furthered their education there. I walked in and took a seat near the front behind several other people. They turned around in tandem and realizing that I was a newcomer, introduced themselves and welcomed me. I was aware that I had enrolled late and that I had missed the first two sessions, but was assured that all I had missed was camera talk. That was all that I was looking for; advice on upgrading my equipment. Seven more people arrived and settled in behind me just as the instructor took his place at the front. A woman of about my age entered and apologised for being late. She looked around for a place to sit. I moved over to the next desk. She smiled and thanked me. As soon as she was seated she introduced herself as Martina Winfred.

The instructor noticed me and walked over to me saying that he was Farron Meade. I stood up, shook his hand, and at his prodding told him who I was and what I did for a living. He asked what my interest was in photography. I told him that it was a new pastime of mine having only recently picked up the camera, which was somewhat of a relic. He welcomed me and said he would have me fixed up in no time.

After the hour and a half talk on still and video equipment and a short film, the session was adjourned. Martina invited me to accompany her and four others across the street to a little café for coffee. That became a pleasant diversion for the next few weeks. All who were interested had been invited to a photo event on Saturday, May 3rd, by the instructor. We were to meet at Langford Ferry Terminal at eight a.m. with our cameras for a quick ride to Saturn Island where we would disembark on the photo safari. I was definitely up for it.

I had a session with Virginia on April 24th. I was settling into my new life I thought rather well. I had some new friends who shared my enthusiasm for photography and I had Padre Emilio and his family, and the people who had welcomed me into their fold in Little Portugal. Virginia was happy for me.

I went home and told Jilly about my session with Virginia. I told her that I missed her and that I loved her. I kissed her picture and went into the sunken living room, her favorite room, and fell asleep with the television on and her picture in my arms. I was moving on.

The weeks seemed to fly by, and suddenly it was June. I had attended several evening prayer services at Arcadia with Padre Emilio at the pulpit in May. I was always uplifted by his sermons, and came away with renewed optimism that my prayers would someday be answered. I kept going to the photography meetings mainly for the company. I had learned all I needed to about taking pictures, and had purchased a new camera. Besides the Saturn Island trip there had been several other group shoots around the city. They were all educational and enjoyable. I looked forward to Tuesday evenings and the friendly coffee chats afterwards. Besides me, the after class group consisted of five men, and three women all from different professions. Martina was a retired insurance agent. Two of the men were divorced, one was a widower, and the others were happily married as were the two women. Martina was a widow, twice over. I hadn't wanted to go into details regarding the state of my marriage at first as I wasn't even sure what it was. I had said that my wife and I were estranged. However, one night we were discussing a strange case of a recent overnight kidnapping of a prominent political figure that had been negotiated successfully. I had mumbled something about wishing that I had of had the opportunity to negotiate, and of course that led to me confessing Jillienne's disappearance. So now my new friends knew the real story of my marriage status. There was much empathy expressed regarding my unresolved situation. I appreciated it, but part of me wished that I had kept it a secret. On May 27th, one week later, I gave Martina a ride home as her car was undergoing an overall. She had taken a taxi to the meeting and was about to phone for a pick-up after coffee when I intervened and offered to take her home as it was only a few blocks out of my way. Our conversation was mainly about our children and grandchildren. I knew she had two grandsons as she spoke of them and their escapades often. She mentioned that they kept her very busy attending their soccer and baseball games. She said that she hoped her car would be ready by Friday as that was their first game in a soccer tournament. I told her that Lannah, my sports minded granddaughter, had taken a hiatus from soccer and other sports this year. I was missing watching the youngsters and that perhaps I could tag along to a couple of the games with her. It wasn't that I didn't get my fill of sporting events as there was always something going on in the high school gym or on the field. I tried to put in an appearance two or three games a week, but it wasn't always possible with my schedule. I quit attending evening games as it just wasn't the same without Jilly.

Martina said she would delighted if I was to join her. I gave her my home phone number telling her to call me as soon as she knew their schedule. I offered to pick her up, and that is how our friendship evolved, and that is all it was ever supposed to be…just a friendship.

I saw Virginia only once during the month of May. I let her believe that I wasn't in trouble anymore so there really wasn't much to talk about. She wanted me to check in with her once a month as she didn't want to lose touch with me. I told her that wasn't going to happen, but I didn't want to take up anymore of her valuable time. I suggested that maybe we could meet for coffee sometime. She liked that idea and we made a date for June 21st which was a Saturday. I finished up with the years school end supervising some late exams on June the 20th. I cleared my desk and drawers of mementos that I had accumulated over the past ten months. Last thing into the box was Jillienne's photograph. I went home and changed clothes for my dinner with Martina.

Although I had accompanied her to half a dozen of her grandsons' soccer games, this was the first time we would be dining together. I did not consider it a date. I had met her daughter Irene and husband Gerard at one of the games. They were a rather uptight couple, but were happy that Martina had a new friend to attend their boy's games with as they weren't always available.

I didn't ask why, but they ran a wholesale business together so I presumed it was work that prevented them from attending regularly. I was glad to fill in as I enjoyed the games.

Martina had made the dinner reservations at a new seafood restaurant on the waterfront. She had asked me if I would like to accompany her to its opening, and I had said, "Sure, why not."

It was a pleasant enough outing and she asked if maybe we could do it again when I got home from my family visit to Shelton. Again, I couldn't see why not.

I met Virginia the next day downtown in a little outdoor café. It was supposed to be just for coffee but we ended up having lunch. I had mentioned that Martina and I had gone out to dinner the night before.

"So you are officially dating then?" She asked.

"Do you consider *this* a date; you and me having coffee?" I replied.

"No, of course not!"

"Then neither was my dinner with Martina."

"Sorry, it has been so long since I had dinner with anyone that wasn't associated with business that I guess I forgot that friends can dine together without it being anything but platonic."

"She knows I am still in love with my wife so I don't think she expects anything else."

"Don't be too sure of that Dan."

"Enough about my non love life…now, why is it that you don't have one?"

She laughed. "Love is not on my bucket list. I was in love once, really in love. I thought it would last forever; just like you and Jillienne. His name was Jim. We were young, and we had plans for our future. We even talked about what we would name our children…"

She paused and took a deep breath. "Yes, I once wanted children, but it never came to be. I was in college and Jim was in the army. He went out on maneuvers one day, and never came back. The army brass concluded that he had gone AWOL. I never accepted that as his plans were to have a career in the armed forces. He left everything and everyone he loved; his parents, his siblings, his dog, and me. I guess he got cold feet or else he never truly loved me. He was a really nice guy and wouldn't want to hurt me so he probably thought that disappearing would solve the problem of how to end it with me. But then, on the other hand, he had to know what it would do to his parents, and he wasn't a coward, so the door is still wide open…"

"Jesus Virginia, why didn't you tell me this before? My case is so much like yours…why did you even take me on as a client?"

"Because you needed me, and my job is to try and heal, and I don't let my personal life interfere with my client's welfare. Yes, maybe our lives are parallel, but what happened to me was twenty five years ago, and I have long been done with it. Maybe it's the reason that I have pushed you so hard regarding Jillienne's physical and mental health. I may have ignored signs that Jim was emotionally unstable…I was studying to be a psychologist so I should have seen that he was struggling, but I was in love, and love is blind."

"Is it possible that in trying to solve Jillienne's disappearance you were hoping to disentangle Jim's illogical departure also? Maybe he was the one who was abducted or met with foul play, or was there another woman? How often have you asked these questions, and how often has my situation triggered your memories? Has there never been any word from his family?"

"His parents both passed away a few years back. I hear from one of his sisters periodically; she says there has never been any word regarding Jim's disappearance. I believe her as she has no reason to lie at this stage in the game."

"Besides that marriage, the one with the bratty kids, has there been no one else?"

"Oh sure, there has been five or six attempts, but they were all doomed from the start. You can't build a new relationship with someone else when you are still living in the past."

"I thought you said you were long done with that?"

"Oh yeah, right. I'm hungry, do you feel like eating? May I buy you lunch?"

"Sure, I could eat."

We had a glass of wine with our salads, and kept the conversation light. I picked up the check before Virginia could.

She smiled and asked me if I would like to get a room. I arched my eyebrows and looked at her in complete astonishment.

She broke out in laughter. "I wish you could see your face Dan Landon! You didn't honestly think that I was serious did you?"

I grinned. "Jillienne warned me about women like you."

"I just bet she did. We have a unique relationship Dan, and I would never do anything to jeopardize it. You know that don't you?"

I said, "Let's get out of here." I walked her to her car. "I might need you again if I find myself in trouble, but right now I just need you as my special friend. I find myself in the strange situation of having two women friends in my life. The concept is new to me as you very well know, but I don't think Jillienne would object to my choices, at least not to you. My heart is not open for any other options, and I don't see that changing anytime soon. Part of me will always be empty without Jilly, but I am reasonably content right now. I want very much for you to find your soul mate; he is out there somewhere you know."

"How about you bring me one back from Shelton? Surely that little town produced more than one Dan Landon?"

I smiled and kissed her on the cheek. "I'll see what I can do, but it's going to be pretty hard finding someone who is worthy of you. I love you in a very special way…you know that don't you girl?"

"I do, and I can guarantee you that the feeling is mutual. Drive safe and call me soon."

I closed the car door and watched as she drove away. I took the long way home driving by Oleander Park. It was one of Jillienne's favorite places to walk as there was a large man made pond that was home to ducks, geese, and sometimes swans. We usually brought our own treats and would sit on one of the benches and feed the fowl. Why the park was named after a poisonous plant had always been a mystery to me. I hadn't visited the gardens in over two years, but I thought; what the hell, you can do it Jordan. I was pleased to find a young lad peddling birdseed as vendors were usually only there on the weekends. I gave him five bucks, and found a secluded spot to throw the grain to the open mouthed feathered friends and tossed a handful to the doves and pigeons on the ground. There was no one sitting next to me on the bench, there was no one holding my hand and pointing to the hilarious antics of the geese. There was no one telling me to make sure I kept the peanuts separate as we would most surely see a squirrel or two on the way out. How many times… how many times had she said the same thing? It had never got stale, never.

"Oh Jilly Baby, what I wouldn't give to hear those words one more time, just one more time."

I needed to hear her voice and the only place that was possible was at home. I dumped the rest of the feed in the water, and threw the few peanuts I had found into some shrubs. I was home in fifteen minutes, and was sitting in the dark in the basement watching and listening to my Jillienne. I was on one of the last home movie when Hope found me. She cuddled up beside me and we watched Jilly running the bases in one of our family baseball games at the elementary school a few blocks away. Jilly was a very good hitter. It was always boys against girls so I was always at a disadvantage because Faith was so much younger, but it was good wholesome fun. Quite often, other kids from the neighborhood would join in. They were usually boys so Jilly would pick the biggest one first and give me whoever was left, whether it was one, two, or three. We watched her pretending to be surprised opening her Christmas presents and coloring eggs for Easter. She made her own dyes with onion skins or beets, and the like. She always had red hands for days after. We laughed at her imitation of the Wicked Witch of the West when she chose to become her one Halloween not so long ago. She had me dress as the scarecrow that year just in case the little kids who came to the door were frightened of her. She scared the hell out of me as she had the cackle down pat.

The last movie was of our twenty fifth wedding anniversary, the actual one that fell on July10th. Jillienne's brother Clay was operating the camera while we were dancing. Our brood, including Hope and Craig, each holding one of the infant twins joined in along with Sandie, and hers and Clay's two children, Diana and Eric. We went from room to room forming a conga line. The second time around the dining room table I stopped and dipped my fingers in the gooey icing of our celebratory cake. I turned to Jilly who was right behind me to give her a taste, but she turned and the icing ended up in her hair. Well, the fight was on. She returned the favor in kind, only smearing me with twice as much. The kids cheered us on helping out a little as we continued with the blitz until we had demolished one whole layer. Sandie rescued what was left of the cake, and cleaned it up so it was edible. I took my sticky frosted wife into my arms and told her I loved her.

"It's a damn good thing I love you more than life itself Jordan Ford Landon or you would be in big, big trouble!"

The screen went black.

"See Daddy, she really did love you." Hope sniffled.

"I know she did Honey, I know. Come on, let's go upstairs and have a cup of tea."

It was then that I found out that Craig and Hope had decided to spend some time apart. I asked her what that actually meant. She said that Craig was married to his job and that it was more important to him than his family. I told her that was bull.

"I know if Mom was here she would take Craig's side, but I never expected that you would."

"I am not choosing a side Hope, but if I was, it would be yours. I am merely saying that Craig is devoted to you and the girls. He hasn't finished his internship yet so he has to keep the hours he does. It will be over soon; can't you hold on until then?"

Hope plunked two cups down on the table. "For your information, he was finished two months ago, but nothing has changed. What kind of tea do you want?"

"I didn't know that…how come we didn't celebrate? I'll have that green tea, the one your mother liked."

"That was a bone of contention. He didn't think I knew, and when I confronted him on it he said he needed more hours. I asked him why and for what, but he didn't have an answer that made any sense to me. You know we were going to rent a recreational vehicle in July and take the girls on a two week camping trip don't you?"

I said that I did.

"Well, that is all shot to hell as Craig can't get time off as he is filling in for a senior colleague. He asked me if we could do it in the fall instead…yeah sure, when the girls are in school. I told him he needed to think about his priorities which at the moment were not me or the twins. After a half hour or so of a heated argument he said he had to get to the hospital, and left. I had a suitcase packed and waiting outside the door for him when he returned. I told the girls that their father was going to be putting in a lot of overtime and that he wouldn't be home much so he was going to live elsewhere for a while. They didn't understand. How could they, I didn't understand myself. I just know that our marriage is not working, and I am terribly unhappy."

I got up and put my arms around her. "I'm sorry Honey. Let me talk to Craig, there has to be a way out of this."

"It's too late Daddy, he already has an apartment. Aunt Sandie was over yesterday. She had run into Craig somewhere and he told her that we were having a trial separation. I asked her not to tell you because I wanted to myself. Anyhow, it appears as though Diana's husband is going to Seattle for some training session for firemen, so she suggested that maybe Diana and the kids would like to do something together, so we are. We are taking the kids to Disneyland."

"What did Craig have to say about that? I thought you were planning a trip there together at Thanksgiving? It's going to be so hot there in July Hope."

"I haven't told him yet."

"Well, I think you had better. When did you send him packing?"

"Don't make it sound like it's all my fault Daddy as it was a mutual decision."

"It doesn't sound like it was."

"It was his choice to work long hours over summer, so he made his bed, and now he can lie in it, alone." Hope said bitterly.

"This does not sit well with me. Do you still love Craig?"

"Of course I do!"

"Well then get off your high horse and make amends! Surely you can live another two months with things the way they are. Do you know what I would give to have your mother back for even a day so I could hold her and tell her how much I miss and love her…do you? And, here you are throwing away a perfectly…"

She cut me off. "I knew you would bring that up, and yes I know that you would give anything to have Mom back, but our situations are completely different. I don't want to argue with you so I am going to go."

I followed her to the door. "I guess I have done a piss poor job of looking after my family. For thirty one years I thought your mother was happy. We started out life with nothing, but we turned it into something and I thought that we made a pretty good life for you kids. It was all her though. Sure, I brought the paychecks home, but it was her who made all the sacrifices. She was only seventeen when we got married, and you were born just before she turned eighteen. She was so young, but we were madly in love so age didn't matter. I had years on her, but I didn't have her wisdom. We lived in a small trailer for almost four months in a strange town where she had no friends or family. We moved six times before we ended up here. She scrimped and saved and ran the household and single handily raised you kids while I worked. She spent many an evening and weekends alone when I had to work on school projects, and then there were the two years I went to summer school to get my PHD. There were three of you then so it must have been overwhelming to her, but she never complained or asked for anything but my love. Two years, three months and seven days ago, she decided to make a life for herself, and left me. I failed her somewhere along the line, but my rose tinted glasses never let me see that she was unhappy. Rusty can't stay in a relationship for more than three months; Conner's marriage is surely going to end in divorce. They blame me for their mother's departure, and now you and Craig are separating. All these years, and what do I have to show for them…my wife left me, you kids are all suffering… what about poor Faith, is her relationship doomed to fail too?"

"Oh Daddy, none of this is your fault. We were brought up in a loving home; you and Mom were, and are the very best parents. The only time I ever saw you two seriously disagree was over that stupid sewing machine. She never stopped loving you, never. Every day I saw the way you two looked at each other, and I prayed that someday I would have a marriage just like yours. Maybe I do, but it is going to take a little work, but we will work it out so don't worry, okay? Faith and Cree are solid, so no worries there, and the boys… well, how they have treated you is disgraceful, and they can work out their own lives. Their problems have nothing to do with anything you did, and neither did Mom's leaving. I am convinced that she has something she has to work out, just as Craig has told us all along… she will be back as soon as she has resolved whatever it is. Just half an hour ago, you said that you knew she loved you, but now you're questioning it again…why?"

"No, I knew that she loved me for a very long time. You can't fake love like that, but something happened, and I may never know what it was, so no Hope, I don't think she is coming back. What could possibly take this long to sort out…she either loves me or she doesn't. It's time I accept that she no longer wants to spend the rest of her life with me. I'm sorry, but I am afraid she is gone forever."

She put her arms around me. "I will never believe that Daddy, and I don't believe that you do either. There is Faith's theory that she went away because she was sick…suppose that is true?

"We've been over this a thousand times Hope; there is nothing to support that theory, so let's just put it to bed, at least for the night, okay?"

She nodded. "I love you Daddy. Please don't be angry with me."

"I'm not angry, just worried, that's all. I love you too Honey. I don't know how I would have managed to get through these last few years if it wasn't for you and Craig, and Faith."

She smiled, though not very enthusiastically. "We'll always be here for you Daddy. What is it Mom always used to say, "It'll all come out in the wash", or something like that?"

"Yeah, right; we'll talk tomorrow okay?"

I barely made it to the kitchen when there was a heavy knock on the back door. It was Craig. I let him in. He walked in looking very lost, and asked where she was. I told him that Hope had just left. He said he knew that as they had passed on the road.

"Who do you mean then Craig?" I asked confusedly.

"Jill, where is she? I need her Jordan; she wouldn't let this happen. I haven't done a damn thing wrong except try to provide for my family, and look what it has cost me. Hope told you didn't she? She kicked me out, and I don't know if I can make it right before it's too late."

I put my arm around his shoulders and told him to sit. I asked him if he was on duty tonight. He said no, and wasn't it ironic that he had a Saturday night off and no one to share it with. I went to the liquor cabinet and grabbed two glasses and an aged bottle of whiskey.

It was raining when I had closed the front door behind Hope so I had thought I would grab my rain gear and head for the beach. Jillienne had fallen in love with the sand and the tides, and the fog just as I had. We had spent many an evening strolling up and down the shorelines when we lived on the island. We had discovered several semi secluded beaches not far from home here on the mainland, and we frequented them often. It seemed a fitting end to my day, but Craig was here, and he needed me. I had leaned on him many times in the last few years so it was payback time. Jill would want me to… look at me, calling her Jill.

Two hours later I ordered a pizza. We adjourned to the sunken living room and I found a John Wayne movie on the television. One minute Craig was talking to me and the next he was sound asleep. I covered him up, shut the TV off, picked up the empty pizza box and dirty dishes. Brunch had been cancelled for tomorrow even before this latest chain of events so I didn't bother tidying up the kitchen. I found Craig's car keys lying on the table. I put them in my pocket, poured myself another glass of whiskey and retired to the bedroom. I picked Jillienne's picture up and sat on the bed.

"Damn it Jilly, your family is falling apart; where the hell are you anyway? It's time for you to come home…come home Baby, we need you, please come home."

I was awakened the next morning by the pungent aroma of coffee. Craig was standing over me holding a steaming cup of brew.

"I think you need this more than I do Dad." He said grinning.

He always called me Jordan. "How familiar did we get last night anyhow?" I asked.

"Just dad and son, nothing to worry about." He nodded at Jillienne's picture lying on the pillow beside me. "I see you are still sleeping with my girlfriend."

"Yeah," I said picking it up, "and I've got the scars to prove it. I have broken the glass at least five or six times."

"I think it's time that I put an end to your torturing."

I asked him what he meant by that.

"Nothing, just that I can have it laminated for you so that you don't keep cutting yourself on the glass. Let me know whenever you're ready to let her out of your sight for a few hours. Have to go as I want to stop by and see the girls as I'm on duty for the next three nights so won't get another change before they take off on their trip."

"Don't let on that I told you okay?"

"I won't, but thanks for the heads up. I promise to act surprised and not too disappointed that I won't be joining them. Thanks for the company and chatter last night. Talk to you in a few days okay? Oh yeah, did you see where I put my car keys?"

"Hand me my pants… I thought they were safer with me than with you." I said fishing the keys out of my pocket. "I needed last night just as much as you did. Tell Hope that I'll be over later, and Craig, get working on that plan to get you all back together okay?"

"I'm going as fast as I can."

CHAPTER 5

Trouble With Women

Aunt Flo's Cheesecake Shop was closed and so I stopped at a grocery store and purchased six cheesecakes for the potluck lunch after the church service. Apricot cheesecake was Jillienne's favorite. Flo's cakes were superior to any others. I hoped the ones I had bought would taste as good as they looked.

Emilio's service was heartwarming as usual. After the luncheon I stopped at Martina's just to say hello. She asked me if I would like to join her for dinner; she was making lasagna. I accepted the invitation and then spent an hour with Hope and the twins. Hope asked me how my talk went with Craig. I hadn't much to tell her except that he had pretty much assured me that they would be back together before summers end, and that she would be happy with his plans. She said that we'd see about that.

Dinner with Martina was enjoyable. She made a mean lasagna; every bit as good as Jillienne's. I felt a twinge of guilt having compared Martina's cooking to my wife's.

After the clean-up, we had a few games of crib. Again, a little guilt as that was also Jilly's favorite card game. As I was leaving Martina asked me if I would like to go to a Neil Diamond concert with her on the twenty-sixth of July as she had bought an extra ticket hoping I would say yes. I wondered if I had told her that he was one of my favorite singers. I heartily accepted, and told her that I would call her after I returned from Shelton. Now, in retrospect, even though I had no intention of doing so, my having a cozy dinner with her at her home, and accepting the concert invitation, I wondered if I was encouraging her to believe that our relationship was advancing past friendship.

I left for home on June 25th as I wanted to beat the rush of the July long weekend. I asked myself why I still called Shelton home as there certainly wasn't a home to go back to. I pulled into the Family Motel at two in the afternoon planning on having a nap before going to the retirement home. I was greeted gleefully by the woman in reception.

"Hi Jordan, I was hoping you would be checking in before my shift ended. I am so happy to see you..." She said coming out from behind the desk. "Would it be all right if I hugged you?"

She had caught me completely off guard. What could I do but return her embrace though somewhat stiffly. "This is a surprise Marlayna...what on earth are you doing here?"

"Thank heavens you still remember me." She said laughing.

"You haven't changed much." I answered.

"I'm afraid that isn't so, but look at you...still the same rugged, handsome and robust Jordan. The reason I moved back is because of Donna; she is ill and needs me, and I don't have much of a life anymore, and so I came back to look after her."

"What about your husband and children?"

She laughed nervously and invited me to take a seat on the divan. "Which husband? I've had two or three you know, and the children are grown and have moved out of London. There are no grandchildren, so there was nothing holding me there. An old friend needed me, so here I am."

She hadn't changed, she was still unpredictable. Donna and she had been close friends many years ago, but their friendship had suffered when she had returned to England leaving her life here behind. That life had included me. Donna and her husband Cole were old school mates. They had introduced me to Marlayna, and were going to stand up for us at our wedding. As providence would have it, there was no wedding: I was eternally grateful for that. I went on to fall in love and marry Jillienne, and never looked back. Cole had told me a while ago, even before Donna became sick that Marlayna was planning on coming back for a visit, and had asked about me. I had thought nothing of it, but here she was sitting next to me, and acting as though it was nineteen seventy two, and that we were still lovers.

She placed her hand over mine; a gesture I did not appreciate.

"Jordan," she said woefully, "is there any word on your wife's whereabouts? I feel so badly for you and your family. I understand that she left without telling you where or why she was going?"

I did not want to discuss Jillienne's disappearance with her. I removed my hand from under hers. "Perhaps you should be focusing on the family you left behind instead of mine. Take it from me; you should cherish what you have for it could all vanish in an instant."

"Don't get me wrong Jordan, I love my children, but my marriages just didn't work out. Truth is; I never let go of my feelings for you." She said wistfully.

I stood up. "That was a long time ago, and I am sorry that your marriages…was it two or three, didn't work, but mine did. It is still intact and always will be. Now if you don't mind, I would appreciate my room key."

"I didn't mean to insinuate anything Jordan. I really just want to catch up. Do you think we could meet later for coffee or a drink?"

I had planned on a short visit with Donna and Cole, but that was out of the question now. Periodically, Jillienne and I would meet up with them when we came up to visit our parents. Secretly, I think Donna resented me for not patching things up with Marlayna. She and Jilly never really hit it off. I had not heard that she was sick and so was curious as to what her illness was. Marlayna said that she had recently been diagnosed with MS. I said that I was sorry to hear that, and that it must be pretty severe if she required a full time nurse. Marlayna said that she was not here in the capacity of a nurse so much but more so as a friend.

"I wasn't aware that you two had remained close." I remarked as I took the key from her. "Tell her that I wish her the best." I picked up my duffle and turned to leave.

"Why don't you tell her yourself?"

"Perhaps I will. I'll see how my time goes."

"And, that drink?"

"Probably not going to happen. Take care."

I had no intention of ever seeing her again, but she had other ideas. I arrived back at the motel after dinner with Jilly's and my parents. I was taking them on a little excursion the next day and then there would be all the July festivities so I planned on being very busy. I had no sooner turned on the light in my room when there was a knock on the door. I opened it to find Marlayna standing there wearing tight blue jeans and a low cut blouse, and a big smile on her face. She was holding a bottle of bourbon and two glasses.

"I thought I would take the chance and see if you could refuse me twice."

"I'll have a drink with you Marlayna just for old time's sake, but only one, and not here." I practically pushed her out the door. "We can sit downstairs by the pool."

I tried steering her away from any conversation that was leading up to discussing our ill-fated relationship. I was not very successful and I ended up leaving her in tears.

"I have no desire to go back there and rehash what went wrong. We were never going to work out in the long run. Just because you are in between marriages, and my wife is AWOL, does not mean that we are going to take up with each other again. I am not ripe for any kind of relationship, especially one that was a disaster, so you can quit coming on to me. You tried this once before remember…it didn't work then and it isn't going to work now. The reason I didn't give you a second chance then was because I was already in love with Jillienne, and she is still the reason why there will never be anyone else. I am still in love with her, and I always will be; no one can ever take her place. Please take your peace offering and go, and don't embarrass yourself anymore. I do wish that you find some happiness, but it can't be with me. Goodbye."

Jillienne did not know about Marlayna. There was no reason for me to have told her about a failed relationship that happened long before I even knew she existed. I can honestly say that I had never thought about Marlayna once in all the years that Jilly and I had been together. Perhaps I had fudged the truth a bit telling her that I was already in love with Jillienne when she had returned to Shelton and wanted me to give her another chance, but it didn't matter anyhow. I was done with her then, and seeing her again meant nothing to me. I wanted to get home and find my wife waiting for me.

I spent the next few weeks attending to things that I had been neglecting around the house. The garden plot was overgrown with weeds, the rose arbor was falling apart, there were cracks in the sidewalk that needed filling, and the pool needed cleaning. I made the pool a priority as I had promised the twins that I would get to it as soon as I got home from Shelton. This was the third summer without Jilly. The first year without her had been the worst. I hadn't been able to carry on with our Sunday brunches or summer barbecues around the pool. I had no interest in keeping the yard up so had hired someone to do so. Last summer I was partially able to get myself back on track. This year I was going to make it all about my granddaughters. It was painfully obvious more and more every day that my sweetheart was not coming back so I best get on with life without her. I wished myself good luck with that project.

Faith had ended up staying another week in Drumheller. I picked her up from the airport on July tenth. She talked non-stop all the way home filling me in on all the things she had done with Cree, and how much fun it was going to be working with him in Peru. I told her I hoped she wouldn't be too disappointed if that plan fell through. She said that she was going one way or the other, but she was pretty sure that her application was going to be accepted. For her sake, I wanted it to be so, but it was just going to be another heartache for me. She asked how things had been going for me and how was my trip to Shelton. We had talked on the phone a few times while she was away, but not in any great detail. I informed her that Hope had enrolled in some summer classes and that I had volunteered to look after the twins so I had been keeping busy.

The first thing she did when she walked into the house was check the mail to see if there was anything for her from the university. I told her that I would have called her if there had been.

"Did you check any of these messages on the answering machine Dad?" She turned it on and replayed two messages from Virginia, two from Clay, one from Rusty, and six from Martina. She asked if I had returned any of the calls.

"Of course; I talked to Clay, but never connected with Rusty. I guess he's out of cell service."

"Why so many calls from Martina; have you seen her?"

"No Faith, I have not seen her and I don't know why she keeps calling."

"And Virginia, have you seen her?"

"I told you I have been busy, and maybe I don't feel like talking."

She said that I should call Virginia. I told her I would tomorrow now that she was home to help with the twins. I did manage to catch Virginia the next day and had a brief conversation with her. I assured her that all was well and that I was keeping busy entertaining my granddaughters. She was on the run as she had a plane to catch as she was going on a much needed vacation to Europe with a colleague. I asked her if her friend was male or female. She had laughed and said that she was still waiting for me to drop her off my double. We planned a luncheon for August.

I had no sooner placed the phone back in its cradle when it rang. Thinking it was Virginia, I answered by asking her what she had forgotten.

"Well, I certainly haven't forgotten you Dan…but perhaps you have me."

It was Martina. "Sorry, I was just finishing up a conversation with my daughter." I had no idea why I had lied to her. "No, I have not forgotten you."

I explained about my situation with the girls and apologised for not returning her calls. We chatted for a few minutes before she asked me if I was still going to the Neil Diamond concert with her. I told her that I was looking forward to it. She invited me to dinner, but I declined citing family obligations for the next two weeks. She was disappointed and said that if I changed my mind the offer stood for any night should I find myself free. I thanked her and said that I would be in touch before the concert.

The rest of July went by in a flash. Every day was a new adventure with Hannah and Lannah. We visited cultural landmarks like the indoor tropical gardens at the Bloedel Observatory in Queen Elizabeth Park and the Vancouver Planetarium. Other days we'd take in a matinee or spend it at Playland trying out different carnival rides. We even took the ferry and spent two nights in Victoria and had afternoon tea at Jilly's favorite hotel, the Empress. We spent one evening with Connor and his wife Beatrice, and my fifteen month old grandson, Joshua. The visit went exceedingly well. Connor asked me if I would help him with something which was just a way to ask me questions about Jillienne without upsetting the twins. There was nothing new so there was nothing to tell him. In a round-about way he apologised for the accusations he had made regarding my fidelity to his mother. He then asked me if I was seeing anyone. I told him I hadn't given up totally on his mother yet, so no, I was not romantically involved with anyone.

As it so happened I ran into Martina at Sear's shopping centre the following Saturday. The twenty year old dishwasher was acting up so I thought that I may as well replace it before it ceased working completely. I enlisted her help in choosing a new one. Afterwards I invited her for coffee. Instead we decided to share a banana split, and that is how I was caught by Hope and the twins.

"I didn't expect to see you here today Dad." Hope said rather tersely.

"I decided to shop for a new dishwasher and Martina was kind enough to help me out…oh sorry, introductions are in order." I guiltily introduced my daughter to the woman I was sharing ice cream with. She acknowledged Martina rather coldly, and then said that she was under the impression that she and I were going to go dishwasher shopping together. What could I say, but that it was done and she was off the hook. I asked them to join us but Hope declined in spite of the twins protesting.

"Thank-you, but we're just going to grab a quick bite to eat, and we don't want to intrude."

I told her they wouldn't be intruding, but I could see that she was uncomfortable, and so I didn't insist they stay. It was later in the week that she brought Martina's name up. The girls were in the pool. Hope sat down beside me and asked me bluntly how far my relationship with Martina had advanced.

I poured her a glass of ice tea. "I will tell you the same thing I told Connor. I am not romantically involved with her or anyone else… any more questions?"

"I know it is just a matter of time before you completely give up on Mom and look for companionship with another woman. I'm just looking out for you Dad; I don't think Martina is right for you."

"I am curious as to how you came to this conclusion?"

"I don't know Daddy, it's just a feeling."

"One five minute meeting, and you made up your mind that she is all wrong for me…based on what pray tell?"

"Intuition I guess." She shrugged her shoulders.

"Well Sweetie, I am going to a concert with her next weekend, and then I will continue to have dinners with her, and go to the movies, and when I decide to take our relationship to the next level, I will be sure to tell you ahead of time." I winked at her. "How is your sex life going without your husband? Are you lonesome? Do you talk to his picture before going to bed, and do you cry because you wish he was still here…oh wait, he is…" I got up dismissing her by shaking my head, and called to the girls that it was time to get out of the water.

"Daddy, please…I'm sorry." Hope pleaded. "I know you are lonely; I just don't want you making a mistake with the wrong woman."

"Obviously you have no idea what lonely is or you wouldn't be sleeping alone. Go home Hope, and see to your own affairs." I walked away. I had never used that incensed tone with my daughter ever before.

Two days later Craig stopped by to see me. After a few minutes of idle chit-chat he said that Hannah and Lannah had told him that I had a girlfriend, and did that mean that their Gramma was really dead. That pulled at my heart strings. I assured him that I didn't have a girlfriend and that I would talk to the girls about their fears. He asked me how long I was prepared to wait for Jill. I told him forever.

"Just a few more months Jordan…three years, can you give it that long, three years, just another six or so months, can you do that? Promise me that you will come and talk to me if you find yourself slipping…can you do that Jordan?"

"Forever is a lot longer than three years Craig. What's with this three year thing?"

"Just a number, just a number…"

"You still believe that she is working something out don't you? Never mind, I know it's just a feeling. Speaking of working things out, how is your plan coming along."

He said things were coming together. I saw him to the door and told him to get some sleep. I picked up the phone and thought about calling Martina and asking her out for dinner. I put the phone down as I realized that I was just reacting to what Hope had said. I had never asked Martina out before; she was the one who made all the plans and I just went along with them. Jillienne had been my date for thirty one years, and I wasn't sure if I would ever be able to ask anyone else out without believing that I would be cheating on my wife, even if I didn't know whether she was still alive.

I arrived an hour early at Martina's the night of the concert. We exchanged pleasantries over hors d'oeurvres and cocktails. I had never been a fan of canapés or mixed drinks, but I was too polite to have refused her offer on the phone.

I surprised myself by cheering and whistling along with the crowd. Martina had obtained seats that provided us with a perfect view of the stage and Neil Diamond. It was just what I needed even though many of his songs reminded me of Jillienne.

Martina invited me in for coffee and dessert. Not wanting to ruin a somewhat perfect evening, I accepted having no idea that the dessert she was offering was herself. We were sitting on the couch waiting for the coffee talking about the concert when she changed the subject abruptly, and asked me if I would stay the night. I was shocked; not only by her invitation but by my stupidity for not recognizing that she had been flirting with me all night. As I was searching for a delicate way to say no, she stunned me further.

"I find that I have fallen in love with you Dan, and I want to show you just how much."

"I wish you hadn't said that Martina."

"Why?"

"I think you are just reacting to the moment. We had a wonderful evening, and you don't want it to end, but end it must. I enjoy your company, but there can never be anything more."

I started to get up, but she took my hand and asked me to hear her out. I made eye contact with her, but it was very unsettling. I withdrew my hand from hers.

"I have been in love with you for quite some time Dan; it's not just a passing fancy. I know you still love Jillienne just as I still love both of my husbands, but they are gone…they are all gone, and we owe it to ourselves to find a little happiness. Please give me a chance Dan. I promise you that you won't regret it. I know I could never take Jillienne's place…"

I interrupted her. I stood up and looked down at her. "That's right; not you or anyone will ever take her place. She's locked in my heart forever, and you saying that you love me makes me very sad. I can never return your feelings, and so I think it's best that we don't see each other anymore. Good-bye Martina."

"Just like that; I mean nothing to you? You're just going to walk out on me? It's that simple for you?" She beseeched.

I turned and looked at her and nodded. "Yes, it's just that simple."

I was a little disturbed that I hadn't felt anything one way or the other about her admission. I was just emotionless. I went on with my daily routines, and dismissed the incident from my mind as it had meant nothing to me. Virginia called me a few days later. We made a date to have lunch and met down town on Saturday, August ninth. After a brief grilling from her about my recent activities I managed to steer her away from my "love life" as she called it. I had laughed and said that it was still non-existent, but that I was interested to know how hers was. She elaborated on the many pleasures of her holiday which did not include any romantic encounters. She made a suggestion that if Jillienne didn't return in ten years and she had not found a suitable partner that maybe we could form an alliance of our own. I had laughed.

"It's a deal, where do you want to meet; perhaps the Empire State Building? I'll be seventy by then so I hope there's an elevator."

She kissed me on the cheek as we parted. "Sounds good to me."

The summer was winding down; only three more weeks until school resumed. Of course I would be busy before September 2nd, undertaking operational tasks such as timetables and the curricula, interviewing and welcoming new teaching staff, and catching up with the old. We had retired two seasoned teachers last summer, and one had moved to Alberta, so there would be three new staff members to meet. I was particularly interested to see who the board had hired as the new drama coach as it would be very difficult to replace the one who had retired. It might prove to be a very interesting year. I was looking forward to getting back into routine. I seemed to have managed to keep the personal turmoil of my life hidden from my professional duties for the last two years so there was no reason for me to believe that I couldn't keep up the charade.

In the meantime I had some final plans for excursions with Hannah and Lannah. I rented a small trailer and we spent a week exploring Vancouver Island, beach combing, hiking, surfing, and making memories. Hannah remarked one evening when we were sitting around the campfire that her grandmother should be with us. She asked me if I had ever done this trip with her, and why didn't the two of us go on holidays except to Shelton.

"You know your grandmother didn't like to fly or travel very far from home. I wanted to take her to places I had visited like Greece and Ireland. She promised that we would one day, but that day has come and gone. I put things off thinking there would always be a tomorrow so let that be a lesson to you two, tomorrow may never come."

They both hugged me and Hannah said she was sorry that I was so sad without Gramma, but they were too. Then they asked me if I thought their parents would get back together. I told them that I was pretty sure they would.

August 15th

Hope arrived to help us clean the trailer before I returned it. She was much more cheerful than she had been before we left. I could only hope that it was because of Craig. There was a note from Faith saying that she was spending the weekend with Cree's parents in Olympia, Washington. I guess I was on my own again. I started the washing machine, grabbed a beer, said hello to Jillienne, and settled down in the sunken living room to catch up on a weeks' supply of newspapers. The phone rang. It was Irene, Martina's daughter asking me if I had seen her mother today. I explained to her that I had been away and had not talked to her mother for several weeks. She said she was sorry to bother me but she was unable to get through to her mother and was very worried about her. I asked her "why", and she said that Martina's brother, Lou had died and that her mother was taking it very hard. They had returned from the funeral yesterday, but she hadn't heard from her mother since and she was not answering her phone. She explained that both her boys were sick in bed so she couldn't leave them alone and her husband had left on a business trip. She went on and on crying loudly until I told her that I would go and check up on her mother. She thanked me and made me promise to call her the minute I got there.

I skipped the elevator, electing to take the stairs to Martina's fifth floor apartment. I guess I was just delaying the inevitable as I was sure there would be crying and carrying on. I could see a glimmer of light coming from under her door and I heard the faint sound of music. She did not come to the door when I rang the doorbell, so I knocked; still no answer. I knocked a little harder the third time and called out to her that it was me. She opened the door and asked me what I was doing there. I told her Irene had called me and was worried about her as she wasn't answering the phone.

"Well, as you can see, I am perfectly fine so you can leave." She said defiantly.

I had to put my foot in the door or she would have shut it on me. I didn't think she was fine at all. She was dressed in jogging pants and a shapeless off the shoulder sweater, and her hair was uncombed. She was always so immaculately outfitted that I was a little stunned, but then, I knew what grief could do to a person. I asked her if I could come in.

"Suit yourself, but there is nothing here that you are interested in."

She walked away and sat down on the sofa in front of a half empty bottle of vodka. I asked her why she wasn't answering her phone. She said that her land line wasn't working and that she had lost her cell phone. I handed her mine and told her to call Irene. She told me to call her myself. After I assured her daughter that she was fine and explained the phone thing, I sat down beside her and asked what I could do for her.

She laughed. "You could get me some ice and have a little drink with me and then you can leave like the good boy you are."

One drink couldn't hurt. That was my first mistake.

I got up to get the ice. "I think I'll make some coffee while I'm here. When is the last time you ate or slept?"

"Who in the hell knows or cares? I don't. There is no one left who cares a flying fig about me."

"That isn't so Martina; you have Irene and your two delightful grandsons. They love and care about you very much. I am very sorry for your loss as I know Lou was very important to you."

I passed her the ice and she added some to both our glasses that were already half full of vodka. She was quiet for a few minutes. When her glass was empty she looked at me with tears in her eyes. "Why does everyone leave me Dan? My parents left me when I was fourteen and Lou took me into his home and raised me, and now he is gone, and all my friends are dead. I have been widowed two times over, and you left me too."

"I am here now, aren't I? Tell me what I can do for you?" I asked warily.

"Are you Dan? Are you really here for me?"

I didn't actually answer her but told her that I had make coffee and that I would make her something to eat. She said she wanted to lie down. I said I would help her into the bedroom.

"Are you going to come with me?" She asked suggestively.

"I'll stay with you to make sure you eat and until you fall asleep, okay? Whoa there, you're a little tipsy." I said catching her before she fell back unto the couch.

She took me by surprise throwing her arms around me and kissing me passionately. That was my second mistake…not breaking the kiss off sooner.

I removed her arms from around my neck. "You're not playing fair Martina! I gave you an inch and you took a mile. We've talked about this before; are you too inebriated to remember?"

"No, you are wrong; **we** have never talked about this. I tried, but you walked out on me."

"There is really nothing to talk about. I'm married and I still love my wife even if I don't know where she is. Those are the cold hard facts and…"

"I love my wife, yak, yak yak," she mimicked me as she stumbled towards her bedroom.

And, that was my third mistake…following her. In my own defense, I just wanted to make sure she got into bed before falling down. Instead she sat on the edge of it and patted a spot next to her inviting me to sit. I did not accept the invitation, but stood rigidly in front of her.

"Okay, suit yourself. You talk about the cold hard facts, but I don't think you have addressed them realistically. What is this therapist doing for you anyhow? It's been two and a half years Dan… Jillienne is not coming back. No one leaves for that long without

sending some sort of word to her family and the man that she loves…
no one. Is it possible that she didn't love you the way you say she did?"

"She loved me." I said blankly.

"Of course she did. I'm sorry, I shouldn't have said that. I know you are never going to forget her or replace her. You will love her forever just as I will always love my husbands, but they are gone Dan, they are gone and so is Jillienne. Don't we deserve some happiness? It may not work out for us, but I am willing to take the chance… please, just give me the chance."

She stood up and slipped her joggers off and pulled her sweater over her head. "I'm not so terribly hard to look at am I?"

An image of a seventeen year old Jillienne was clouding my mind.

I mumbled something about not being prepared for anything to happen between us. She took it the wrong way. She laughed and asked if I was worried about getting her pregnant or was I worried that she wasn't pure. She was talking, but it was Jillienne's voice that I heard. She opened up a drawer and extracted a Trojan condom. She was saying that she could take care of me. Why was my head so fuzzy? What was Jillienne saying about being pure…of course she was. I felt hands unbuttoning my shirt and caressing me, she was whispering my name, telling me that she loved me, pulling me into the bed…

It was like waking from a bad dream, a **really** bad dream. Someone was saying my name, over and over…who was Dan? Who the hell was Dan? Where the hell was I…oh God, no! What have I done? She was asking me if I was okay as I was scrambling to find my clothes…*she* was not Jillienne. No, no, this didn't happen. How did I get undressed…I had no recollection.

"Dan, what's wrong?" She was asking.

The only words I could get out were: "My name is not Dan."

I couldn't get out of the room fast enough. I found my shoes by the front door where I had left them. I had no idea where my socks were. I ignored the pleas coming from the bedroom and fled down the back stairs cursing all the way. Keys, where the hell were my car keys? I fumbled in every pocket; no keys. Damn it, I must have laid them down on the coffee table. There was no way in hell I was going back to get them. Phone, where was my phone…on the table with my keys. There was a convenience store two blocks away. Surely it would still be open…who the hell was I going to call? How could I explain to Hope or Clay why I had lost my keys? I caught my breath at the Mom and Pop store. They were closing but let me use the phone. I called a cab and had him drive me home to pick up my spare keys and then back to my car. Thank God Faith was in Olympia. How long had I been at Martina's? I needed to figure it out…how much time had I spent with her? Why couldn't I remember? I only had one drink…Christ, how did that saying go, "screwed, blued, and tattooed." Yup, I had crossed over the line. How was I ever going to explain it to Jillienne?

I arrived back home at nine P.M. I wondered if Hank had noticed my comings and goings. I tripped going up the back stairs and cursed loudly when the outside light blinked on. I felt like I was a teenager sneaking in the house after curfew. I heard a faint meow. Sorry Lionel, you'll have to wait until tomorrow. Lionel…what the hell was the matter with me? He was Jilly's cat and he had been gone almost as long as she had.

I stripped and threw my clothes in the washing machine along with the rest of the laundry and restarted the washer. I must have showered for half an hour, but I still felt dirty. I picked up a bottle of rye and the picture of Jillienne and crawled into bed. I confessed my infidelity to my wife begging her to forgive me.

I was jarred awake by the jangling of the phone. I ignored it thinking it was Martina.

"Where are you Jord ole boy? Why aren't you answering your cell?" It was Clay's voice on the answering machine.

I reached for the phone. Oh hell, I was supposed to have breakfast with him and Sandie. My head was pounding. "Sorry Clay; met up with an old buddy last night and tied one on. I'll have to take a rain check, apologise to Sandie for me will you?"

He laughed. "Been there, done that, no need for apologies. Call me later and give me the details…hair of the dog boy, hair of the dog."

I hung up. The empty bottle was on the floor. I couldn't have drunk the whole thing could I have? The answer was clear when I slipped on the wet floor. I pulled on a pair of chinos and staggered into the kitchen and put on a pot of coffee. Bathroom next, I need aspirin. Just a minute, just a damn minute…something was wrong. I went back into the bedroom and straight to the dresser. Jillienne's picture was missing. Did Craig take it to be laminated? No, he wouldn't do it without telling me. I went to the bed and pulled down the blankets. She was lying there all crumpled with shards of glass covering her face. I supposed that was why my arm was bleeding. I salvaged what was left of her. "I broke you for good this time didn't I sweetheart…I broke you, and I broke me too."

I wallowed in self- pity for the rest of the morning trying to remember the events of last night and wondering why my head hurt so much. I managed to pull myself together before Faith got home. After three frantic phone messages from Martina I seriously thought of unplugging the phones. I talked myself out of it because what if Jillienne phoned? She may not remember my cell number, but she would never forget our home number. For about the thousandth time I wondered what had happened to her mobile phone. Surely if she had taken it with her she would have called if she was able to. Supposition, supposition…where had it gotten me in two and a half years?

Faith was a ray of sunshine. She had me laughing in no time. I was going to miss that girl when she goes off to Peru with another man.

I had everything in order for the start of the new school year by August the twenty fifth. I was through with my consultations with the old and new faculty except for the new Drama coach. I was reading her credentials when I heard someone speak my name.

"Hello Jordan, are you waiting on me?"

Who was this woman calling me by my first name? I didn't know any Janelle Short.

"May I come in?"

I stood up. "Certainly, please pardon me. Have a seat, Ms. Short." There was something vaguely familiar about her.

She offered her hand smiling. "You don't remember me do you Jordan?"

I shook my head. "Give me a moment…Nell, Nell Chalmers? Well, I'll be damned! You're the new drama teacher?"

"Surprise!"

"So when did this all come about, you finishing school and all? I thought you were going to live off your parents and bum around Europe for the rest of your life. Sit down please; we have a lot of catching up to do."

"Surely you don't want to go back to the last time we saw each other? I'd rather forget that if you don't mind. I understand from a mutual friend that you did marry that girl you ran after that day, so it all turned out all right after all, didn't it?"

"How long has it been since you last talked to this "mutual" friend?"

"No secret, it was Barrie Brown. You may or may not know that he was killed in an automobile accident five years ago, so not since just before that."

"No, I hadn't heard, but then I don't keep in touch with any of the old crew from college. I will make this brief because you are going to hear it via the Q.E. grapevine anyway. I did marry Jillienne. We have four children and as far as I was concerned, we had the perfect marriage. Two and a half years ago, she left home and has not been heard of since. We do not know if she is alive or dead. I don't want to embellish anymore, but I am sure that gossip runs rampantly through the hallways so you will have no problem forming your own conclusion as to why my wife left me." I said conclusively. "Now, let's talk about you."

She appeared to be genuinely distressed and uttered her sympathy, but I was an expert on expressions of pity so I had already tuned her words out. We spoke no more of Jillienne.

I found my cell phone and my keys in the mailbox when I got home that afternoon.

Faith informed me that her Aunt Audrey had phoned and wanted to talk to me about her mother's worsening condition. She was afraid that she had Alzheimer's. I told Faith that I had no intention of discussing her grandmother's health with her aunt and that Jillienne and I would look after it as soon as she got home.

Faith stared and me. "What's the matter with you Daddy… Mommy is not coming home. She is most assuredly dead. I thought you had accepted that. You're regressing, and you are scaring me… please Daddy, please, you need help."

I pulled her into my arms. "You're right Honey, I'm sorry, but you know I don't accept that she is dead; she is just *gone*. The guilt is eating me up, and sometimes it is overwhelming and I don't even realize what I am saying. I miss her so much Faith."

"I know you do Daddy; we all do, but we've told you a thousand times that you have nothing to feel guilty about."

She had no idea what guilt I was referring to. I phoned Virginia's office to see if my old time slot was available; it wasn't so I made one for the following week. I had no sooner returned the phone to its cradle when it rang startling me a little. I always let the answering machine get the calls these days. I picked it up as soon as I heard Virginia's voice. She asked me if I could come in tomorrow at noon. I said I could and could I bring her lunch. She said I knew what she liked.

I stopped at the Deli and ordered her favorite; pastrami and Swiss cheese on rye, and a little custard éclair. I wondered to myself if it was odd that I knew what my therapist's food preferences were. Her receptionist was not at her desk. I supposed she was on her lunch break. I knocked on Virginia's door. She opened it immediately with open arms. I did not return her hug, I handed her the deli bag and sat down on the sofa.

"Oh oh, something's wrong." She said intuitively. "What's happened? Have you heard something regarding Jillienne?"

"Nothing new, but it does involve her." I answered solemnly.

She pulled her chair up opposite me. "How so Dan?"

"I wish you wouldn't call me that."

"What do you want me to call you then?"

"Oh, I don't know…cheater, adulterer, liar, martyr, betrayer…I am sure there are a thousand words to describe me, take your pick. You can't call me Dan because he is someone I don't know, and you can't call me Jordan because that guy doesn't exist anymore."

She offered me her hands; I rebuffed her again. I got up and walked over to the window so that my back was to her. "I crossed over the line that I had drawn so firmly. I was unfaithful to Jillienne… I broke our marriage vows."

I heard her intake of breath, but she didn't say anything. I turned to face her. "So what do you think of your golden boy now?"

"I think no less of him than I did before he walked in my door and made a confession that is eating him up. All the values that he placed on his marriage promises and his morals have somewhat dimmed, but I promise you that they are not lost. You are human, and so you stumbled a little, but you have not fallen off your foundation. Please come back and sit down and we can talk about it."

"You want to know about my disgusting act of betrayal?"

"I think you need to talk about it so it's not all so consuming. Will you let me help you absolve yourself of what you feel is unforgiveable? Are we talking about you and Martina?"

"There is no me and Martina. I never want to hear her name or see her again."

"Okay, got you. Had you been out on a date?"

"I told you before that I don't date!" I said emphatically. "I went over to her apartment because her daughter had called me saying that she was worried about her because she wasn't answering the phone. Mar…her brother had died, and she was taking it pretty hard. Irene, that's the daughter couldn't go so good ole what's his name here said he'd go and check up on her. I should mention that I hadn't seen her for weeks because she had told me she loved me and wanted to have sex with me."

"She said that specifically, that she wanted to have sex?"

"Okay, if we are splitting hairs, she said she wanted me to stay over. I told her that was never going to happen, and I walked out never planning or wanting to see her again."

"You're a kind and caring person Dan…sorry, what do you want me to call you?"

I ignored her question. "Yeah, so this kind and caring guy went to check on her. She was fine and drowning her sorrows in a bottle of vodka. She told me to leave. I wish I had. Instead I made some coffee and had a drink with her. Next thing I am in the bedroom with her and she takes her clothes off and starts on mine. I remember nothing else until it is all over with."

"So you let her undress you…"

"I told you I don't remember!"

"There must have been kissing and touching…"

"What part of "I don't remember, don't you understand?" I bellowed.

"You're getting awfully testy with me. Do you want me to know the details or not?"

"I followed her into the bedroom to make sure she didn't fall as she was pretty much plastered. She had already plied me with kisses which I guess I didn't actually refuse. There, are you happy. I told her again that I was still in love with Jillienne, and she said she still loved her husbands, but they were dead, they were all dead and never coming back. It was at that point that I felt a little woozy. I remember her offering me a condom."

"Did you put it on? Did she help you?"

"Don't know."

"You are not going to like this next question, but I am going to ask it anyhow. Sorry, but did you have an orgasm?"

"You're right, I don't like the question, and I don't like you very much right now either."

"Well, I am not here to win any popularity contest. Do you want to talk or not?"

"Maybe I would rather you just be my friend right now."

"Okay, but I am still going to ask you the same question."

"I will answer it the only way I know how… I don't remember, but there was evidence."

"And, I believe the reason you can't remember is because you were drugged."

"You think Martina drugged me? That's a little far-fetched don't you think?"

"How else do you explain your lack of recall?"

"I can't, but I'm not some teenage boy who was lured into bed by a conniving older woman Virginia. We are talking about two sixty year olds here."

"Oh, so now you are saying it was consensual?"

"I don't know what the hell I am saying."

"Then let me say it for you. You went to Martina's apartment solely to see if she was okay, am I right? You just wanted to comfort her. You made coffee and accepted a drink from her, right?"

"Yes."

"Did you see her pour the vodka into your glass?"

"No, but that doesn't prove that she slipped me a ruffie."

"You are right, it doesn't. Has this ever happened to you before… complete lack of recollection? I have observed you over the past six months, and I know that you have the capacity to recall total conversations from thirty years past. This sudden lack of recall is rather disturbing to me. The night in question was two weeks ago?"

"It was a Friday, August 15th."

"So, ten days ago approximately. It is a little late for a blood test, but some drugs do stay in the blood stream for a long time, but there is another way to find out what really went down."

"You want to hypnotise me?"

"I want you to ask Martina if she drugged you."

I laughed vulgarly. "You what? You want me to come right out and ask her? That would mean I would have to see her again, and that is not going to happen!"

Virginia shrugged her shoulders, closed her notebook and got up. "Suit yourself and live with wondering what really transpired between the two of you for the rest of your days."

"It's not going to consume me Virginia."

"Then why are you here confessing to me? Do you want me to absolve you of what you consider was a sin? Sorry, only a priest can do that. Perhaps you should be having this conversation with your friend the Padre?"

"Okay, okay, you have made your point. I'll call her and ask her."

"That's not good enough; you need to see her reaction to your question, you need to be looking in her eyes when she answers you. A person can lie their way out of anything over the phone. No, you need to be front and center with her."

"I guess I can come up with some excuse to see her."

"Do you have any feelings at all for her Dan…is it Dan or Jordan, what name do I call you?"

"I guess I am still Dan; I'll be Jordan when Jillienne comes home. She was a friend, someone I could have dinner with, and go to functions with. I never expected anything else from her but friendship."

"So, you don't hate her for taking advantage of you?"

I shook my head. "You think I am really naïve don't you? You think I let a woman lure me into her bedroom without me suspecting what her motives were? Suppose if it is all a ruse and I knew exactly what was happening, but I just can't accept that I cheated on Jillienne, and you are right…my confessing to you will make me feel better, and the guilt will all go away?"

"I think we both know you better than that. So, what are you going to do?"

"I will give your idea some thought. I will have to come up with a damn good reason why I haven't returned any of her phone calls and suddenly want to see her again."

"I have no doubt that she will accept anything you tell her. I also doubt this will make you feel any better, but you did not commit a sin. Jillienne has been gone for a very long time. I don't want to agree with Martina that she is dead, but as for her returning is very doubtful, and I thought you had come to terms with that. I do not consider what transpired between you and Martina as cheating on your wife. Most men would have moved on a long time ago. Don't be so hard on yourself Dan."

"Well, I am not most men as you have been so fond of telling me time after time, but then most men don't have a wife like Jillienne."

Faith and I picked Cree up from the airport for the Labor Day weekend. They kept me busy rushing me from celebration to celebration. Sometime during the weekend I decided that I would make the dreaded call to Martina. Part of me was hoping that she wouldn't be home. She answered on the second ring. Without apologising I asked her if she was still talking to me. She said yes, and that she had been hoping I would call. I asked her if she would like to go to dinner on Saturday night. Why hadn't I just asked if I could come over? Did I figure that I would have the answer to whether she had drugged me in the first few minutes of seeing her, and then there would be no reason to go out to dinner? She accepted enthusiastically.

I then called Virginia; she wasn't home. I left a message on her machine saying that I hoped she was having a pleasant holiday, and that I had thrown down the gauntlet and was seeing Martina on Saturday. I chose not to call her cell as I didn't want to interrupt whatever she was doing. I hoped she was on a hot date…or did I?

I had a message from her on my home phone when I got home from the first day back at school on the second. She said she was sorry she had missed my call, but that she had taken a quick trip home to Windsor to see her parents. I hadn't known they were still alive, but then why would I? I guess I should have asked. She asked me if I could come by for lunch the next day. I left a message saying that it wasn't possible, but I'd see her early next week as planned.

Faith had gone back to Drumheller with Cree as she had not enrolled in any classes for the semester due to her up and coming wedding. She had left me strict instructions to feed "the cat" every night just in case it was Lionel. I hadn't the heart to tell her that I was pretty sure it wasn't, but I put food out anyhow. I was doing so when I thought I caught a glance of a busy tail exiting the back yard when I heard the phone ringing. I caught it just as the answering machine was picking up, and I heard Virginia speaking.

"I guess we have been playing phone tag; what did we ever do before answering machines?"

I laughed. "I have no idea. I'm here now though." I was happy to hear her voice.

"Oh good! I'm sorry, I forgot about school, damn it. I kind of wanted to talk to you again before you see "her', but I guess not, and I know you are busy with the family thing on Sunday, but for sure I'll see you on Tuesday right?"

I told her she would regardless of the outcome. We made small talk for a few minutes. I asked her about her visit with her parents and she asked if I was happy to be back at school. I said I was as it took my mind off a lot of things. I apologized for not being able to have lunch. She said she understood.

"Unless…" I left the thought hanging in the air.

"Unless what Dan?"

"Nothing, my mind was just wandering, sorry I best be hanging up. Be good okay?"

"Good luck on Saturday Dan…be careful okay? You know you can call me any time right?"

"I know; thanks." I set the phone down.

Jordan Landon, you stupid ass, what the hell is the matter with you? You know damn well that you wanted to ask her to go out… out on a real date. Isn't it time you quit pussy-footing around and took the plunge? She can always say no, you know. Oh yeah, that's the problem…you are pretty sure that she won't say no, and then what? How the hell would it work? She knows all about Jillienne, she knows that you are still in love with her, she knows everything. Hey, she's just a friend…yeah, a friend that you've been thinking about more than you should. Damn it! What was stopping me from calling Virginia back and asking her if she would like to have dinner with me? Was Jillienne in the room with me or just in my head? Did I just imagine that I heard her say, "It's not the right time Jordy, don't do it, don't do it."

CHAPTER 6

There's Always Another Song

Saturday, September 6*th*, 2008
Four P.M.

The stereo greeted me loudly as I walked in the back door. I yelled at Faith asking her why she had it turned up so high. I was a little surprised that she had left it on the Country Classics channel. As I reached for the volume control, one of my all- time old favorite singers, Sonny James, came on offering his rendition of Empty Arms. I listened for a second familiarizing myself with the words. I turned it down and walked away saying out loud, "Yeah, if you would just walk through that door Jillienne, my arms wouldn't be empty anymore."

Apparently, Faith wasn't home. I was going to have to lecture that girl again about leaving the doors unlocked. I turned the shower on while shedding my highly scented sweaty clothing. It was always a workout with Clay on the tennis courts. I was cutting it pretty close time wise with my date with Martina. Date…why was I referring to my meeting with her as a date?

I came out of the bathroom to hear Chrystal Gayle belting out "When I get Over You." I walked over to the stereo and turned it to an easy listening channel. Johnny Mathis was singing "I'll Be Seeing You." Every word reminded me of Jillienne, and only enforced my feelings of loneliness without her. I shut the stereo off; enough was enough.

I had done a lot of soul searching in the week that had led up to my calling Martina. I had almost convinced myself that things weren't as appalling as I had made them out to be. Perhaps I had been a willing participant in the "episode", but I just couldn't accept it. Now weeks later I had come to realise that the aftermath wasn't as earth shattering as I had once believed it to be…after all, Jillienne was most definitely not coming back to me. Everything and nearly everyone said so. I had vowed to make a conscience effort to move on for everyone's sake, not just my own. My first step was to quit listening to sad songs.

I found myself whistling as I pulled my Vancouver Canuck jersey over my head. It was number 14, Alex Burrough's number; he was Jillienne's favorite. We were great fans of the team, but I had not attended a single game since her disappearance. Perhaps it was time I bought season passes again. Martina shared my love of the game, but no, it wouldn't be with her. I don't know with whom it would be then… or did I? It might be a mistake to even think about it, and it would be yet another betrayal to Jilly's memory. I was getting ahead of myself again.

I picked up Jillienne's photograph as I might not feel like talking to her later. I sighed.

"I've lived two and a half years without you Honey…that is if you can call it living." I touched my fingers to my lips and placed them on hers. "Sorry Baby, but I've decided to try and move on. It's taken me all this time to get to this point, but I am pretty sure that you are never coming back to me, so it's time I let you go. I am not looking forward to coming home to an empty house every day. Faith will be gone soon and so there will be just me and this big empty house, this house that you and I made into a home. I'm not sure I can live here by myself; I don't know. Maybe I should sell it; what do you say? Would you be all right with that? I hope you will understand whatever I decide to do. One thing is for sure though, I will not be moving anyone else into our house…no, that would be sacrilegious. This Martina that I told you about says that she in love with me, but I feel she has deceived me so I don't know what my feelings for her are right now. After tonight I am hoping it will be perfectly clear. There are a few questions I need answered about what happened "that night" before I can move on, and I am pretty sure it will be without her as a friend as that is the only way I ever thought about her. I cannot see myself falling head over heels in love with anyone else like I did with you. I will never feel that kind of love ever again. No, that ship sailed the day you walked out on me. I could never replace you, but I need to find some peace of mind, and maybe I will if I can finally admit that you are never coming back. I'm just so lonesome, lonesome for physical contact, holding hands, kissing soft lips, holding someone in my arms and telling them how much I love them…them, what the hell? There is no them, it's you and only you! Can anyone else ever fill that void? I think I need to try before I wither up and blow away. Are you wondering if I have someone on my mind? I can't answer that for sure, but there is someone who is very special to me, and I just might take the plunge. Hell Jilly, I don't even know what I am saying…you've been by girl for so many years, I have no idea how to even ask someone out. I just don't know if I can do it. I may just change my mind, and wait for you forever. One minute I tell myself that it truly is time to let you go, and then the next, I'm telling myself to wait…wait just a little bit longer. You're right my love, I'm a little bit crazed, hell, maybe I'm fully submerged! Sleep peacefully my sweet; there will always be an empty space in my heart without you. I will miss you all the days of my life and I will never forget you, no matter what." I ran my fingers over her beautiful face. I was feeling especially vulnerable, but I didn't know why.

The phone rang. I knew Faith was home because she had yelled saying she was home, and asking what was for supper. I guess she had forgotten that I was going out. She had never met Martina, but she had already formed an opinion of her and it wasn't favourable. She never answered the house phone so I picked it up and said, "Hello." I thought it was either Virginia or Hope. I couldn't have been more wrong.

A little voice said, "Jordy, is that you?"

I had to sit down. My heart was racing. Only one person ever called me Jordy. No, it couldn't be… I must be having some sort of hallucination because I had been talking to her and I was still holding her picture.

"Jordy, are you there?"

I found my voice. "Jillienne, my God, is it you?" I was angst-ridden that it was her and scared to death that it wasn't.

"Yes, it's me Jordan; will you come and get me?"

Come and get her…I would go to the ends of the earth to get her. I managed to ask her where she was and she said she was at the airport… she was at the Vancouver airport in Melody's Coffee Shop, and did I know where it was.

"You're here? My God, Jillienne, where have you been? Are you all right?" I stammered.

"I will tell you when I see you okay? Can you come now?"

"Yes, yes I will find you. I'm on my way, half an hour maybe more, depending on traffic. Stay put, don't go anywhere Jillienne."

"I won't Jordan."

I heard a noise at the bedroom door; it was Faith munching on an apple.

"Who was on the phone Dad? Was it Hope?"

"You heard it ring?" I wasn't actually sure that it had.

"Well you answered it…you had better hang up as the operator is telling you to do so."

I looked down and the phone and Jilly's picture were still in my hands. I passed them to her and grabbed my keys and a jacket. I touched Faith on the shoulder affectionately.

"Call your sister and tell her to get over here! Your mother is home. I'm going to the airport to pick her up."

"Dad…Dad, what are you saying?"

"You heard me, your mother is back!" I slammed the front door with her voice echoing in my ears. I cursed all the way to the car because it was raining again…raining raining… just like the night Jillienne had come to me so many years ago. Please let her be coming to me again.

I must have went through every emotion possible; joy that my baby was home, fear that it was some prank, anger because she had left me, apprehension…what would I say to her, how would I react when I saw her, disgust because I had been unfaithful. She would know it because guilt was written all over my face. Then I would rotate back to being angry with her again, but I still loved her…oh, how I loved her. I was driving myself crazy anticipating of how it would feel to hold her and kiss her. Just a minute, just a minute, who said she was coming home to you? All she asked was if you would come and get her. Anger again; she was going to tell me she wanted a divorce. Yes, she really had left me for another man…another man… suppose if it was a woman, the woman she had last been seen with? Would I let her go just like that? Was my love for her greater than the animosity I felt for anyone who had stolen her away from me? Calm down Jordan, calm down, give her a chance and let her explain… suppose if it really is a prank?

I turned the radio on hoping to drown out the voices in my head. Frank Sinatra was crooning "Some Enchanted Evening"; yeah that was going to calm me down. That was Jillienne's and my signature song dating back to the first day our eyes met across a crowded room. Maybe, just maybe, that was a good sign.

How I managed to arrive at my destination completely unscathed was a miracle in itself. Now, please God, let there be another miracle waiting inside for me. I pulled into one of the 15 minute loading spaces thanking my lucky stars that there was one available. Anxiety had taken over my exhilaration again as I raced through the airport. After a few agonizing minutes I realized I had no idea where I was going. Breathing hard I asked a security guard for directions. I couldn't remember where Jillienne had said she would be. He told me to relax and that we would figure it out. He rattled off a few names of cafes and coffee shops. When he got to Melody's, I stopped him. He directed me and I was off and running again. He yelled at me to slow down. I took the escalator two steps at a time, took a right and carried on until I saw an overhead arrow pointing the way. It was an open area with a few tables and chairs and a counter where a man sat reading a newspaper. There was a young couple sitting closely together at a table playing on an electronic device, and a lone older woman at the back. She was stooped over the table and her head and shoulders were completely concealed by a large flowing shawl; I guess it was what Jilly would have called a pashmina. Anyhow, it was not Jillienne; she was not here. Disheartened I started to leave. Something made me turn around and ask the gentleman at the counter if he had seen a petite, middle aged woman with long auburn hair. He said no one like that had been in the cafe that he had seen. I thanked him and was about to walk away when he said that I might want to check with the older lady at the back table as there had been another woman sitting with her up until just a few minutes ago.

A little voice was whispering to me. "She may not look the same Jordan." I turned and took a step towards the woman. At that precise second she lifted her head… a faint smile crossed her face. Peeping out from underneath that oversized scarf were my Jillienne's dark brown eyes. I had a lump in my throat the size of a grapefruit; my legs felt like lead.

"Hi Jordan." It was the same voice I had heard on the telephone less than an hour ago.

I crossed the floor and knelt down beside her. I took her hands in mine. "Jillienne, Jillienne, is it really you? I never thought I would ever see you again…where have you been? My God, what has happened to you?"

"It is me Jordan, and I'm all right, I'm all right now."

How could she be? She was but a shell of herself. Under the heavy Cossack coat and long cloak- like scarf she was wearing I could tell something was dreadfully wrong. What atrocities had she suffered? Was she fleeing from someone or something…why else would she be dressed the way she was? She was almost unrecognizable.

She touched my face with soft, cold fingers. She was shaking. "I'll tell you everything Jordan, everything. Can we just get out of here?"

"Yes, yes of course."

She started to get up, but faltered. I caught her before she fell. She thanked me and asked if I could get her cane for her which had fallen to the floor. I passed it to her and asked her where her luggage was. She pointed to a wooden handled fabric bag on the floor. I picked it up wondering how that was all she had to show for two and a half years of her life. I put one arm around her and took her hand with my other. She told me she was going to be a little slow. I told her it didn't matter because we had all the time in the world. I was euphoric, but my heart was breaking as I knew something terrible had happened to her. God only knew what it was.

Her eyes were moist and her voice was sad. "Maybe now we do Jordan… maybe now we do."

What unspeakable horrors had she endured? Had she indeed been held captive? Had she been starved, or someone's sex slave…oh God, please don't let it be so! I hoped I had the fortitude to mend her and understand whatever had taken her away from me and be her hero again.

She stopped abruptly at the escalator and shook her head. "I can't Jordan, I can't."

"It's okay Honey; I'll see if there's an elevator."

"No!" She protested. "I can do the stairs."

I held on to one hand as she carefully placed her cane on the first step, then one foot and then the other. It was slow going, but we made it. She apologised for being so slow. I wondered why she had objected so vehemently to taking the elevator.

I was pleased to see that my car had not been towed. I opened the door for her and helped her in. I reached around her and buckled her up. It had become a habit of mine ever since she had been pregnant with Rusty. I would snap the buckle in place and then kiss her and she would smile. I had continued that ritual right up until she had gone away. I looked up at her now. Should I kiss her; was she expecting me to? She touched my face again and I kissed her fingers. There were tears in both our eyes. I quickly rose before I lost what was left of my self-control. I tossed her bag and cane into the back seat and climbed in behind the wheel unsure of what to do or say next.

She asked me where I was taking her.

"Home, of course." I replied.

"It's not my home anymore Jordan. I gave up those rights a long time ago." She said remorselessly.

"It's still your home Jillienne, and it always will be."

"Do you live in that big house all alone Jordan?"

I knew what she was asking without actually asking it outright... she wanted to know if I had moved another woman into the house.

"Faith still lives with me, at least for a few more weeks anyhow."

"Where is she going?"

"She's getting married."

"My baby's getting married? Do I know him, is he a nice boy?"

"You'll like him, he's a charmer." I looked at her. "You are going to be here to see her get married aren't you? You're not going to go away again are you?" I asked nervously.

"I'm sorry Jordan. I know you will never be able to forgive me." She said sorrowfully.

I reached out and squeezed her hand. "I will hold off passing judgement until I know what drove you away. Do you want to wait until we get home to talk? We can't sit here for much longer, but we can drive down the road a ways and park in the hotel lot if you want."

"Okay, because I don't want you to be driving when I tell you, and you need to know before we get back to the house."

CHAPTER 7

The Arcadia Project

I didn't like the sound of that. I started the car and she asked me how Hope and the girls, and the boys were. I said they were all fine and would be so happy to see her. She then asked about Clay, and our parents. I did not tell her about her mother's dementia. She did not ask about her sister, Audrey. There was so much bad blood between those two, and it had never mellowed through the ages. Audrey had called me periodically to ask if there was any news about her sister. She invited me to dinner several times, but I always declined. Then there was that call about her mother which I hadn't returned. To be perfectly honest, I didn't trust her. She had never married, but did like someone on her arm and in her bed, and I was not about to fall victim to her conniving ways. Jillienne didn't ask about Craig. Sometimes I thought she loved him more than her own sons so I thought it was odd that she hadn't asked how he was.

I parked near the front where there were lots of lights as I wanted to be able to see her face, I hadn't even turned the engine off when she spoke and shocked the living daylights out of me.

"I had a brain tumor Jordan."

I wasn't sure I had heard her correctly. I turned to face her. "What…"

"I had a brain tumor. It was inoperable and terminal." She said without emotion.

"A brain tumor…I don't understand. Why wouldn't you have told me…wait a minute…you said it was terminal, and yet, here you are sitting next to me… how is this possible? "I was dumbfounded.

"I was offered an experimental treatment and I accepted it. That's why I went away. If I had of stayed, I would have been dead within weeks. It would have been an unusually painful death and you would have had to watch me suffer, so I took the 11-14% chance that the treatment could work. I'm here as you stated, so I guess it worked."

"My God Jillienne, why didn't you tell me?"

"I couldn't; I couldn't tell anyone. The facility, which is called Arcadia, is an underground treatment centre. It is an experimental clinic…no, that is not right as it is actually a hospital. Incurable diseases are treated differently there. Conventional and alternative treatments are both utilised, but the emphasis is on alternative and experimental. I don't want to get into that now as it is too detailed. If word ever leaked out about its' operation thousands of lives would be in jeopardy, and the dedicated doctors and staff that run Arcadia would be criminally investigated for performing illegal treatments and operations. I made the choice to accept the terms because I chose to live."

I reached out and took her hand. The name Arcadia dazed me for a second… was it just happenchance that I had stumbled upon the church with the same name? "How did I miss that you were so ill? I let you go through this hell all on your own…I just can't understand how you kept it from me…"

"I didn't even know how bad I was until four days before I left. I didn't have any of the many symptoms except I was tired all the time, and I had those relentless headaches. There were days I would sleep for hours. After you left for school I would lie down and wouldn't wake up until you called me at noon. It got so bad that I took a timer into the bedroom and set it so it would wake me up after two hours. I ignored the pain in my head because Dr. Quale had told me that it would go away eventually, or I would learn to live with it. By time I chose to seek out a neurologist, it was already too late. I was given something for the pain which was also supposed to keep me from having anymore seizures. I had to administer those injections myself every eight hours that whole weekend before I left. That is how I was able to keep up the pretense that nothing was wrong. I was not entirely alone though."

"Good God Jillienne, how did I miss that, and what do you mean you weren't alone?"

"How far did you track me Jordan?"

"You told me not to look for you remember?"

"How far Jordan?"

"To the ferry and the bus where we lost you…"

"Did you notice a woman with me? That was Gayle, and she was…**is** my guardian angel."

I felt like an idiot. My wife who had been gone for two and a half years had just come home, and I hadn't held her or kissed her or told her that I loved her. "Can I come over there Jillienne?"

"What do you mean?"

"I want to hold you…is that okay?"

She said that it was. I climbed out of the car and made my way around to her. I unlocked her seatbelt and swung her around to face me.

"Can I take this scarf off…I want to see your face." I started to undo it, but she put her hands on top of mine.

"I am not very pretty Jordan."

"I hardly doubt that."

The oversized scarf slid down onto her shoulders only to reveal another tied at the back of her head in a knot. I undid it, and removed it slowly knowing full well what I was going to find underneath.

"Hi Beautiful." I said cupping her face in my hands. "There's my girl, there's my Jillienne."

She placed her hands on mine again. "I am so sorry Jordan." She whimpered. "I lost it; I lost it all, it's all gone; the hair that you loved, it's all gone."

I kissed her forehead and then the long incision scar, and the three cavities that were obvious drill holes. "I loved your hair; there is no denying that, but I loved what was under it more." I pulled her up and into my arms. "Thank-you for being so brave and for coming back to me."

"I wasn't so brave Jordan. I was scared to death and I missed you so…"

"And, I have missed you, oh, how I have missed you, but no more, no more Jillienne. Promise me… promise me that you will never leave me again."

She sobbed something inaudible. Her coat was so heavy that I couldn't get a feel for what she was hiding underneath, but I was pretty sure that there wasn't much left of her. She just stood there leaning against me. Her breathing was very shallow. I asked her if she was hurting. She said she wasn't, but that she was very tired. I asked her where she had journeyed from.

"I don't know where I was, and even if I did, I couldn't tell you."

I told her that I understood, but I didn't really. I didn't understand anything at all.

"Let's get you home then so you can rest. The girls are waiting for you." I lowered her back into the car and buckled the seatbelt again. She lowered her head. I guess she didn't want me to kiss her, but I wanted to so I tilted her head up and did so. It was just a brief touching of the lips, but it was enough to satisfy me for the moment. Just before I shut the door she thanked me and said that she was sorry again. What horrors were her sad, dark eyes hiding?

I climbed back in behind the wheel and reached for her hand. "You have nothing to be sorry for; you did what you had to do, and if you hadn't, I wouldn't be sitting here holding your hand now would I?" I tried my best to smile and put her at ease, but I failed miserably.

"What will I say to them…do they hate me?"

"They love you Jillienne; just tell them what you told me. I can promise you that they will understand. How could they not?"

"I can't tell them everything Jordan…I just can't. I don't know if I can even tell you."

"Let's not worry about that right now Honey, but I can guarantee you that they are going to be overcome with emotion when they see you, just as I am."

"I kept a diary, but I should have burned it."

"Why would you want to do that?"

"Because there is nothing in it but sadness. I wanted to keep a day by day account of my feelings and treatments, but there are many empty pages in the beginning because I was either completely unaware or in too much pain to do so. I guess that word "empty" pretty much says it all. Later, I realized that I was probably going to live, but wasn't sure if I wanted to. I convinced myself that you had given up on me and found somebody else. I hated myself and what I had been forced to do. Six months ago I realized that I had been given a second chance for some reason and decided that I would give life another chance and face the consequences of my actions. I relived my life with you over and over again. My remembrances gave me hope that all may not be lost, and that you might still want and love me."

I was pretty choked up visualizing the suffering she had endured. I squeezed her hand and managed to say that I had never stopped loving her and that I too had relived our life together practically every day. I asked her if she would let me read her diary. She said, "Maybe" and changed the subject rapidly asking me when I had bought the new car and what had I done with the old one. I told her that I had given it to Faith.

"And my car, what happened to it?"

It was such a strange question as she never cared to drive, and didn't like the car in the first place. She always said it was too big for her.

I was surprised that I could laugh a little. "It gave up the ghost, but there is a very happy ending to it as that is how Faith met Cree. I will let her tell you the story."

"Cree…that is a strange name."

Without missing a beat she asked if we were still married.

Again I was astounded. "Of course we are; why would you think that we wouldn't be?"

"I thought perhaps that you might have me declared dead, or divorced me so that you could marry someone else. I know you are too principled just to move someone in with you."

"There is no one else Jillienne. I never ever considered divorcing you or having you declared dead. I was empty and broken, but I never felt that you were lost to me forever." I answered wondering how she was going to react when I told her about my infidelity. I knew I had to. I was sickened by the thought of it.

"Umm, I wonder if that is something that one can feel. I always knew you were alive."

Curious, she said knew, and not felt; how would she know that? Was someone in touch with her and reporting to her of not just mine, but everyone's going ons and well-being? Well, that would mean that she already knew about Martina, wouldn't it? The guilt was running off me like perspiration.

I had to change the subject. "You don't have to go into detail about the treatments you received or anything, just tell me that your tumor is completely gone…it is, isn't it?"

"For all intents and purposes it is, I guess. They told me that what was left was dried up so that it couldn't feed on tissue anymore, and that one couldn't harm me anymore."

"That one…are you saying there are more?" I asked fearfully.

"No one knows what awaits us Jordan." She said calmly. "I have looked death in the eye on more than one occasion. I am no longer afraid of the unknown or of dying. One should not be afraid of dying if it is their time and they are prepared to go. If they are not ready, then they should just leave the place they are in and go to some place where there is hope. I was not ready, and so I went to Arcadia. There were times when I thought I might never leave there, and that I would never see you or my family again, and then I would hear your voice and I would be full of optimism once more."

Her take on dying was a little disturbing, but it wasn't for me to question her rationality. Instead I told her that I talked to her every night and it was comforting to know that she had heard me.

"You didn't talk to me silly, you sang to me." She said matter of factually.

"I sang to you? What kind of drugs were you on anyhow?"

"Lots." she giggled ever so slightly. "I particularly like your renditions of 'Fallen Star' and 'The Waltz You Saved for me', and 'Gone' even though I was the one who was gone."

She made me want to cry, but I forced myself to laugh a little. "So Ferlin Husky sang you to sleep every night…I'm going to have to talk to that guy about carrying on with my wife."

"Is he still alive Jordan? I'd like to thank him for keeping me company and subbing for you."

"I don't know Honey, but I am sure we can find out. I could never hear what you heard in his voice, but if it reminded you of me then I am glad you found some comfort there. I am assuming that you were listening to radio-free Europe?"

"Of course you couldn't hear your voice in his; we don't sound the same to ourselves as we do to others. Who said I was in Europe? I really don't know where Arcadia is, but I can tell you that it is very far away. I don't remember the trip as I was sedated very heavily on the trip over because the air pressure in the airplane would probably have killed me. I know that we left Victoria in the light of day, and

I arrived at Arcadia in the dark…the clock on the wall said three forty five. I sort of recollect travelling by train, but I can't be sure. It makes perfect sense though as there is a railroad that ends at the castle…I mean hospital, and I have ridden in it many times. Sometimes I thought I was in Austria or Switzerland, and then other times I thought perhaps it was Yugoslavia or Transylvania… I just don't know."

"Castle; was that just a slip of the tongue, or was there a castle nearby?"

"You don't miss anything do you?" She said tersely.

"It's my job, remember?" I made an attempt at laughter.

"How could I ever forget that?" She exclaimed, and then carried on. "Yes, some Baron or Marquis or Grand Duke built the castle in the seventeenth century. If I remember correctly, his name was de le Roux."

"Sounds French so I am thinking he was a Marquis."

"Of course you would know that. Are you ashamed of me Jordan?"

"What…why would you ask such a ridiculous question?" I asked mortified.

"Because I have no formal education. I didn't even graduate high school, and I never made any attempt to do so. I never contributed to our finances. I suppose all your colleagues wondered how you could be married to someone like me."

"They wondered all right…they wondered how a jerk like me ever managed to snag such a beautiful and intelligent woman like you! They were all envious of me, and though they sympathised with me when you left, I'm sure they thought that you left because of some terrible thing I had done. I have never been ashamed of you; not one day in my life. You have more smarts and compassion than anyone I know. Just because education is my vocation doesn't by any means make me smarter than you. Who have I been going to for advice for the past three decades if not you? You always set me straight and show me the best way to approach the problem, and just because you didn't have an income, you were no less valuable. You may not have a paper diploma, but you carry all of life's wisdoms in your heart and that is more valuable than any old certificate."

"You're just prejudiced."

"You think?"

"Well, don't nominate me for Sainthood just yet. There is a lot more to this story that even you won't be able to justify."

"Are you trying to scare me?"

"No Jordan, I just want you to prepare yourself…there are things you are not going to like, and I might say things that will shock you."

"It won't be the first time that you have shocked me Sweetie."

She laughed cynically. "We'll see. Now where we…oh right, I was telling you about Arcadia. My room was on the fourth floor. I was very groggy that first night, but I remember Gayle telling me that as she got me ready for bed. She told me that I had a very nice view, and she was right, I did. My room was about the size of the boy's rooms. There were two windows that both looked out onto a green sea of lawn and gardens that boarded on a dense forest. You could not see beyond that. I awoke the next day to a blinding headache and my treatments began immediately. That was the last day for many months that I have any memory of. Just before I was put into one of many medically induced comas Gayle asked me if I would like a television in my room. I told her that I didn't, but I liked music so could I have a radio or some sort of music device. She asked what kind of music I liked and I told her country and that Ferlin Husky was my favorite. I have vague recollections of listening to him and Waylon and Conway Twitty, and others those first six months or so. But, back to your question regarding a castle…the first time I had a view of Arcadia from below was a year later. It was the first time I had been allowed outside for more than a few minutes. Once I could tolerate sitting up an orderly would take me for a little spin into the courtyard when the weather was agreeable. One day Gayle had taken me down the road for a ride in a golf cart. I think it was in May. As I looked back I realized that Arcadia was housed inside the walls of a medieval castle, and that was when I learned a bit about its' history."

I had wanted to question her about the comas, but she just kept right on talking so I didn't interrupt. I wasn't entirely sure I wanted to hear about her gruelling treatments at the moment anyhow so I asked her if she was ready to go home. She said she thought she was. I started the car. "What made you think you were in any of those countries that you mentioned?"

"Peoples' accents I guess. Arcadia is a smorgasbord of cultural differences which I was not aware of the first year as I was pretty much a vegetable. All I remember are faces…many different faces, usually masked. But then there was Gayle, and your voice."

She turned away and huddled up into a little ball. I reached for her. "Its okay Honey, we're going to get through this. I hate what you went through and that I couldn't be with you, but I am here now and you just have to lean on me, just lean on me Baby."

"I might be more then you can handle Jordan."

"Never, you will never be too much for me, do you hear?" I demanded an answer.

"Well Darling, there is not very much left of me and I am damaged, so…"

She was being flippant, but she had called me darling even if it was a little sarcastically.

I asked her if Doctor Quayle had referred her to the neurologist. I thought it was an innocent enough question even though I knew he didn't.

"I think you know that he didn't Jordan, but I'll play your little game. I picked the neurologist's name out of the phone book; I closed my eyes and pointed. I don't even remember his name because as luck would have it, and I do mean that, I never got to the floor he was on. I passed out on the elevator and a patient of Dr. Ben Casey's found me and helped the staff get me into his office.

I woke up on the examining table and was told I had suffered a seizure probably due to a brain tumor. I would most likely have been turned away if not for that seizure. I guess I owe it all to fate."

I wondered if that was the reason why she wouldn't ride in an elevator. "Dr. Ben Casey eh?"

"Is that all you got out of that?"

"No, and I want to hear more, but really Honey, is it just a coincidence that your neurologist shares his name with an early television doctor?"

"Well, you can't know his real name, so Dr. Ben will do. I have a lot more names for you too."

"I just bet you do." I was glad and concerned at the same time that she was able to make light of her dilemma.

"Yes, my favorite is Dr. McIntyre, and then there was Dr. McCoy, Hardy and Banner."

"I don't know what this says about me, but I recognize McCoy from Star Trek and David Banner from the Hulk. I'm not sure, but is Dr. Hardy from your soap, General Hospital?"

"Very good Mr. Principal."

"Thank-you. I don't recognize the name of McIntyre though, and why do you say he *is* your favorite and all the rest you speak of are in the past tense?"

"Because I will still be seeing him and Dr. Ben too. Maybe you know McIntyre better as Trapper John from Mash?"

"Aha, your old boyfriend; who was the actor who played him? You had a crush on him even before me, didn't you, and didn't he leave Mash to become a seedy private eye?"

"I think he would take exception to the word seedy. His name was Wayne Rogers. I wonder if he is still alive."

"I'm very glad you had all your heroes to keep you company, but I wish it had of been me." I said kneading her shoulder.

"Thanks for making this so easy for me Jordan, but you are the only hero I have ever needed."

How much longer could I keep up this pretense that all was well in the Land of Oz? It was almost as if she had read my thoughts.

"What did you think happened to me Jordan?"

"At first I thought you had been abducted, but Hank had seen you get into a taxi, and then Craig's detective friend Marty Reagen, tracked you to the ferry so that theory was pretty much awash. After eliminating other so called possibilities, the only conclusion I could come to was that you just simply quit loving me and left. Faith said you went away to die…I guess she wasn't too far wrong was she? Hope always believed that you would come back. Of course that was mostly because Craig kept saying that you had to have a reason, and that you would be back as soon as you dealt with whatever it was. I must say that he became more positive as time went on. I really believed that he was just trying to convince himself that his best friend couldn't possibly desert us all. Rusty and Connor believed that you left because I had clipped your wings and that you found out I was having an affair. I almost disowned them on the spot. Faith ordered them out of the house, but as usual, Craig was the voice of calm, and he managed to salvage an inkling of my relationship with them."

"I'm sorry; just one more reason for you to be disappointed in them I guess. I never once stopped loving you Jordan."

I squeezed her hand. "I'm glad you didn't Jillienne. But just because Connor opted out of college after one year, and Rusty chose to leave home at seventeen before even finishing high school, doesn't mean they were a disappointment to me."

"Like mother, like son, I guess. Apparently you have chosen to forget that their life decisions caused you to become dangerously close to a nervous breakdown."

"Was it so wrong that I wanted our children to have a good life, and I don't think I was anywhere near a breakdown."

"No, you weren't wrong, but you can't live someone else's life for them. They simultaneously leaving home is not a time I like to remember either. It was the one and only time you shut me out. I guess I just got even with you."

I could tell that she was withdrawing into herself again. We were only blocks from home. I reached for her. "I'm sorry Jillienne, I was an idiot. You didn't leave because you wanted to hurt me; quite the opposite, right?"

"It's all wrong Jordan." She mumbled.

"What do you mean Honey?" I asked hesitantly.

"Everything…Arcadia's need for secrecy, the subterfuge of research, the dubious clinical trials, government interference, pharmaceutical companies, the whole bloody world…it's all fucked up."

She shocked me a little as she had never used that expletive before except in the privacy of our bedroom. "Sweetheart, I cannot even begin to imagine what your journey was like, or what atrocities you endured at the hands of strangers in a foreign land, but if you will let me I would like to continue the rest of the journey to complete healing with you. In turn you will be healing me too. Shall we take a few minutes again?" I asked her pulling the car over to a wide spot.

"No, I am fine. I am sorry that I caused you any distress, but there is no need to sugar-coat your feelings by calling me sweetheart. You never call me that, so don't start now because you want to console me." She said flatly.

"Oh, I am pretty sure I call you sweetheart, and I do want to comfort you." I wondered if she was aware of how suddenly her moods changed and if they were a consequence of her illness.

"No, a woman knows what her husband calls her. It's either honey or sweetie, the same thing you call the girls. Sometimes you call me baby."

I got out and walked around the car and opened her door. I knelt down. "Look at me Jillienne; you are the only sweetheart I have ever had. You are my sweet, funny Valentine every day of the year. I thought we had the perfect life and marriage. You weren't just my wife and mother to my children, you were my best friend, my lover, the woman I held in my arms every night, and woke up with every morning. I adored you and our life. But then one day you were gone, gone without reason, gone without a trace, gone, gone, gone. I was left wondering why, what had I done?"

"Did you hate me Jordan?"

"I hated what you had done, but no, I never hated you. I told myself night after night that if you would just come back to me I could forgive you for anything. But this Jillienne, this nightmare that you faced all alone doesn't require any forgiveness as you did nothing wrong. You said Gayle was with you, but it should have been me; it should have been me. I'm sorry as hell that it wasn't, and I am sure I will understand more as the story unravels. For now I want you to know that you are without question the bravest person I know. I loved you then, and I love you now. The question is… do you love me?"

She nodded and said tearfully that she did. I held her face in my hands and kissed her. "We are all set then; love will see us through. Let's go home and see our girls."

"You do recognise that these strangers are responsible for saving my life aren't you? My objections are with the bureaucrats who control the health system and force places like Arcadia to operate under clandestine conditions."

"I do, and I will forever be grateful to the doctors who saved your life."

She wasn't quite through with her sermonizing. "Every minute of every day, all over this planet, there are clinical trials being conducted, but not everyone with a life threatening illness can participate or gets to make a decision as to whether the treatment should be made available to them. How often have you and I sat through a documentary or a newscast that heralds a cure for one disease or another, but it "might" be available to the public in two or three years? What about those people who are dying waiting for this treatment? What about their hopes and fears and frustrations? And, why was I selected to participate in the experiment? Why was I chosen from a million others? These trials are heavily screened; there are too many regulations and guidelines that deal with fraud and misconduct by the pharmaceutical companies and interference by the government. They aren't considering the well- being of the patients. Ha! If they only knew what goes on behind closed doors in private clinics. Arcadia is free from commercial interests. There is no support from any industry. It is funded completely by donations, and their research is conducted in an independent manner free from government interference. And, what about the researchers who have made these medical breakthroughs; they may never live to see their discoveries be implemented and applauded? It all sickens me, but I will tell you one thing Jordan, I will spend the rest of my life fighting the injustices of the unenlightened practices of medicine, and seeking to find a way to make places like Arcadia accessible to everyone and their families."

I had never heard Jillienne be so verbose before. It was clear she had done her homework. I told her that I would be her advocate, but secretly thought that we probably couldn't do anything because she didn't even know where she had been. It was then that I decided that I could never tell her about my infidelity. My intentions of a romantic tryst with Virginia would be my dirty little secret. I squeezed her hand again.

"I thank God that you were one of the chosen few Jillienne. There must be criteria for selecting applicants and maybe your condition was a priority over others."

"I did not apply Jordan; I was just offered the chance. I think Gayle was the reason…"

She didn't finish her sentence. I asked her why she thought that. She said that we should just leave it at that. She knew a hell of a lot more than she was willing to admit to or discuss.

As we rounded the corner to our street Jillienne said that she didn't think she was ready to face the girls. I told her that I would be right beside her, and that she had nothing to worry about. We turned into the driveway and the lights shone on a figure sitting on the front steps. It was Hope.

"Stay put Honey; I want a moment with her first." I cautioned.

Hope ran down the steps and tried to open Jillienne's door; she yelled at me to unlock it. I opened my door and and cautioned Hope. "Your mother has come a long way; she is very tired and fragile…"

"**Open** the door Daddy; I'm not going to hurt her!" I sprang the lock. Hope was crying, "Oh Mommy, Mommy, where have you been? Are you all right? Let me look at you…oh Mommy, what has happened to you?" She hugged Jillienne crying all the while.

After a few minutes I pried Hope away from her mother and told her to get her mother's belongings from the back seat. I reached down and picked Jillienne up. She was very light.

She insisted that she could walk.

"Not on my watch." I said explaining that the grass was slippery.

Hope ran ahead of us and opened the front door. I sat Jillienne down on the Parson's bench and unbuttoned her coat. Hope undid her boots and massaged her feet a little before sliding them into a pair of Sandie's knitted slippers. We stood her up and removed her heavy coat.

"Oh Mommy, you've lost so much weight!" Hope exclaimed.

"You know how I always said I wanted to lose weight…well, be very careful what you wish for. All that extra weight may just have been a Godsend though as it helped sustain me through the toughest months of my treatments when I was not able to consume soluble food."

We sat her between us on the sofa in the living room. I asked Hope where her sister was. She said that she was sure she would be with us shortly. Jillienne took a few minutes getting reacquainted with the room. She said it smelled like home. Then she took our eldest daughter's hand and told her briefly why she had left us all. She did not go into great detail like she had with me. Hope was very disturbed but kept quiet and kept nodding until Jillienne quit talking.

"I knew it had to be something horrible that took you away from us, but this…oh, my poor Mommy. I want to see you; will you let me?"

"Please don't be too shocked Sweetie." Jillienne warned as she removed her scarves. Hope didn't flinch.

"Does your head hurt Mommy?"

Jillienne said it didn't but that it got cold. Hope gently touched the scars and kissed her mother's maimed head just as I had.

"You are so very beautiful Mommy, so very beautiful and brave… isn't she Daddy?"

"Yes Hope, she is. What can we get for you Jillienne, are you hungry, tea, coffee?"

God, this was my wife, not some stranger. Why did I sound so indifferent?

"If you have any, I would like a little drink of brandy. I became quite fond of it at the convent and shared a dram or so with the Sisters every evening."

"What's this about a convent? Was Arcadia Catholic and run by nuns?"

"No Jordan, I went to Three Sisters Holy Alliance to convalesce."

I said that I was pretty sure there was still a half bottle of brandy left over from the last time she made Christmas cakes. I went to check out the liquor cabinet and found Faith hugging the banister half way up the stairs. I motioned to her to come and see her mother. She shook her head. I loaded a tray with four glasses, just in case, with brandy and sherry, and returned to the living room. Hope was telling Jillienne that she had failed terribly at her attempts to recreate her recipe for Christmas cake. She said she must have missed some important ingredient.

I passed Hope her sherry and told her that I thought the missing ingredient was all the love her mother put into making them. I put the small crystal glass in Jillienne's hand and closed mine over hers for a few seconds. She smiled and said that I was right. I asked her to tell us about life in the convent.

"I much prefer that then talking about Arcadia even though Arcadia saved my life. It is with God's mercy that I have not many recollections of the first five or six months." She had told me in the car that she would not speak of the torment that she had undergone with the girls. "Yes, there are many stories to tell." She turned to Hope. "Do you know the meaning of Arcadia?"

"It means salvation doesn't it?" Hope asked. "Isn't that the name of the church that you have been going to Daddy?"

"Church, you're going to church Jordan, and it's called Arcadia… that can't be right. Hope must have gotten the name wrong." Jillienne said looking at me inquiringly.

"No, she's not wrong; quite a coincidence isn't it? It's not a word one hears every day, but here it is front and centre, and has made an impact on both our lives. We'll talk more about that later. When I think of the meaning of Arcadia, I think of Elysium. It is an ancient Greek conception I believe of a place or state of perfect happiness… in other words, paradise, heaven on earth, celestial. Is that how it felt to you Jillienne?"

"Your father is so knowledgeable; it's obvious that you all got your "smarts" from him. But no, it did not feel like heaven to me, not at first. I was somewhere far away from the people I loved, unable to contact them, and pretty certain that I was never going home again. Sometimes when I closed my eyes I would wish that I never woke up; nothing was worse than being away from all of you. I hated Arcadia and its' strict, secretive doctrines. It was all so inhuman."

"Oh Mommy, their rules were so cruel, but they saved you so we have to be thankful for that. Maybe we did get some of our intellect from Daddy, but we got our lust for life and love, and moral values from you." Hope said hugging her mother. "I hate that you were all alone in Arcadia. Did you become friends with any of the other patients?"

"Yes, after a year or so I was able to carry on a conversation and get around a bit. An orderly or Gayle would take me in a wheelchair to the common room where I met many people, some in worse condition than me. Some of them did not make it." Her eyes clouded over, but no tears fell. "I met Erica and Maureen the Christmas of 2007. They were on a different floor but we shared the same affliction and were undergoing the same treatments. Erica is from the Netherlands; she went home in July. Maureen is from Ireland. She had been admitted six months before Erica and me so she was discharged last April. The three of us were considered "miracles" as we had all near death when we were admitted. We were the subjects of many studies as to why our bodies tolerated the treatments and others didn't. One theory was that we were all from a northern country, and that somehow the colder climate benefited us. I never considered myself as being from the "north." Anyhow, I have their addresses and I suppose I will correspond with them one day. I was never alone Hope."

We all heard footsteps on the stairs and a second later appeared a sobbing Faith leaning up against the archway. She just stood there crying.

Jillienne reached out her arms. "Come here Baby, come to Mommy."

Faith ran and fell down at her mother's feet and laid her head on her lap. "I'm so sorry Mommy, I'm so sorry."

"You have nothing to be sorry for my darling." She patted Faith's head trying to soothe her.

"I do, I told them all that you were dead, and I didn't even tell you that I loved you that day. I did something wrong didn't I? It's my fault…"

I lifted her up off the floor. "Nothing is your fault Faith. Come and sit by your mother, and you can tell her you love her now."

I pulled a wing chair up beside the chesterfield and listened to the three loves of my life console each other for five minutes or so. I passed them a box of Kleenex. Jillienne took them from me and asked Faith if she had heard anything that she had told Hope. Faith blubbered that she did, but that she still didn't understand why it all had to be kept secret. Jillienne repeated the whys for the secrecy over again for Faith's benefit. Every now and then she would look at me and I'd smile and nod my approval, and yet I was struggling with something. Why did everything she was saying sound so rehearsed? She couldn't have made the whole story up could she have? It was pretty far- fetched, but who could ever prove her wrong? Was she really somewhere else and maybe with some man? I could see her losing all the weight in two years, but shaving her head, and what about those scars on her head? Snap out of it man! How could you even think that she was lying, what the hell is the matter with you… it's the guilt isn't it?

"But, we should have known Mommy; we wouldn't have told anyone would we have Daddy?"

"Your mother had to make the difficult decision to accept the 'deal,' so to speak, immediately. She had to consent to complete confidentiality to protect Arcadia's existence. Many lives were at stake, not just hers'. She was only given an 11 to 14 % chance of survival; it took a great deal of courage to consent to the terms. To be perfectly honest with you Faith, if she had of told me, and only me…I don't know how I would have reacted. I would have wanted to go with her that's for sure, and I guess that would have negated her eligibility for treatment. Knowing what she was going through may have been worse than not knowing anything. Your mother made the right decision no matter how barbaric it may sound to you, and we need to say thank God she had the courage to do so." I reached over and squeezed my wife's hand. She smiled ever so slightly.

I needed a minute to collect my thoughts and put a check on my emotions. I let go of her hand and asked to be excused for a few minutes while I got something out of the freezer. "Don't carry on without me, okay."

"I won't Jordan."

I needed a moment all right…what the hell had I been thinking? For a fleeting moment I had thought that she fabricated the whole thing. I stuck my head in the freezer. It was my own guilt that was taking hold of me, and it wasn't even about Martina; it was what I had been planning on putting into motion with Virginia. What had stopped me from phoning her last week and asking her out? I could have been fully involved with her right now because I knew she wouldn't refuse me. There was no doubt in my mind that when she had asked me after lunch that day if I wanted to get a room that she was serious. She had laughed it off when she saw the stunned look on my face. I was still in love with Jillienne then so nothing was further from my mind. Just a minute, I *am* still in love with her, so whatever it was that had kept me from calling Virginia I had my lucky star to thank. Now I better get my ass back upstairs and dismiss all those silly notions as the love of my life was waiting for me. I threw the loaf of bread on the kitchen island and returned to where I belonged… next to my wife.

"Now," I said to her, "you were going to tell us about life in a convent."

"One day, ten months after arriving at Arcadia, I awoke from an induced coma to find a young lady sitting by my bedside. She was dressed all in white, and so of course I thought she was an angel. She was quick to dispel that notion. Her name is Sister Margret Mary; she along with three other nuns are teachers at the school. I should mention here that there is a whole village that houses the families from Arcadia. It is called Woodland, I guess because it is surrounded as is Arcadia, by dense forests. I was told that it was originally known as Dasos, the Greek name for forest. I don't believe anyone who is not connected to the hospital resides there. What happens to the children after they becomes teens is another secret, but that is a whole other story. Sister Margret continued to visit me every day. She would read and pray with me, but more than that she made me laugh. One day when I was stronger she took me to meet the rest of her family at Three Sisters' Holy Alliance Convent. There was Sister Maxine, Sister Yvonne, Sister Karen, and Mother Georgette. I guess it was very unusual for one of the Sisters to become so personal with a patient and Margret was admonished for doing so, but our friendship continued. When I was in one of my last months of treatment I could have been moved to a convalescing ward in the hospital, but I asked if I could live at the convent. Of course this was unheard of, but Sister Margret lobbied for me. After many negotiations between my doctors and Mother Georgette, I was allowed to go on a weeks' trial period. I guess I set a precedent as others will be allowed to recuperate there now. Of course Arcadia was only entering into its' fourth year of operations when I arrived there so everything was still relatively new."

"Wasn't it cold and dark there Mommy?" Hope asked.

"The bedrooms were, but there is electric lighting and lots of fireplaces. Remember this was spring and summer; I imagine it is much chillier in the winter. The kitchen and prayer rooms have a southern and eastern exposure so are sunny and warm. There are lots and lots of beautiful glass stained windows that reflect the light like a prism. I would not have petitioned to recover there if it had of been morbid and dark." Jilly said.

She related a few stories, some of them quite amusing, regarding people she had met the past summer. They included the cook at the convent whose name was Gretchen, Petter, the delivery man who supplied produce, dairy, fish and chickens, and Delores who belonged to a nomadic group who camped out in the Woodlands every year. They came in late spring and stayed until autumn growing vegetable gardens and grazing their livestock, working and selling their wares and performing for the residents of the village and Arcadia. Delores was a fortune teller and became Jillienne's good friend.

"I don't understand Mommy…I thought Arcadia was a private institute; how were strange people who sound like gypsies to me, be allowed in? Was it not guarded, and wasn't it possible that its' existence would be compromised by these migrants?" Faith asked probingly.

Jillienne looked uncomfortable. "I can't answer that Faith. All I know is that they had been coming for hundreds of years. There must have been some sort of agreement with the owners."

"The owners…I thought it was owned and operated by the doctors?"

I was about to intervene and tell Faith to save her questions for another day when she shrugged her shoulders and said that it didn't matter, and that she was just curious. Instead she asked her mother if there were phones at Arcadia, and if there were why she hadn't called them to let them know she was still alive.

I stood up. "That's enough Faith! You know damn well that she couldn't reveal where she was. Did you miss that part where she said she was sworn to secrecy?"

"No, but…I'm sorry Mama; I just need to know why you couldn't call us? We never found your cell phone…did you take it with you?"

I was about to reprimand Faith again, but Jillienne halted me with her hand.

"I never saw a phone, but of course they existed. Up until last May I didn't even know if I would ever be returning so there was no need to call anyone. Why would I want to give you all false hope? No, I did not take my phone. Gayle knew I had it with me the day we left. She suggested that I should resist temptation and the way to do that was to throw it overboard. I just hope that I didn't maim a dolphin or a sea otter in doing so."

Hope laughed. "I don't think you did Mommy, but you did take some things with you didn't you? We thought that you took a family picture, the book of poetry that you had given Dad, and the pearl bracelet that he had given you for your birthday. Why it and not your wedding rings?"

"I didn't know what the tumor could do to my memory if the treatments were successful. I needed a picture of you all if I wouldn't be able to recall what you looked like anymore. I took the book because your dad had written notations in it about me and I wanted to be reminded of how he felt about me. I would read it every day when I was lucid. His words reminded me how he had loved me, and I would hope…hope beyond hope that he might still love me."

My mouth was dry, but my eyes weren't. "Every word is still true Honey." I said emotionally.

She smiled and carried on. "I didn't take my rings because I really had no idea what I had consented to. I might lose them or maybe they would have been taken away from me or stolen. If I made it, then I wanted them here waiting for me. The bracelet was new and I had not formed any attachment to it yet, and I was pretty sure it was worth a few bucks. I took it because I thought I might have to hawk it to get passage home."

"Oh Mommy, I can't imagine what you went through that day; it must have been agonizing."

"It was Hope. I didn't want to go, but I knew I had to take the chance. Not telling you all was the hardest thing I have ever had to do. If I held onto your dad and sister much too long that morning it was because I truly had the feeling that I would never see them or you, or the rest of my family ever again."

I had never been at a lack for words before, but this woman, this woman who I loved more than life itself, the mother of my children, the woman who had gone to hell and back to get home to us had just left me speechless. All I could do was get up and pull her into my arms and whisper her name over and over again. The girls were crying again…still; I don't think they had ever stopped. We all just stood there rocking together until Jillienne pulled away and told us all to sit down. I sat on the coffee table in front of her and kept hold of her hands.

"I need to say this and then it can be done. You are all I lived for and worked so hard at rehab for, but then I took a real honest look at myself last April. I barely weighed eighty pounds, my complexion was that of a ghost, I could barely walk, and I was weak and tired all the time. Why would I want to burden you? I might never recover completely, and you probably already thought I was dead…that was then I decided to ask for sanctuary at the convent."

"But when you recuperated, your plan was to always come home wasn't it?" Hope probed.

"No, not always. I didn't believe that I had a life to come home to. I was pretty sure that you had all written me off, and that your father," she locked eyes with me, "had fallen in love with someone else, and I decided to partition the church to accept me as a novice."

Hope and Faith gasped.

Jillienne looked so forsaken that my heart was breaking all over again. I squeezed her hands. "Never, never was that ever going to happen. I was never going to fall in love with anyone else; do you hear me Jillienne, never!" I wasn't just telling her this, I was telling myself also. It was time to put a stop to this. I pulled her back up and into my arms. "I think the day has caught up to you Honey. You've come a long way and you have been answering our questions for the better part of two hours; it's time to call it quits. I want you to let the girls take you into the bathroom and let you freshen up, and how about getting out of this heavy dress?" I lifted her head up. "Whatever or whoever changed your mind I will be eternally grateful to them." I kissed her forehead and led her into the bedroom, and told Hope to get the boxes from my closet.

As I sat her down on the bed; she spoke sombrely. "It was Delores. She said that my fate was written in the stars, in the tea leaves, in my palms, and in the crevasses of my cranium…she said my destiny was here with you. Three days ago she told me that I had to get home right away. I thought something terrible had happened to one of you. I called Gayle and she said that yes, I needed to go home. She made all the arrangements, and here I am."

"I think I like this Delores very much." I said emphatically. "Now how about you open one of these boxes and see if you like what is inside?"

She looked up at me; her eyes were telling me she loved me. I don't know who was more vulnerable at that moment, her or me. "Are these for the three birthdays I missed? Did you carry on with your yearly ritual even though I wasn't here?"

The answer was obvious so I didn't need to answer. I passed her the middle box saying that I thought she would like it the best. She opened it tossing the ribbons and wrap to the floor. She held the apricot colored negligee and dressing gown up to her body and said that she loved it.

"I haven't felt anything this soft and luxurious in a very long time; thank-you Jordan."

"Open the jewellery case Mom." Faith coaxed her. "Let's see what Daddy got you."

Jillienne's face lit up when she extracted the orange garnet infinity necklace and earrings that had a ruby red heart inset. If she had of been here for her fiftieth birthday she would have scolded me for spending so much. I would have explained to her as I did every year that she was my prize possession, and if I wanted to spend a whole years' salary on her then I damn well would. She would shake her head and say that she loved me. She said no such thing tonight, only that she might have to force the earrings on as her piercings had closed. Delores had offered to redo them but she had declined. Faith said she would take her to the mall to have them done by a professional whenever she was ready.

"Come on Mommy; let's get you cleaned up and into these beautiful get-ups." Hope said helping her mother up. "Faith, will you get that new lavender lotion you bought?"

Jillienne said that she needed to take her medication and asked Hope to get her bag. I brought her a glass of water and said I was going to get started on supper. The phone rang. I told Faith I didn't want to talk to anyone so she should just let it ring; she usually did anyhow. She surprised me by picking it up. She said "Hello, just a minute." She handed it to me.

"What did I just tell you Faith?" I said curtly.

"You need to take this Daddy…she's already called twice while you were out."

I cursed. I waited until I thought I heard the bathroom door close before I took the phone from her. Faith whispered. "You need to end this with her *now*!" She walked out of the room.

I took a deep breath. "Hello Martina…"

CHAPTER 8

Confessions and Forgiveness

Hope all but pushed me into the bathroom and shut the door quickly.

"Come over here Mom; sit on this little stool that Daddy made for you."

She undid my dress and let it fall to the floor. "Oh, this is different, where did you get it?"

She was referring to my undergarment. "It is called a petticoat; an underskirt and bodice all together. I haven't worn a bra in years. This is less restricting. Gayle got it for me."

She took my straps down and washed my back with a soothing warm face cloth, and then moved to my front. She laughed. "Well, I see you still have the need for a bra!"

"I asked a couple of doctors why I was still so bosomy and their reply was that I shouldn't question why, but just be thankful that I would be going home with something that I came with."

"That's a very strange answer, don't you think?"

"Well Hope, Arcadia is a very strange place. Your father has a girlfriend doesn't he?"

"Damn, I'd hope you hadn't heard that!"

"Well, I did, so the cat is out of the bag. Who is Martina, and how long has it been going on?"

"Nothing is going on Mom; she is just a friend. He met her at this photography class he joined. A bunch of them would go for coffee afterwards, and she was one of them. He went to some of her grandson's sports events with her. Lannah isn't playing soccer or ball this year and I guess Daddy missed watching the young kids. I think they went to a concert and a couple of dinners, that's all. She's not his girlfriend. My God, she isn't even his type!"

"So you have met her…what does she look like?"

"I only met her once. Dad was out shopping for a new dishwasher and he ran into her, and she helped him pick one out. She's average, no great beauty; she has short greyish hair…"

I interjected. "At least she has hair."

"Oh Mommy, you are more beautiful than most women who have hair."

I patted her hand. "It's okay Honey; I just want to know what I am up against. There is not much left of me to fight…"

"Don't say that Mommy; Daddy loves you, and only you! You have nothing to worry about."

I wasn't sure about that. Jordan had told me that he still loved me, but I supposed he had been lying to me because after he found out what had happened to me he figured he had no choice but to say so. I did not want his pity.

"Here's the lotion…oh, you look beautiful Mommy! I'll rub some on your legs and Hope can do your arms, and I found a brand new lipstick; it's a peachy color just like you like, and look, I found this terry-cloth turban and a package of underwear, do you think they will fit?" Faith said as she opened the door interrupting my conversation with Hope.

"They will be fine Faith, much better than what I have been wearing. Yes, I like the turban."

Five minutes later my daughters paraded me out to their father.

"What do you think Daddy?" Faith asked.

He smiled. "I think she is as gorgeous as ever. Do you feel refreshed Jillienne?"

I said that I did. He then asked the girls if they would do him a favor. They said of course they would and what was it? He took what looked like two credit cards out of his wallet and handed them to Hope.

"I want you girls to go to the mall and buy your mother some new duds; a couple of dresses, a pair of slacks, stockings, under things, whatever she needs. Will you do that for me?"

"Jordan, that is not necessary! I can make do with what I have… if I have to I can take in a few things, and I have all those muumuus so there is no need." I stated emphatically.

"Did you learn to sew while you were away?" He said teasingly.

I glared at him.

"Sorry Honey, that was very insensitive of me, please forgive me." He pleaded.

I said I would think about it and told the girls not to go. Faith said it would be fun, and that they wouldn't be long. Hope measured me by putting her arms around my waist and hips.

"I think you are about three or four sizes smaller than Faith." She said nodding.

A few minutes later they were ready to go. I was still protesting. I wasn't going to win so I told them not to bother with any slacks as I was much too thin to wear any and the longer the dresses the better as my legs were ugly and skinny like a chickens'. The door closed behind them. I asked Jordan why he had sent the girls away.

"Because I wanted you to feel good about yourself and having something that fits you might make you less self- conscious about your body image, that's why. And, maybe I wanted to be alone with you so I could tell you how much I have missed you and love you." He replied leaning over me.

"And, what about Martina, do you love her also?"

He straightened up and looked down on me frowning. "What did Hope tell you?"

"Hope never told me anything, just that she is a friend of yours. It was you who told me she was someone special to you."

"She isn't, and I never mentioned her name, so where did you get that from?"

"I heard you on the telephone." I said emptily.

"You heard me say what?"

"I heard you say: "Hello Martina"; it was the way you said her name in that deep sexy voice of yours that was once reserved for only me. You didn't say, "Hi Martina or Hi Marty, if that is even what you call her… you said, *Hello Martina.*" It was long and almost seductive. Hope closed the door so don't worry, I didn't eavesdrop on your conversation, but I imagine you told her that you couldn't see her tonight because your wife had come home, and she had been through hell so you didn't feel right leaving her alone. Am I right?"

"No, I did not tell her you were home. You only think I spoke to her seductively, but I can guarantee you that there was no such inflection of the sort in my voice, and if I do have what you call a deep sexy voice, it is still only reserved for you."

"Why wouldn't you tell her that I am back? She knows about me doesn't she? Do you still want to carry on with her? There must be something going on between the two of you…why else would she be calling you at this time of night? Oh God, you had a date with her didn't you, and I came home and put a damper on that just like I did with you and Eleanor all those years ago." I was near to tears, but I told myself to suck it up.

He walked over to the window and pulled the drapes over the blinds. I had only seen him do that once before…a night so very long ago, but still fresh in my memory. He hadn't known how to answer me then, the night I had come to him on my seventeenth birthday, and I guessed he didn't know quite how to answer me now. He turned and took a few steps towards me, but decided to keep his distance and stopped.

"To begin with, I have no idea who Eleanor is. Martina is a friend, just as Hope said, but it stops there. I honestly don't know why I didn't tell her you were home. I just wanted to get rid of her, and so I told her something had come up. Anyhow, I didn't want to talk to her about you. She means nothing to me Jillienne, and I am certainly not in love with her. I have never loved anyone but you. She wanted more than I was willing to give her so things became awkward between us. Something happened and I have been sick over it…"

I heard him talking, but it was like I was in a void as nothing was registering. I felt the sensation of queasiness in the pit of my stomach; it was rising quickly. I tried to force it back down, but I couldn't. What was Jordan saying? I tried to concentrate on his voice…not now, not now, please, not now. It was too late, the nausea was in my chest, in my throat, and any second it would be in… too late, it was already there. I clasped my hands over my mouth and ran for the bathroom, gagging as I went. The last words I heard Jordan say that resonated with me was that he had been unfaithful to me.

I didn't stop. He was calling out to me following me saying he was sorry, over and over again. I couldn't speak. All I could do was gesture for him to stay away. I tried to get my peignoir off but couldn't. I managed to throw the turban into the bath tub before immersing my head in the toilet bowl and retching. The dry heaves continued to wrack my body in burning waves every few seconds. I wished I could pass out, but no, I had to endure every second of torture. I was vaguely aware that Jordan was still talking, begging me to tell him what he could do. I couldn't answer. He put a cold cloth on the back of my neck and rubbed my back and shoulders. After what seemed like an eternity, I felt the spasms lessen, and then stop. My mouth was parched and my throat felt like it was on fire. I managed to get out the word "water." Jordan was gone and back in a half a minute. It was funny that we had the same phobia about drinking water from the bathroom…funnier that I should think of that right now. I drank the whole glass, and pushed myself on my rump over to the small partition between the shower and the Jacuzzi, and rested my head against the wall. Jordan was staring at me with puppy dog eyes asking again what he could do and saying that he was so sorry again. I was afraid he was going to start crying.

"It's not your fault Jordan; it's nothing you said. You don't have to take credit for me being sick. It's not like this has never happened before. I know better, and yet I still took my meds on an empty stomach…I was so happy, I wasn't thinking." I managed to croak.

"Don't try and make me feel better about what I did or said…"

I put my hand up to stop him from blubbering on. "There's a little silver box in my bag, can you please get it for me, and another glass of water?"

He returned with it saying that it looked like a cigarette case from the fifties. I asked him in a mocking voice how he would know about that. He answered that he had watched enough old movies with me to know one when he saw one. He asked me if I had taken up smoking. I told him to open it while I downed the water.

"Oh, medicinal cannabis?" He questioned.

"Sure, can you give me one?"

"Are you hurting?"

I shook my head. He asked if I was still nauseated. I shook my head again. I took the joint and lighter from him and started to get up. He asked me where I was going and I said, "Outside to smoke." He opened the window and told me that I could smoke right here. I offered him one.

"I think not. One of us has to keep a clear head, and I promised the girls I'd look after you."

"Of course," I replied taking a long drag, "Mr. Righteousness, what was I thinking offering you weed. I guess adultery doesn't fall under your moral jurisdiction. OH God, if you could see your face! Sit down, take a load off. Look, it's not like I wasn't expecting this. I guess I just didn't think your confessions would come so quickly…I mean I did ask you in the car if you had found someone else and you said no, so I guess you lied, and you lied when you said you loved me."

"That was not a lie, I do love you, and I have not found someone else."

"Okay then, maybe you do still love me, or think that you do, or that you have to. Look, I know I kept you on a pretty tight leash, and as far as I know you were faithful to me for thirty one years." It was more a question, but I didn't let him answer. "How long did it take you to hop into bed with some pretty and sew your first post-marriage lusts?" I held up my hand to stop him from answering. I didn't want to hear his denial. "Let me guess…three months, six, and how many willing slutty women have you satisfied… two, six, am I getting close, maybe a dozen or more?" I took another long drag closing my eyes.

"You never heard a word I said in the bedroom did you?" His voice was without emotion.

"I heard enough. I'm not chastising you Jordan…hell, I probably would have done the same thing if the tables had of been reversed. What I am trying to say is that it doesn't matter what you did while I was gone. For all you knew, I was dead or had run off with someone, so good for you for continuing on with your life. I hope you didn't break too many hearts along the way." I winked at him.

"You are completely off base, and the pot is probably fogging your senses. You need to get some sleep and clear your head. Here, give me that thing."

"No, I'm not finished yet!" I held my joint away from him, "There is nothing wrong with my head…oh yeah, I had a brain tumor so I guess I am crazed. Sober or not, I am still going to tell you that it doesn't matter to me how many women you have screwed, and if this Martina is the one you have settled on, then good for you because I probably can't give you what she can anymore any way. If you haven't already started divorce procedures, you can get on that right away. I won't stand in your way, and I will ask for nothing."

"Maybe you are a little crazy or they really did take away your brain because the woman who left here two and a half years would never say anything like that. She would never have just passed me off to another woman." He said pathetically.

"Well, my darling, I am not the sweet, little innocent virginal wife that left here two years ago. I have locked horns with the devil. I would have sold my soul to him just so I could come back home to you, but he wanted my first born so I would not deal with him. I barred the grim reaper from my door more times than I can remember. I even denied the angel of mercy because I was not ready for deliverance into heaven. So, I'm not your sweet housewife anymore. I drink, I smoke pot and I curse, and I have no expectations that our lives will ever be the same again. You are free to walk out that door and go to the woman you are fucking; it's no concern of mine, and I will not fight for you."

"I think I can deal with the dram of brandy at night and the medicinal pot, but I'll have to clean up that potty mouth of yours, and *my darling*, there was never anything innocent about you. Now come on, you're going to bed." He said taking the butt out of my hand and flushing it.

I wanted to wipe that smirk off his face. "You are not the boss of me Mister!"

"We'll see about that." He snapped as he picked me up and threw me over his shoulder like I was a sack of potatoes. I protested all the way to the bedroom.

He attempted to put me on the bed. I pounded on him. "There is no way I am getting into that desecrated bed that you have shared with God only knows how many women." I yelled.

"God, you are incorrigible!" He groaned plopping me down in my old easy chair. Then he cautioned me. "Don't say it, don't you dare say you don't know what the word means!"

"Well, I don't." I answered glumly.

He cautioned me with his hand. "And, don't pout because it is not going to do you any good. I have listened patiently as you made up stories about my depraved non-existent love life, and now you are going to sit there quietly while I tell you the truth. Firstly, no woman has ever shared that bed with me except you. In fact, no woman has even been in this house that wasn't related to me in one way or the other since you've been gone. I am not, at this time or any other time having an affair. Is that clear?"

"Yes Sir, if you say so." I bit my tongue.

"Good, now can you let me talk without interrupting…I know it's going to be hard."

"And suppose if I don't? Are you going to put me over your knee and spank me?"

"Don't tempt me young lady."

"Aye, aye Mr. Principal, I wouldn't dream of it." I said defiantly.

"I will start at the beginning again seeing you weren't listening the first time…sorry, I think you just tuned me out because you were fighting being sick. I will make this as short as I can without leaving anything out. It's as Hope told you, I met Martina at a photography class I joined. She and half a dozen others would go for coffee afterwards and I was invited to join them. It was just a friendly little group. Weeks passed before I felt comfortable enough with them to tell them about you and how you had disappeared. I supposed they pitied me, but I pitied myself so no big deal. One night after coffee I gave Martina a ride home as her car had broken down. We talked about our grand kids. Lannah had decided to give up sports this year, for what reason has never been clear to me. Anyhow, I mentioned to Martina how much I missed watching the youngsters play soccer and ball and she invited me to her grandson's games. I went, and it became a weekly thing. One night she invited me out to an opening of a new restaurant. I enjoyed her company, but that is all it was ever supposed to be, just dinners and a few movies with a friend. I was not looking for any other kind of relationship. One night after a concert she invited me in for a night cap, and that is when she told me that she had fallen In love with me and wanted me to spend the night. I told her that was never going to happen and left."

I put my hand up. Jordan grinned and said, "Yes?"

"Permission to speak?"

He nodded yes.

"Who was performing at the concert, and was that the first time she had invited you in?"

"No, I'd had dinner at her place a couple of times, and we played cards after. There was never any hint that she was interested in anything other than friendship. It was a Neil Diamond concert. I should not have accepted her invitation; I thought about you the whole way through it. I never intended to see her again after that night, but fate had other plans for me. One evening, two weeks later, her daughter called me asking me if I had seen her mother. I told her that I had not as I had been out of town which was not a lie as I had taken the twins camping on the island for a week. Irene, the daughter, informed me that her mother was not answering the phone and she was worried about her. Martina's brother had died, or maybe it was her uncle, and she was taking it very hard. Irene was unable to go and check on her mother. She asked me if I would, and I being the pillar of virtuousness said I would. I had a bad feeling about the whole thing. At first she wouldn't let me in. I should have left, and God I wish I had of. She was three sheets to the wind already having drunk half a bottle of vodka. I called Irene as she wouldn't and put on a pot of coffee. She asked me to have a drink with her, just for all times sake; I did. Things got a little foggy after that. I know she plastered me with kisses, and invited me into her bedroom. I fought her advances off and followed her only because I thought she was going to fall down. I told myself I would see her settled in bed and leave, but that didn't happen. She started kissing me again and said something like she would look after me if I was afraid she wasn't pure enough. She opened a drawer and pulled out a condom."

"What...was she worried that you would get her pregnant? Oh my God, she's young isn't she?"

"She's sixty two. She's been married and widowed twice and has had a few boyfriends so I guess she was just looking out for me, yeah sure, that was it, she was just looking out for me." He laughed almost vulgarly. "I am vaguely aware of her taking her clothes off and starting to undress me. I remember nothing more until I awakened to what I thought was a nightmare as I was in her bed."

"Do you really expect me to believe you blacked out?"

"Virginia thinks Martina drugged me."

"What…who the hell is Virginia?" I asked angrily.

"She's my therapist." He said calmly.

"You have a therapist? Why?"

"Why do you think Jillienne? Because of you…because of you."

"How long have you been seeing her, and why did you choose a woman therapist over a man?"

"It was Hope who made the initial appointment; she booked it a day before your birthday last year which also happens to be our anniversary, if you remember. She didn't think I would make it through another one without you."

"Of course I remember Jordan! Are you still seeing her…of course you are or how else would she know about the night in question? You talk about your sex life with her? Have you told her about ours?" I was not at all comfortable that he may have related very personal things about our love life to another woman.

"First of all little girl," he said through clenched teeth, "I have not had a sex life in your absence, and yes, she knows everything about you and me, right from day one!"

"Well, isn't that just honkey-dory!" I replied in my most sarcastic voice.

"Virginia has helped me in more ways than you can imagine. With her guidance I have been able to return to a somewhat meaningful life without you even though I have missed you every single day I don't blame myself so much for your leaving anymore, but that I was the cause is always there at the back of my mind."

"Yes, I just bet she has helped you in more ways than one!"

"What the hell does that mean? Are you insinuating that our relationship is more than that of client/patient?"

"If the shoe fits…"

"Well, it doesn't! When did you develop such a vulgar suspicious mind?"

"About ten minutes ago."

"I will take credit for that then, but Virginia and I are only friends."

"Do you take her to dinner and the movies and visit her at her house just as you did Martina?"

"No, we have had several lunches, and talk on the phone, but that is all. I have been to her house once. Before you jump to conclusions, and I can see that you are going to, Hope and Faith were both with me as it was a musical event for the underprivileged. Do you have anything against that?"

"I wouldn't know so how could I understand? I have never had a friend of the opposite sex to commiserate with. How long has it been with you and this Martina?"

"There hasn't been *anything* with her. We met last May sometime. You've never had a relationship with anyone of the opposite sex eh?"

"I guess I can take some consolation in knowing you waited two years to replace me."

Jordan said that he hadn't been looking for someone to take my place because no one could do that. The phone rang. I asked Jordan if he was going to answer; he said no. I asked him he was afraid it was Martina calling. I wanted to say "your girlfriend", but bit my tongue again.

The answering machine turned on. "Grampa, why aren't you answering?" It was the twins.

Jordan picked up the phone. "Hi girls, I'm right here. Your mom is out on an errand right now…oh, it's your grandmother you want to talk to is it? I think perhaps that she would like to talk to you too." He handed me the phone.

"Hello my angels." We talked for a few minutes expressing how much we had missed each other and couldn't wait to see each other at brunch. Hannah said her dad wanted to talk to me.

"Hi Jill; I am *so* glad that it is finally over and that you are home. Is everything okay with Jordan?"

"I'm glad too Craig…I'm not sure yet."

"You can't possibly know how relieved I am. I don't know if I could have held out much longer. Things have not been easy."

"I am sure they haven't, and I am so sorry…"

"No, no, no, don't go there! You beat the odds, you cheated death; there are no regrets. Nothing was ever your fault. There was a reason though that things happened the way they did, but I am still not sure what it was. I can hardly wait to see you, but maybe we won't tell Hope that I am coming to brunch tomorrow okay?"

"Why would she think that you weren't coming?" I looked over at Jordan. He shook his head and mouthed something I couldn't understand.

"Sorry Jill, I thought she would have told you. We have been living apart for a few months. It's not her fault, it's mine. She just got sick and tired of me being married to the ER. Not to worry though, it's all being taken care of. I'm going to let you get back to Jordan; see you tomorrow. I love you Jill."

"I love you too Craig." I handed the phone back to Jordan.

"I rest my case." He said all too smugly.

"What does that mean?"

"You, not having a friend of the opposite sex, that's all."

"He's my son-in-law for God's sake!"

"There is a special bond between you and Craig, and you can't deny that. I'm pretty sure you share a secret or two, but it doesn't bother me because I love him too. My relationship with Virginia is not that connected; she is more like the sister I never had, but I don't expect that you will be able to accept that, but your home so I never have to see her again."

"I didn't come back to interfere in your life Jordan. I have no intention…"

He cut me off. "Life, do you think I had anything remotely resembling a life without you? You are my life, damn it, don't you know that Jillienne?"

He was yelling which was not like him at all. I had to try and appease him. "I was your life, and you were mine, but things have changed Jordan. It's obvious that I put my own welfare above yours. I didn't trust in your love for me enough to confide in you; I should have, and I will be eternally sorry for that. You have made new friends now, friends you would never have found if I had of been here. I kept you in my own little prison thinking that you didn't need anyone but me. You never stopped off for a beer with your colleagues, or joined a bowling league or went fishing with your buddies because you didn't have any. I kept you from doing all those things that a man needs to do. You always came home to me, your jailor. We were always together, just you and me. I don't think that was healthy."

"I came home to you because I wanted to, and if you think you held me hostage then it is what I wanted. I don't regret one single day with you."

"It's your time now Jordan. I will not be the albatross around your neck. I need to see if I qualify for a disability pension. I need to find another doctor who understands my plight and can work with Dr. Ben. I need to find a physiotherapist and a massage therapist, and I need to find a little place of my own. I need to learn to stand on my own two feet. I would ask that you let me stay here just until I get my strength back; it might be a week or so, would that be all right? I hate to ask, but I will probably need to borrow some money from you until things get settled… I really don't want to be a burden to you or the kids." I tried to sound positive and not pathetic.

Jordan turned his back to me. I thought he was going to walk out of the room. Instead he went into the hallway between our bedroom and the closets. I thought I heard the safe opening. He returned with wads of bills and proceeded to throw them in the air. They landed on the bed, on the dressers, on the floor in front of me.

"**Money**, you want **money**? This is yours, it is all yours, every last dime, the bank accounts, the bonds…it's all yours! You are the one who scrimped and saved to put the kids through college, you made sure every bill was paid, you started a retirement fund for us… for you and me. It's no good to me without you. You don't need to go on welfare or anything else as there is enough to keep you for the rest of your life. I will help you, if you will let me, in every step of your recovery, but you **will not** leave this house! I will be the one to leave, and I will go tonight if that is what you want. I guess the boys were right; I kept you high on a pedestal and clipped your wings so that you were unable to fly…fly away from me. You don't want or need my help because you can't stand the sight of me and you don't love me anymore. You will never be able to forgive me for what I did. I hate myself for what happened. I wish I had never told you, and I had decided not to because it meant nothing to me. Maybe you would never have found out, but then there would have always been this elephant in the room with us, and me being this highly principled jerk that I am…well, I had no other options. I want you to be perfectly clear on one thing though, and that is that I have never stopped loving you for even a second, and I will never ever stop trying to win your trust and love back. This night has gone from being the miracle I have been dreaming of to a bloody, freaking nightmare! I have had to tell you of my infidelity, I have betrayed your trust and broken your heart, and in doing so, have broken my own again. I have yelled at you on your first day back…I guess I don't deserve you after all. I am going to go and fix you something to eat now. I have nothing else to say except I'm sorry."

He turned with shoulders slumped, and headed for the bedroom door. I felt remorseful.

"When I heard your voice on the phone, my heart sighed. All the guilt and anger and pain flew out of my body when you said my name, and I heard music. Then you said you would come and get me and I had a glimmer of hope that you might still love me." The tears were running down my face like rain. I tasted them, and they were sweet. For the first time in what seemed like an eternity, I was cleansed. "I never stopped loving you Jordy; I have loved you all the days we were apart. I loved you when I left, and I love you now, and I will forever."

He turned; I could see that he was battling his own emotions. "Jilly…are you saying what I hope you are?"

"I am." I threw the quilt off my lap, and held my arms out. "Come to me Jordy, come to me."

He crossed the room and knelt down at my feet. Silent tears were running down his face. He took my hands in his. "Say it again Jilly; say that you love me; tell me that you will be able to forgive me."

I caressed his face. "I do love you. I don't need to forgive you because you have done nothing wrong. I'm sorry I accused you of multiple acts of betrayal without hearing the full story. I warned you, remember? I told you I was not totally stable, but my God Jordan, I was gone a very long time! You had no word on whether I was alive or dead so I don't need to forgive you, but if you need me to, then yes, I forgive you my darling. I do need you and I don't want to take another step without you."

"And, you never have to." He pulled me up in his arms and kissed me all over my face and my head. Our tears united and we became one through them again.

"I am so tired of pretending that I am holding you in my arms dancing with your picture every night. I have the real thing in my arms now and I never intend to let her go again. Will you grant me the pleasure of letting me hold you in my arms and dancing with me?"

"I might be a little wobbly Jordan, but I will try. I see you had my picture laminated."

He laughed. "Craig did that for me just a few days ago. I can't tell you how many times I rolled over on you at night and cracked the glass."

"Oh Jordan, you big boob!"

"Yeah, that's what Faith calls me. She used to stand at the door and watch me dance around the room with. Hey, hey, no more tears okay? Let's see what's on the radio, oh, this is just perfect, one of our favorite songs."

I agreed that it was. He held me tightly as we swayed to the Righteous Brothers singing Unchained Melody. Tears were still escaping and running down my cheeks in memory of the first time we had danced to it.

"This is the first time I have been able to cry in a very long time. I guess all the injections dried up my tear ducts. I used to sit in a chair by the window and in my muddled mind, day after day, I would imagine that you were at the edge of the forest waiting for me. You would beckon to me to follow you. I would try and get up, but I couldn't. Eventually you tired of waiting for me, and ran off with a damsel with long black hair…does Martina have long black hair Jordan?"

He hugged me tighter. "No, she doesn't. I never stopped waiting for you, I never gave up on the dream that you would come back some day. If I could have just heard your voice…"

"Every day I wanted to call you, every day, but what good would it have done me? I didn't know what my future held, and I could not, would not, give you hope. I convinced myself that you were better off thinking I was dead, and then I just couldn't do it anymore. I had to come home and face the consequences."

"There are no consequences, not one, not one Jilly. We are together and together we can face anything. I just need you to trust me and believe that Martina means nothing to me."

"I do Jordan, and I think that maybe Virginia was right. I think that you were drugged and for your own peace of mind you need to confront her."

"Maybe someday; but not now. All I want is to concentrate and rejoice in you."

"Are you sure? I am but a shell of what I once was; my arms and legs are freakishly scrawny, my face is chubby like a chipmunk's, I don' have one single solitary hair on my body except for eyelashes and scrawny eye brows. I might always be this way. Are you sure you want to take that chance? And suppose if I can never be your wife again? I don't know what all those drugs have done to me."

He laughed. "I don't care if you weigh two hundred pounds or ninety three, if you have hair or not…I'm in love with the essence of you, your spirit, your heart, your soul. Everything else is just window dressing." He kissed me tenderly. "Now what do you say, do we have a deal?"

"Yes, we do. Now I need to go and wash my face and find my hat before those girls get back."

"Oh yeah, those girls, and I guess I better get busy with supper."

"Yes, you had better, but not before you clean up this room Mister."

"I guess we don't want the girls to see this money all over the place as they would be sure to ask questions." He patted my bottom as I left the comfort of his arms. "You don't know how good it feels to have my old boss home."

I washed my face over and over again. I picked up the hand mirror and looked solemnly at the image in it. "Mirror, mirror, I never was the fairest, but my husband thought I was, but now, what does he really see in me?"

I was unaware that Jordan had followed me. "He sees what he always has…the most beautiful doll in the world and she's his for all time."

I laughed. "I'm a doll all right, a kewpie doll."

He squeezed my chubby cheeks. "All the more for me to love."

"I never thought I was vain Jordan."

"You're not Honey."

"Then why do I want my hair back? I want my long, thick auburn hair back…I don't feel like I am me without it?"

"Then we will get you a wig, hell we'll get half a dozen, each one in a different color, what do you say about that?"

"Maybe, we'll see. Now what are you doing here; I thought you were cooking?"

"Thought that I had better check to see if you had developed any new food allergies?"

"Not that I know of, just my usual dislikes. Now, off with you; I am very hungry."

I found the turban and returned it to my head, and applied a new layer of lipstick. I opened my silver cigarette case and wondered if I had time…

"Mommy, we're back; where are you?" Hope called out.

I took a deep breath and went out to meet them.

"Did you have a little rest Mommy…eek, what is that smell? Did you use some of Daddy's horrible spray?"

Faith laughed. "Oh, you are so square Hope! That smell is 'pot'."

"Pot…oh, marijuana. Are you taking medicinal marijuana Mom…does it help?"

"It used to help with the pain and nausea, but now I don't have much of either so I think I am just using it to unwind. I should really quit."

"Don't be silly Mommy; if it helps, it helps. What did Daddy say?" Faith asked.

"Not much. I think he is all right with it. Now, show me what you bought."

They were pretty excited over their purchases so I feigned delight also. Truth of the matter was that clothes were not on my list of importance. I really just wanted to be back in Jordan's arms. Faith tossed all the personal items like panties aside and extracted two dresses from a large bag. One was elephant patterned, long, black and white and didn't appear to be too form fitting. It was made of rayon which had always been a favorite material of mine. The other was a shorter red and orange cotton flowered frock. It would probably come down to my knees. I said that I would wear it tomorrow. They had also decided to get me a pair of tan linen-like slacks, and a long forest green top and jacket. Hope produced four head wraps. She explained that the black one was a sleep turban, the blue flowered lace beanie may be what I would chose for outdoors. There was also a peachy colored bandana head wrap, and a grey cotton snood. I love them more than any of the clothing, and donned the snood right away saying that the peach colored wrap would go nicely with the flowery dress and I would wear them tomorrow. I hugged them both, and thanked them. Jordan appeared at the doorway and said that dinner was on the table.

He apologized that it wasn't much, but if he had of known that I was coming, he would have baked a cake. I laughed a little. Faith said that I would be very surprised to see what a good cook he had become. They sat down at the table while I wandered around the kitchen touching the counters and opening up a few of the cupboards. Jordan asked Faith what she thought she was doing. I looked over and saw that she was sitting in the chair next to her father, the spot where I had always sat.

"Your mother is home now Honey, so you are going to have to relinquish her seat."

Faith laughed. "Of course, I wasn't thinking. I kept your place warm for you Mommy, and everything is just as you left it."

"I can see that. I always loved this kitchen, and thanks for keeping your dad company while I was gone. Now, will someone please let Lionel in?"

"Oh Mommy, Lionel is not here anymore; he left home shortly after you did. I'm so sorry."

"Well, then who is that sitting on the patio table? He sure looks like Lionel."

The three of them rushed to the window that I was looking out and all exclaimed in delight when they saw our family cat. Faith ran to the door and picked him up scolding him for running away and worrying them. She gave him to me and I sat down with him on my lap. His purring was a great comfort to me.

"I told you I heard him didn't I Daddy?" Faith said with tears in her eyes.

"Yes, you did, and that's why I went out and bought his favorite food. I have been putting it out every night and every morning it is all gone, but I never saw him so I figured it could be any stray cat. I did hear a mewing one night though and hoped that it was him."

"He knew you were coming home Mom. The twins are going to be so excited. Is his bed still under the steps?" Hope asked.

"Yes." Jordan answered, taking Lionel off my lap. "There is plenty of time for you two to get reacquainted, but right now you need to get some food in your stomach Jillienne. Faith, will you take him to his bed? I'll get him a dish of food."

I let Jordan take him a little reluctantly. He had claimed that cubby hole underneath the upstairs steps for his own just as Faith had years ago. She had just turned three when we moved into the house. Only two of the four bedrooms on the top floor were finished so the boys had to share a room as did the girls for the first year. The master bedroom was only framed in, and the kitchen had nothing in it but a few wooden crates used for cupboards, and a single sink. It was like a three ring circus that summer as Jordan's and my parents set up trailers in the back yard so that they could help us make the house livable. Our fathers built temporary kitchen cupboards until we could afford to have some custom made. Jordan's mom and mine did the cooking and helped with the children while Jordan and I hammered and dry walled and painted. It was one of the happiest times of our lives until the day

Faith went missing. We searched up and down for her, but she was nowhere to be found so while Hope stayed in the house, just in case Faith magically appeared, the rest of us took to the streets. Some fifteen or so minutes later with no sign of her we decided we had to call the police, and headed back to the house. We were met at the door by Hope holding her sister. Faith had found the cubby hole that was at the back of the stairs which was concealed by boxes that had not been unpacked yet. Somehow she had managed to squeeze between them and had taken her blanket and two dolls and had fallen asleep. Hope heard her crying and managed to find her. Apparently, Faith had closed the door behind her and the latch got stuck so she couldn't get out and was oblivious to our calling for her. Jordan immediately removed the doors. It remained a favorite place for Faith to play and take a nap. She introduced Lionel to it the day we brought him home. He had taken to it immediately.

Faith sighed deeply as she sat down beside me. "At last, everyone is home."

"But you won't be for much longer will you Honey?" I asked trying not to sound too woeful. "I want to hear all about Cree, but first I have two questions. First, what happened to all the house plants, and when did you two start eating white bread?"

Faith and Jordan looked at each other as if they were partners in a conspiracy.

"First of all, we had to toss all the plants because they got some sort of disease. Hope thinks we over watered. We still don't eat white bread, but Daddy buys it every Friday just like he always did for you from that bakery that you like. He buys it just in case you came home. On Saturday evenings when he realizes that you aren't coming he puts the loaf in the freezer. I'm guessing that he had already put this loaf in the freezer just before you phoned."

I didn't know what to say so I just let the teardrops fall. Jordan placed his hand on mine.

"It's okay Babe, please don't cry."

"That is the saddest, yet most touching thing you have ever done." I managed.

"I had to do everything possible to keep the dream alive Jillienne." He said humbly.

"So, am I to assume that there is a freezer full of white bread?"

Faith said that every three months they would load up the frozen bread and drop it off at the local food bank or soup kitchen, and then the ritual would start all over again. I didn't know if I would be able to swallow because I was so emotional, but I managed to pick up the quartered sandwich and took a small bite.

"Chicken salad…oh Jordan, you have outdid yourself! None of you can possibly know what a treat this is! All we ever had at the convent was heavy rye bread. It always tasted stale, and the only way you could eat it was to soak it in tea or porridge, or I should say, what passed as porridge."

"Was all the food horrible there Mommy?" Faith asked.

"It was summer, so we always had fresh vegetables. On Fridays we had fish of some sort, usually fried, and roast chicken and dumplings on Sunday, and whatever was leftover the next day. Eggs and cheeses were plentiful, and we churned our own butter, and made cottage cheese. There weren't a lot of condiments like ketchup or peanut butter though."

"Aah, your staples, and you lived to tell the tale without them?" Jordan laughed.

"Don't be silly; Gayle bought them for me. I was dependent on her for a lot of things as I had no monies of my own." I lamented.

"Is there any way we can reimburse her Mom?" Hope asked.

I smiled and told her there wasn't. "Now what is this I hear about you and Craig living apart?"

She looked at Jordan crossly. He said, "Don't blame me; your estranged husband told her."

"We are not estranged Daddy!" She responded irately.

"Sorry, but I don't know what you would call it then." He answered.

"We'll talk more about this later Hope, but for now, I would like to hear how Faith and Cree met, okay?" I prompted.

Hope pouted. "I should have known he'd call you."

"He didn't, the girls did. I had a very brief conversation with Craig. He did not know that I hadn't been informed of the situation yet."

"Mommy's home!" Faith said cheekily.

Jordan smiled. "Yes, she is, and I have already found out that she's still the boss. Now you had better hope that she regards Cree the same way she does Craig."

"That's not possible Dad; everyone knows that her and Craig go way back…back to medieval times where they were kindred spirits, or maybe they were even king and queen of some kingdom." Faith stated.

Hope snorted. "Well, that's a theory I haven't heard yet."

I laughed too. "That's very interesting Faith. I have often wondered who I was in another life; thanks for making me a queen. You have the floor my dear; let's see if Cree can give Craig a run for the crown."

"It was December, 2006; I was not in a very good mood to begin with the day I met him. I was not pleased with the last grade I had been given, so I gathered everything I could carry planning on studying hard over the Christmas break. The campus grounds were deserted as practically everyone else had left hours ago. To make matters worse it was trying to snow."

"Sorry to interrupt Dear, but what was the grade you were so upset with?" I asked.

"It was in philosophy. I thought I deserved a 99, but I only received an 87."

That was degrading to my daughter. I did not comment, but told her to go on with her story.

"So, by the time I got to my car, my feet were soaked, and I couldn't find my keys. I placed my books on the hood so that I could search my purse for them. Of course they were at the very bottom and I dropped them in a rather large puddle as I fumbled to pull them out. I guess I swore because when I bent down to pick them up, a voice behind me said that was not very becoming language for a young lady. I did not respond though I wanted to tell this guy behind the voice to take a hike. I opened the door and got behind the wheel. I was attempting to shut the door when he asked me where I thought I was going. Now I was thinking that he was some sort of pervert as I wrestled him for the door. I did not win, and I called him a few choice names. I leaned on my horn hoping to attract attention. He laughed and backed off.

"Okay, got you. I just thought you might require help with that flat tire."

I shut the door and said through the open window that I didn't believe him. He shrugged and started to walk away telling me to have a nice day. I put the key in the ignition; it just went urrrrrr, urrrrrr, urrrrrr. It didn't take a brain surgeon to know that the battery was dead. I had three choices, call Daddy or the Automobile Association, go back inside and see if someone could help me, or ask that stranger if he had jumper cables. I chose to call Daddy, but my damn phone was dead. I guess *he* heard me trying to start the car because he came back and told me to pop the hood and he would take a look. After a few minutes, he closed the hood and admitted that he knew nothing about engines. I probably sighed and asked if I could use his cell phone. He said I could if he had one. I wondered who this hick was. He offered to change the tire and would then find someone who might have jumper cables or he would go inside and call a tow truck. I told him I had AA. I got out still not believing that I had a flat. Well, I did and when we opened the trunk, there was no spare, no jack, nothing! He offered to give me a ride. I asked him if he really thought that I would get into a car with a complete stranger. He agreed that he was a stranger but he certainly wasn't complete yet. He walked back to his car asking if I was coming or not. The only other option I had was to go back into the university as there wasn't another soul around, but I decided to go with him. His car was a little old yellow Volkswagen. When he opened the door for me a dozen or so books fell off the seat unto the floor. He picked them up and threw them into the back seat which was already overflowing with junk. The dashboard was filled with miniature plastic and wooden dinosaurs. I commented that his son or daughter must be fascinated with the prehistoric creatures.

"My dear, I have no children, no wife, not even a girlfriend, woe be it." He said.

He then introduced himself as Cree McFarlan, and said that the dinosaurs were all his babies, and asked if he might know my name. I told him wondering why a grown man would have children's toys all over his car. It was then that I noticed his parking pass from the Royal Tyrrell Museum in Drumheller. I asked him if he was an archaeologist. He said he wasn't, but that he was a paleontologist, and proceeded to tell me the difference. I felt like a dunce because I should have realized that the dinosaurs were a clear indication that he dealt with fossils and not human artefacts. He stopped at the first major business we came to which just happened to be Tom's Tire Store and More. I went inside and called Daddy; he did not answer on his cell or home phone which was most unusual. I called AA, and found out I no longer had a membership there. I then called Hope and hung up before she could answer because I remembered she was at the twins' Christmas concert. Craig was at the hospital. I decided to call a taxi, but Cree told me to go wait in the car and he would see what he could do. I was getting a little antsy wondering what was taking him so long when he emerged pushing a tire. He loaded it and we headed back to the university parking lot. He had it on in no time, and told me I was all set. Miraculously the car started. I had no money on me so I asked for his address so I could reimburse him.

He said he'd take it up with me at home as he was going to follow me just in case the car conked out. So, we get home, and Daddy's car was in the drive. I get out and told Cree I would get him the money, but he followed me into the house. I asked Dad where he had been, and he said he had been home all the time except when he ran across the road to Hanks'. He hadn't checked his phone for messages. I explained what had happened and asked him to settle up with Mr. McFarlan. I thanked Cree and went to shower and change as my clothes were wet and I was cold. When I came out half an hour later, Daddy and Cree were sitting here at the table laughing and drinking coffee. Daddy lectured me a little on not renewing my AA, and for not replacing the spare tire after I vacuumed out the trunk. He then took Cree upstairs to Connor's old room so that he could shower and change into dry clothes. I stood there wondering what the hell had just happened. Not only did Cree stay for supper, but also the night. Daddy said it didn't make any sense for him to drive all the way to his parents place in Olympia in the inclement weather. Much to my disbelief I found myself liking him by the end of the evening. When he left in the morning, he said he would be in touch, and he was true to his word. He called me from his parent's home in Olympia later that day, and we have never been out of touch ever since. He said he fell in love with me two minutes after we met. Even though I had been most rude and obstinate, he said that it was my pluck that endeared me to him. I probably would have written him off as just another pompous male if it wasn't for Daddy's shrewd insights. So, if you don't like him as he is a bit of an odd-ball, you can blame Daddy, but I think you will come to love him just as I do."

"I think I like him already Darling." I smiled at her, and then Jordan. "And, just for the record, your father has always had good taste and judgement. I gather by his last name that Cree is of Scottish descent?"

"Yes, his father is from Nottingham Scotland. His heritage on his mother's side is Native American. His grandmother was a full blooded Cree; hence his name. He thinks of himself as a mixed breed and says that our children will be multi-cultured."

Jordan got up and announced that his good sense was telling him it was time to get me to bed, but before that we should have some dessert. He took something out of the fridge and sat it in front of me. It was apricot cheesecake; my very favorite indulgence. I asked him if he had been buying them like the bread since I had been gone.

"Not as often, but one has to be prepared. I cannot take credit for this one though as the girls picked it up on their little shopping trip."

"It's not from Aunt Flo's though Mom as it was closed, but it looks good."

"I'm sure it is Hope. It will certainly be better than anything I have had in a very long time."

I had a few forkfuls and then asked if I could have it wrapped up along with the rest of the sandwich for later. Jordan took my arm and led me towards the bedroom. The girls told me they loved me at the door, and expressed tearfully how glad they were that I was home. I returned their sentiments, and we had a group hug. Faith asked her father if he wanted her to make up the bed in the den. He shrugged and said, "Sure, if you want to." He winked at her and ushered me into the bedroom, and closed the door.

"Jordan," I scolded, "that was a little gauche."

He laughed, taking me into his arms, and plastering me with kisses. "Gotta keep them guessing…now, where were we earlier?"

I left his embrace stating that I needed to brush my teeth. I returned a few minutes later to find that he had changed into a tee shirt and leisure pants. He was sitting on the edge of the bed waiting for me. He helped me off with my dressing gown and drew back the covers. He looked troubled. I asked him what was wrong.

"Perhaps I am making assumptions that you want to share the bed with me…would you prefer that I slept in the den?"

"You can if you want, but I don't want you to."

"That's all I need to hear, be right back."

He returned with the lotion that Faith had given me, and crawled into bed and told me to turn over. He took down the straps of my negligee saying that it would be easier if I wasn't wearing anything. I told him he could take it off if he promised not to look at me. I automatically placed my hands over my breasts as he slid the gown off.

He laughed. "You're still doing that I see."

"Yes, it's just reflex."

"Well Sweetie, I see you still have something to hide…"

"You noticed?"

"Pretty hard not to; any explanation as to why your perfectly beautiful breasts weren't affected as was the rest of you?"

"Nope, I asked, but no one had an explanation, so I'm stuck with these overtaxed girls."

"You won't hear me complaining."

He continued to apply the lotion to my back and my shoulders in gentle massages. I relaxed and delighted in every caress of his hands. I felt the hardness of his body against mine, and I felt that we were both ready to become one again. I turned over and kissed him passionately. I asked him if he wanted to make love.

"Oh Darling, you can't imagine how much I want to, but it's too soon."

I stiffened up immediately. "I am so sorry, how insensitive of me. Of course it is too soon for you after Martina."

"Oh Baby, that's not what I meant at all! Please don't ever think that. I hate myself for what happened, but even if I did remember, it would mean nothing, nothing! I am only worried about you. My God, you have been to hell and back! Today has been one giant marathon for you. Not only have you spent half a day on a plane, but we have bombarded you with questions for hours. I'm only concerned for you well-being Jilly…if I hurt you I would never forgive myself."

"You won't hurt me Jordan. I am stronger than you think, and more so when I am in your arms. I need to know if I can be your wife in the true sense of the word, but if I can't be I'll just head back to the convent and see if they will accept me as a novice."

"You are just being silly now. There is no way on earth that you could take vows of chastity and obedience!" Jordan exclaimed.

"There will never be anyone else for me but you, so remaining chaste would not be a problem."

"There is absolutely no doubt in my mind that our love life will be just as wonderful…no, let me rephrase that, it will be stronger and more impassioned than ever. There is so much more to our love than sex…just a minute, did you say "go back to the convent"? You told me you had no idea where it was; was that not true?"

"Oh Jordan, shut up and kiss me; you always did ask too many questions."

CHAPTER 9

All the Other Women

I gently removed Jordan's arm from around me and inched my way across the bed. It was very strange to wake up after two and a half years of sleeping alone to discover that someone else was sharing the bed. I picked my night clothes up off the floor and tiptoed into the bathroom. It was three in the morning. I shut the door quietly, dressed, and opened the window, and sat down on the floor with my back up against the wall under the window with my silver "cigarette" case in my hands. I had only taken two long drags when I heard Jordan coming down the hall. He knocked lightly.

"Are you okay Honey?" He asked.

I told him that the door was open. He came in asking again if I was all right. I smiled running my eyes up and down his naked body. He grinned and reached for his robe that was hanging on a peg on the back of the door, put the toilet seat down, and sat facing me.

"You don't have to cover up for my benefit, in fact, I rather like the view. I see you have kept in shape since I have been away. I guess no cheesecakes?"

"Faith bakes now and then, and Hope will pop over with cookies she and the girls have made, but none of it is as good as yours. Are you sure you're not hurting…did I hurt you?"

"I told you I don't have much pain Jordan, and no, you definitely did not hurt me."

"Are you nauseated?"

I shook my head. "Just chilling and musing."

"About what?"

"You; I don't think I believe you."

"What don't you believe Jilly?"

"I don't think your romp in the hay with Martina was as unrewarding as you would like me to believe. You like sex way too much to…"

Jordan halted me by showing me the palm of his hand. "Stop right there little girl! I do like sex, I love it, but with **YOU** and only **You**! Last night, being with you was amazing, and beyond my wildest expectations of what it would be like to be with you again; and you… well, I told you that you had nothing to worry about, didn't I?"

"Yes, but what if someday you remember being with her, and I don't measure up?"

He took my hand. "Oh, you sweet little minx; don't you know how preposterous that is? Everything I told you about that inexcusable few minutes is true. With not much memory of the whole ordeal I may as well have been a robot and she may as well have been a blow-up doll. And, if I ever do remember, it will mean absolutely nothing to me. Honey, I don't know what more I can do or say to assure you of that."

His eyes were pleading for me to believe him. I was amused by the idea of him and a blow-up doll and I told him so. "I told you I forgave you Jordan, and I meant it, and I do believe you."

"Good, because I have never lied to you or kept anything from you in thirty one years, actually, it is thirty three and a half years if we are dealing in facts."

"Actually, that is not quite true is it Jordan?" I was going to hate myself for bringing this up, but I felt compelled to do so. "You've kept something from me for all these years haven't you…a little something by the name of Marlayna Davidge?"

His face didn't register shock or surprise. He just nodded and said that it was funny that I should mention her name at this time. I asked him why. He came and sat down beside me and took my "smoke" out of my hand and put it up to his lips.

"Don't Jordan!"

He took a drag and asked why not. I told him I didn't want him to disrespect his morals.

"Morals…hell, do you think I have any left? I cheated on my wife, I've kept something from her believing that what she didn't know couldn't hurt her, and you talk about making a pact with the devil…yeah, I know all about that. I called on him a time or two offering up my tarnished soul if he would bring you back to me. I would have done anything, anything, even murder, but I guess there were too many more important mortals in line ahead of me. Now, what is it you want to know about Marlayna?"

"I'm sorry Jordan. I don't need to know why you never told me about her…it must be this Martina thing or the pot. I don't want to open up old wounds as it must be very painful for you to talk about her or else you would have told me a long time ago."

"It's not painful at all. We were over and done with long before I met you. There wasn't then, and there aren't any residual feelings for her left. I can't in all honesty tell you why I chose not to tell you. You were, and are this precious jewel and maybe I didn't want you to know about a failed relationship in case it scared you off."

"Nothing would have scared me off Jordy."

"Yeah, I know that now, but we were starting a new life and the old one had been dead for a long time, and it had nothing to do with us. I can only speculate on when and how this made its way to you."

I confessed saying that I had known since I was fifteen.

"God Jilly…why didn't you ever ask me about her?"

"I think that ball was in your court, and it still is."

"You're right; I should have told you that I was engaged to someone before you. I never thought about her so I didn't think I was keeping anything from you. I didn't even think that maybe you would hear about it from someone else. I just never thought about it at all. But, if you have known since you were fifteen…that is the year we first met…Clay must have told you."

"He did. I don't think he knew all the facts, but he said you had given him a rough version of your relationship with her, and that it hadn't sounded like it was a healthy one. He thought that you may still be in love with her, and he was worried that she was going to hurt you again."

"Clay got it all wrong. If I ever was in love with her, and that is a mighty big **if,** I sure as hell wasn't in 1973. Don't look at me as if you think I am just saying this because I think it is what you want to hear. I can say it without any doubt because until you, I had no idea what real love was all about."

"You must have been in love because you asked her to marry you." I said blankly.

"It seemed like the right thing to do…"

I interrupted him. "Oh, just like you asked me to marry you after we had been intimate?"

"Damn it Jillienne; stop putting words in my mouth! Our situation was entirely different and you know it! We had been secretly in love with each other for years…God; you were only eleven or twelve when I had my fling with Marlayna. I didn't even know you existed."

"My love for you was not so secret. Tell me what went wrong with you and Marlayna."

He sighed and took a drag of my smoke. "This doesn't taste at all like I remember."

"Of course not; it's medicinal remember, very little THC I imagine."

"I guess I first met her in 1970 or "71. She had moved to Shelton with her parents from England, for what reason, I can't remember. Donna and Cole Tripp had me over for dinner one night and that is where I met her. She was a Practical Nurse like Donna so they had become friends at the hospital. I guess we hit it off…perhaps we were both ripe for something. We dated throughout the summer until I went back to school. She would work overtime so that she could bank time to come and spend a week with me every so often. Jillienne, look at me …this was way before you and me, you understand that don't you?"

I had stiffened up. "I know; I just don't like to envision you in another woman's arms."

"I know Baby, I know. Let's get this over with okay? We got engaged the next spring, and everything seemed to be a "go" for us to marry the next year. Something was missing, but I was too young and naïve to know what it was at the time. August came and three days before I was to leave for school she informed me that her parents were going back to England and she was going with them. We argued about what the distance was going to do to our relationship, but she promised absence would only make us grow stronger. She was wrong. We talked on the phone once or twice and month and corresponded by mail for a while. By spring, I couldn't care less whether she came back or not. However, she talked me into going to England and I, stupidly went. I had been seeing other women, and I suspected that she had been unfaithful also, a fact she admitted to. I broke off the engagement although she said she would come back with me and we could be married immediately. I didn't trust her, and frankly, I wondered what I had ever seen in her in the first place. So, that is it. She did come back in 1973 she and wanted us to try again. I told her I had seriously moved on, and that I was going to marry the girl of my dreams."

I was near to tears. "Nell?"

He took the squashed butt from my hand, flushed it, and took me in his arms. "No, it sure as hell wasn't Nell! You know damn well it was you!"

I blubbered. "You're just making that up. You knew nothing of the kind back then."

"Are you sure about that? Anyhow, that is what I told her, and I never looked back. I love you Jillienne Marie Connors Landon; are we good?"

"Almost. What did you mean when you said it was funny that I should mention her name at this time?"

"Oh that; when I was in Shelton the July long weekend I ran into her." He answered casually.

"What…she's back? Oh my God, did she know I was missing and came back for you again?"

"She said she came back to be with Donna who was having a hard time dealing with her newly diagnosis of multiple sclerosis. She did want me to have a drink with her, and she did say that she still had feelings for me. I set her straight on that telling her that missing or not, you were still my wife and that I was still madly in love with you, and that I was not in the market for any kind of relationship with her or anyone else. After visiting with our parents I went back to the motel and found her waiting for me with a bottle of whiskey. I told her I would have one quick drink, but not in my room, but at the pool. Apparently, she hadn't got the picture yet that I wanted nothing to do with her. I'm afraid I was rather rude in my rejections to her advances. I left her crying, but I didn't give a damn, and hoped I would never run into her again. Now I guess I had better tell you that Nell is now the new drama teacher at Q.E. It was my job to welcome her and I did. I let the Q.E. grapevine fill her in on the details of your disappearance, and my anguish. By the way, she is happily married and has two teenage boys. End of stories."

He said we were done talking now. I said I wasn't, and he said he expected that the subjects would come up again sometime but it was time to get my butt off the cold floor and back into a warm bed next to him.

"Okay, but I have one last question." I pointed to his hand. "I see you are wearing your wedding band…do you always wear it?"

Without missing a beat he said that he has never taken it off, and then realized my implication.

"Oh God Jilly, I am so sorry." He stammered woefully.

"No, I am sorry for asking. I know you had no intentions of anything happening with Martina. Let's put it all to bed and us too."

He pulled me up gently and kissed me thanking me for being so understanding. I hoped, for his sake that I would be able to keep my word and supress my suspicions that all was not as innocent as he wanted not only me, but himself to believe. But, I knew me, and I had a sinking feeling that the other shoe was about to drop. Not tonight though, not tonight as my husband was promising me a foot massage if I was a good girl.

"I have no idea how I made it through two and a half years without you Jordan."

"One day at a time, just like I did, one day at a time, one agonizing day at a time."

I awoke the next morning to the pungent smell of coffee. I found my negligee on the floor and slipped into it, and wrapped myself in Jordan's soft terrycloth bathrobe. I headed to the kitchen without even stopping to wash my face. It wasn't so much that I wanted coffee; it was that I wanted to see my husband. I stood at the kitchen doorway and watched him beating the pancake mix; he was humming a tune I recognized immediately. It was "Some Enchanted Evening."

"Hey Sailor," I said enticingly, "what does a girl have to do to get a cup of coffee around here anyhow?"

He turned around grinning from ear to ear. "Well, I usually charge six dollars and ninety five cents per cup to all the other dames in the neighborhood, but for you I think a kiss will suffice."

I walked over and into his arms. "Thank-you kind sir as I am an impoverished waif."

He laughed. "And, that is just the way I am going to keep you; penniless and barefoot so that you can never run out on me again."

"Oh sure, and how did that work out for you before?"

He answered me by putting his hands inside the robe and kissing me passionately.

"I see you two up to your old shenanigans **again**? Am I going to have to knock every time I enter a room **again**?" Faith squealed surprising us.

Jordan answered her without hesitation. "Fraid so Honey."

She crossed the floor to us and embraced us. "Oh, thank God; I was so afraid."

Our other daughter entered the room and asked what was going on.

"Mommy and Daddy are still in love Hope." Faith answered.

"Of course they are; didn't I tell you that last night?"

"Yes, but I was still worried."

Jordan asked what she was worried about.

"I don't know for sure. I mean, Mom was gone for a long time, and…"

I stopped her from saying what she didn't really want to. "Were you concerned how I would react when I found out that your dad had a lady friend?"

Faith was stunned. "Daddy told you already?"

I took her hand and sat her down at the table. "Yes Dear, I know all about Martina, and I am not in the least bit upset. I am glad that your father found someone to socialize with."

Jordan and I had decided that no one else ever needed to know anything else about that questionable sordid night.

"We weren't really that worried Mom because she was not his type at all."

"How do you know that Faith? It is my understanding that you never met her?"

"I didn't actually, but I did see her and Daddy together, and I could tell that there was nothing going on between them."

Jordan asked her when that was.

She answered coyly that it was at the Sunshine Sea Festival.

"You mean the one you said you had no interest in attending?" He questioned.

"Yes, I changed my mind after you left and decided to go and track you down. I saw the two of you watching the boat races, and then you went to one of the food booths. I was pretty sure you weren't more than friends because you never put your arm around her or held hands like you and Mommy always do."

I asked her how she knew it was Martina and not some other woman. She said she knew it by the way Hope had described her; tall, grey permed hair, mousey looking and dressed in an outdated pantsuit, and besides that, Jordan only had one other lady friend, and it certainly wasn't his therapist. I asked if she thought Virginia was a more suitable friend for her father.

Jordan cleared his voice loudly expressing his disapproval of our conversation, but Faith answered me anyhow.

"Of course not Mommy; she's his therapist! I can't believe you told her everything already Daddy." She said looking crossly at her father.

"There wasn't much to tell Faith."

Hope sighed. "She never could keep her big mouth shut, but I am glad that everything is out in the open, and that there will be no surprises if one of them shows up at the front door,"

"I thought I taught you girls never to judge a book by its cover. You both condemned Martina because of her looks. For all you know, she is a very lovely woman." I hoped they didn't notice the bitterness in my voice. "Now, I need to go and shower. You girls can help your father with the preparations, and Faith, you owe him an apology for spying on him. And Jordan, that dishwasher is going to have to go."

For once, everyone was silent.

Hannah and Lannah were out of the car and running up the steps before Craig had even turned the engine off. They were in my arms crying and laughing at the same time. I smiled at Craig over their heads. He asked them if they minded if he said hello to me. I told them to go help their mother with the table while I talked to their father. There was no one else in the hallway except Craig and me. A tear slid down his cheek as he fought to keep composure. He pulled me close and whispered that I had no idea how glad he was to see me.

"Oh, but I do Craig as the feeling is mutual." I said kissing his cheek.

"I don't think I would have made it another six months Jill. Thank God you came home early."

"I should have come home earlier, and then maybe none of this would have happened."

He stood back. "What do you mean?"

I could not tell him that I would have prevented Jordan's ordeal. "Maybe I could have prevented Hope and you from separating."

"Maybe, but it was a lesson learned and it's all over now."

"Is it?"

He took my hand. "Come on, I want to see my wife, and I have something to tell you all."

We joined the rest of the family in the dining room. The twins had sweet-talked their grandfather into letting me sit between them. Good naturedly he had given in telling them that it was a "one time thing." He asked us all to hold hands, and said a mushy prayer thanking God for bringing me back home. I said "Amen" before he could launch into anything mawkish. Jordan had always been wishy-washy on religion, but had gained a whole new sense of spiritualism since meeting Padre Emilio. I was looking forward to meeting his mentor.

As soon as everyone was finished eating Craig could contain himself no longer. He reached for Hope's hands. "Wednesday is my last night in the ER. I am opening my own private practice. It will be a nine to five job, five days a week. Can I come home now?"

The twins were out of their seats. "Please Mommy, let Daddy come home."

Hope was apologetic. "I should never have expected you to quit doing what you love Craig. I'm sorry, and I want you to move back in more than you will ever know, but private practice…how is that even possible?"

"First things first; I did love working in the ER, but I love you and the girls more. I know it has been a long haul, but it is over… well, I may still do an occasional shift at the hospital if it is all right with you."

Hope said it most definitely was and asked him again how and where he would be practicing.

"It's not just me. I've entered into a partnership with two other doctors; a pediatrician, and another general practitioner. We have purchased the Hanover Building on Sixth Street. Also on board are a dentist, a physiotherapist, and a massage therapist." He looked at me. "They might be of some interest to you Jill. There are several other offices unclaimed as of yesterday, but we have half a dozen inquiries."

"It sounds wonderful Craig, but how did you manage your share of the cost?"

"Believe it or not, my mother financed me. Actually, it was her idea when I told her about it."

"You shared your plans with your mother and not your wife? I suppose you knew too Daddy…and did you know too Faith?" Hope said accusingly.

"No one else knew Hon. I didn't want to tell you until I was sure, and it was only finalized yesterday. I called you as soon as I finished my shift, but you didn't answer, and then you called me and told me that your mom was home. My news paled with that, and so I waited until today. I'm sorry; I guess I screwed up again." Craig apologised regretfully. "Will you forgive me and come and work with me?"

Hope's voice was strained. "Work with you…what do you mean?"

"I want you to be my assistant."

"To assist with what? I'm in no way medically inclined."

"Well, you would be my aide-de-camp; you know, secretary, personal assistant and partner in the business…what do you say?"

I couldn't resist. "It sounds like a dream job, and if Hope doesn't want it, can I have it?"

Hope looked at me grinning. "No, you cannot Mom! I know just how much you would love to work with my husband, but you already have a full time job looking after Daddy!"

We all laughed. Hope kissed Craig, and said she accepted but if the togetherness became too much she reserved the right to quit. Craig asked if we would excuse them as he wanted to take Hope to see his new office. Jordan proposed a toast and said that we would keep the twins while the two of them had a little alone time. We saw them to the door where Craig asked me if I would do him the honor of becoming his first patient. I agreed enthusiastically as I already knew that he and Dr. Ben could work together.

While Faith and the girls helped clean up Jordan made me comfortable in the front room and placed calls for me to my family. I spent ten minutes assuring Conner and Rusty that I was all right, and that they would hear the rest of my story on Saturday. Jordan explained to me that my mother have become quite forgetful so I shouldn't be surprised at some of the things she might say. I only got to talk to her for three or four minutes as her crying made her speech indecipherable. Dad made the excuse that she was just wrought with emotion, and that everything would be all right when she actually saw me. I wasn't too sure though and even less convinced about my mother's health after I talked to Jordan's mother. She said that she wished they could all see me before Faith's wedding as that was still a month away, but they understood that I was still recuperating. Jordan took the phone from me, and said that as soon as I felt strong enough to make the trip he was bringing me home for a short visit, perhaps as early as next week. I smiled and nodded to him that I would be. Clay had not received Hope's phone call regarding me as he was on a canoe trip somewhere in the Cariboo. There wasn't any cell service so I would just have to wait until he called me. He was due home on Saturday. There was only one call left to make. I made an obnoxious face when Jordan told me that he was calling my sister. She wasn't home so he left a message. Thank God for small miracles.

Three hours later I stood hesitantly in front of the elevators at the Hanover Building. Craig's offices were on the third floor. Jordan said that the stairs would be too much for me and promised me a Wendy's burger if I'd take the plunge. I said, "Okay, but no mustard and no pickles." He told me we had a deal. I did not pass out on the fifteen second ride.

Monday morning I saw my husband off to put in his request for a leave of absence. If it wasn't granted, he was going to quit. I had to do a lot of talking as he was prepared to resign outright. His reasons were me, of course. His intentions had always been to retire at sixty-five. He would be sixty this December so that only meant five more years. I think I had talked him into returning to work and finishing out the school year after Faith's wedding, but time would tell. The last time I had stood at the kitchen window and saw him back out of the driveway was two and a half years ago. I'd had a moment of unease as he kissed me at the back door and said he's be back before I even had time to miss him.

"You are going to be here when I get back, aren't you?" He'd asked.

I didn't know if he was joking or serious so I had just smiled and told him that I loved him. He told me to lock the door behind him.

I wanted to keep busy while he was gone so I thought I'd go through my closets and drawers. I had no sooner dumped the contents of one drawer onto the bed when the front doorbell rang. I sighed and went to answer. I looked out the 'peephole' and saw a young man standing there with a bouquet of white roses. I opened the door. He asked if I was Mrs. Landon. I said that I was and asked him to wait while I got my purse. He said everything was taken care of and told me to have a nice day. I thanked him and relieved him of the bouquet and deposited the roses in the sink while I went to find a vase. The card on the flowers said: "Do you miss me yet?" Thinking that I should have access to money I detoured into the bedroom and searched the closet for the purse I had left behind two and a half years ago. Inside my wallet I found my driver's licence which had expired, and my credit cards which would also be expiring next month. There was also two hundred dollars in twenties and small bills and a handful of coins. It was just as I had left it. I wondered if Faith had taken up my job of supplying her father with lunch money. My wedding rings were still where I had left them. I was disappointed that they no longer fit and went off to find some adhesive tape to wrap around them. I was interrupted by the doorbell again. I put the rings in my dress pocket and went to the front door to find the same young man standing there smiling and holding yet another bouquet. This time they were yellow roses. I thanked him again noticing that his name tag read Tim, and went back to my original task of finding a vase. I nicely had them all cut and arranged in the crystal vase when once again the doorbell chimed. I was not surprised to see Tim again holding red roses. I asked him if this was going to continue all day. He said "No Ma'am, there are just three more dozens." I asked him why he didn't bring them all at once. He said he had specific orders to stagger the deliveries each by ten minutes. I said that was just a big waste of his and my time and to get them all and we could be done with playing my husband's cute little game. He returned with bouquets of pink, lavender and orange roses. There were handwritten notes on all of them just as there had been on the others. Once more I set them all in the sink and set out again to find more vases. I knew there were several in the basement but I decided to wait until Jordan got home as I didn't want to tackle the stairs. I filled a container with water and wedged them all in together and set it in the sink. I remembered my rings were in my pocket, found some tape, wrapped them until I was satisfied that they wouldn't fall off. The doorbell rang. I hoped it was Jordan and not Tim. I found a woman standing on the top step with her back turned to me. Thinking she was some sort of salesperson I asked if I could help her. She turned around smiling and asked if Dan was home. I told her that I thought she had the wrong address as no Dan lived here. She insisted that she had the right address and showed me a piece of paper with the name Dan Landon written on it and our address. She said that she had phoned the high school where he was principal and had been told that Mr. Landon was not in, and so she had taken the chance that he was at home. She asked me if I was Donna. The only Donna I knew was Jordan's cousin. I knew that she had stayed here for a few days after surgery last July waiting for her husband to return from overseas. I looked into this woman's pale blue eyes and knew intuitively that this was the woman who had drugged and seduced my husband. Something evil took hold of me, and I thought I may as well have some fun with her.

In the sweetest voice that I could muster I asked her if she would like to come in and wait for Dan saying that she had taken me by surprise by using Jordan's old nickname. I led her into the kitchen and offered her a cup of old coffee. She looked around and spying the roses in the sink and the counter asked if the roses were all for me.

"As a matter of fact they are." I answered amusingly. I picked one of the lavender roses out of the container and held it up to my face. "Lavender roses have a special meaning for me and my husband as they signify love at first sight."

"That is sweet. When is your husband coming to pick you up?"

"Very soon…he will be here very soon." I continued to smile.

"I hadn't realised that you had returned; was it for a check-up after your surgery? I haven't seen Dan for a few weeks so I'm kind of in the dark."

"Why is it that you haven't seen him; have you been away?" I asked cunningly.

"No, we've both been busy." She held out her hand. "Oh, how rude of me; I haven't even introduced myself."

Before she could say anything else I told her that there was no need as I knew very well who she was. She seemed very pleased and surmised that Dan had told me about her.

"Actually, Dan hasn't said a thing, but my husband has told me plenty."

"Really, your husband and Dan must be good friends then."

"Closer than you can imagine. He couldn't keep the truth from me even though it might kill him to tell me he had been unfaithful."

She seemed very uncomfortable. "What truth? I'm sorry Donna, but what has that to do with me and Dan?"

"Oh, how ill-mannered of me," I put my left hand to me forehead holding my taped rings on with the other hand, "letting you think I was Jordan's cousin!"

She looked confused. "You're not? I'm sorry, I just assumed…"

"Well, you assumed wrong. I'm the wife of the man whom you drugged and seduced several weeks ago. You remember him don't you, or has there been so many that you don't remember?"

"I never drugged or seduced anyone, and I don't know who your husband is! You obviously have me mixed up with somebody else." She rose. "Thank-you for the coffee, but I believe I do have the wrong house after all."

"No," I said sharply, "don't go. I know who you are Martina. Jordan didn't mention your last name, but I will start with mine… it is Landon. I'm pretty sure you have heard my first name; it is

Jillienne, and I am Jordan's wife. The man you knew as Dan was only an imitation of the man he really was, and he died the night you drugged him and seduced him. I am not happy about that at all Martina."

I had never seen a person turn white before, but she did. It was like all the blood drained from her face. She blubbered something about me being dead and started to get up again.

"Oh, stay a while, finish your coffee." I stood blocking her from moving. She outweighed me by forty pounds or more so I hoped push wouldn't come to shove. "I think we need to talk. You admit that you drugged my husband and you can be on your way, but if you don't, then we have a problem. You see, Jordan is the sweetest, kindest person in the whole world, and he is willing to let the whole thing go if you apologise and admit that you drugged him. However, his wife," I put my hand to my chest, "that being me, is not so forgiving. You raped my husband, and I intend to see you suffer just as he has."

She practically spat in my face. "You are not Jillienne! Dan's wife was a beautiful, sweet woman, and you are spiteful and a charlatan!"

"Jordan still thinks I am beautiful because he loves me as much today as he did the day I left. But, you are right; I am a wicked, wicked person, and I will have revenge for the torment you caused my husband." I laughed. "But, let's be honest here, so are you and I have the proof. You do know that Rohypnol stays in the blood stream for up to three days don't you? Well, that was long enough for Jordan to have a blood test and it proved positive, so what do you have to say for yourself now *Martina*?"

"If he took some drug it has nothing to do with me. I wouldn't do such a thing, and besides I wouldn't even know how to get my hands on such a thing."

"Oh, come on Martina, don't play dumb with me, you know perfectly well that you can score any illegal drug in any bar or on any street corner!"

She was very incensed. "I don't know what class of people you have been running with lady, but decent law abiding citizens do not know anything about that! I assure you that if Dan was into something, it was none of my doing. If you are gullible enough to believe that he blames what happened between us on drugs and a loss of memory then you are in for a very rude awakening when he admits that he knew exactly what he was doing."

"So you admit that you know Rohypnol causes a loss of memory?"

"I said no such thing!"

"You kind of did. Anyhow, Jordan has no memory of that sordid night with you except that he woke up in your bed, and had no idea how he got there. When did you put the condom on him Martina?" Seeing the look on her face, I realized that I had hit a nerve. "Was it after he passed out? Did you fill it with some gooey substance like KY jelly and water? Oh my God, he never had sex with you at all did he; you just wanted him to think so. What kind of a perverted mind would do such a thing?"

I thought the top of her head was going to explode. "You insipid little waif... I feel sorry for you, but more so for Dan that you came back! You should have stayed dead, and I am sure that he wishes that you were!" She got up to leave, but I hadn't played my trump card yet.

"We were pretty sure that you wouldn't own up so we filed a police report citing you for the illegal use of a narcotic for the sole purpose of rape. A nice detective by the name of Marty Reagen will be visiting you as early as today, and hopefully he will have obtained a search warrant. You do know that traces of the drug can be found long afterwards don't you?"

This time she was really leaving, but Jordan was at the door.

"Where are you Sweetheart?" He called out.

I winked at Martina. "You may as well say hello." I walked into the foyer and greeted Jordan. He pulled a single lavender rose out from behind his back. I laughed and said that I wondered where the twelfth one had gotten to. He pulled me into his arms and asked if I had missed him.

"Well Darling, I hardly had time to do so thanks to your little game with the delivery boy. You will be pleased to know that I foiled you at your own game, but enough about that for now. Come, you have a visitor awaiting your arrival in the kitchen." I pulled him along.

"I can't imagine who… what the hell are you doing here?"

I don't believe that I had ever heard such animosity in my husband's voice before.

"I think she wanted to make sure the Rohypnol that she spiked your vodka with wasn't still causing you memory loss." I smiled sweetly.

"She's crazy Dan! You won't believe what your wayward wife has been accusing me of if she is your wife at all! She doesn't look anything like her picture."

Jordan turned to me with a twinkle in his eyes. "I'd kind of like to hear that for myself."

"Apparently you didn't have sex with her at all Dear; she just wanted you to think that you did. For whatever reason I have no idea, but I think she had a plan. I'll explain it all to you later. I gave her an ultimatum…she confesses and apologises to you or I make the phone call to Detective Reagen."

Martina was on her feet again. "I don't have to sit here and listen to these fabrications from this woman. I can only imagine what kind of stories she has concocted about where she was and who she was with for two years. Don't be a fool Dan; she's bamboozling you!"

Jordan grabbed her by the arm. "You're right, you don't have to stay, and believe me, we want you gone, but first you will apologize to my wife for every name you have called her, and everything you have accused her of." He gently removed my turban and said he was sorry.

I said it was okay. He directed his anger at Martina.

"It's none of your business, but I'll tell you anyway just so you can see how wrong you are. This little woman here, the love of my life, has spent two and half years in an underground facility battling an inoperable brain tumor. She won the battle thankfully, and came home to me a little broken, but nothing that my love can't see her through. I don't care one iota about what you did to me, but I won't have you call Jillienne a liar so apologise, and get the hell out of here!"

She said she was sorry though not very sincerely, and headed for the door. I said that wasn't good enough and that she had to admit to Jordan what she had done to him. I told Jordan that I would be in the bedroom waiting for him with one hand on the telephone waiting to call the detective. Just before the front door slammed, I heard Martina say that it wasn't supposed to end up the way it did, and he knew how she felt about him so he must know that she wouldn't do anything to harm him.

"Is Jillienne right? Did you just make it look as if I had slept with you?"

I didn't hear her answer, but she was sobbing so I assumed that she confessed. I did hear her say that she had made a horrible mistake by spiking his drink, and asked him to forgive her.

"I'll just die if you don't Dan."

"Then I guess you are just going to have to die aren't you!" He said as he slammed the door.

Jordan found me folding sweaters to donate to the local Salvation Army. He took one out of my hands and put his arms around me.

"I am so sorry Darling that I wasn't here when she arrived. I can't imagine how you felt when she introduced herself."

"Actually, I knew who she was before I let her in the door. The girl's description was spot on."

He laughed although a little uncertainly. "How long was she here before I came in?"

"Not long, half an hour or so."

He turned me to face him. "Oh God," he moaned guiltily, "I should never have left you alone."

"Are you saying that I can't fend for myself against one of your lady friends?"

He smiled provocatively. "Oh, I am pretty sure you can as you just did! I can't imagine what you two talked about for so long?"

"To be truthful, it was probably only a few minutes of idle chit-chat, and her assuming I was your cousin Donna. I am afraid she wasn't very friendly after I set her straight on that. I must admit that I had some fun with her first." I shook my head. "Really Darling, I thought you had better taste in women than that."

"I do, and she is standing right in front of me. Remember, I wasn't looking for a girlfriend. But, how in hell did you get her to confess?"

"I had a hunch and I played it." I reiterated my account of the conversation, accenting heavily on my accusations stating that I was steadfast all along believing that the woman was going to entrap herself, and she did. "The only thing that has any consequence at all Jordan is that you did not sleep with her, and so you can quit worrying about it because it never happened."

"In all honesty, I don't think she would have admitted it to me, so thank-you for putting my mind at rest."

"You are most welcome. One down and two to go before my mind will be entirely at rest."

"Jillienne…"

I winked at him. "Now, let's talk about all of these roses…do you have something to be guilty about after all?"

His answer was to pull me down on the bed and smother me with kisses.

Jordan took me to *his* Arcadia Tuesday morning to meet Padre Emilio. He welcomed me with a smile and open arms that melted my heart immediately. He agreed jubilantly to officiate over the renewal of our marriage vows. Later in the day I sent Jordan to deliver bouquets of roses to our elderly friends Jock and Judi, and Hank and Elaine. I loved the flowers, but six dozens were overwhelming. I put the red ones aside to take to Craig's office on Friday. I wanted to send a bouquet to my young friend Timmy's mother next door, but Jordan said they were in Poland or wherever they had come from for a holiday. He then told me how Timmy had driven him crazy asking about me almost every day so I should be prepared for an emotional reunion.

I answered the phone anticipating that it was my brother. It wasn't.

A melodious voice said "Hi, is that you Faith? Is your dad home?"

I said I wasn't Faith. She asked if I was Hope.

I said no, and did she want to leave a message. There was silence at the other end of the phone, and then an exclamation of excitement. "Oh my God, it's Jillienne isn't it?"

I answered that yes, I was Jillienne. I was most suspicious that another woman was looking for my husband. Without missing a beat she continued talking in a very animated voice.

"I knew there had to be a damn good reason for Dan to miss an appointment, and you are it! He must be over the moon that you are back…oh sorry, my name is Virginia Teal, and I am your husband's therapist. I must meet you Jillienne! I have been waiting along with Dan for the last six months for word from you. I feel like I already know you, but to see you for myself in the flesh would be my greatest pleasure. Is it possible, or is it too soon?"

Jordan walked in as I was saying that perhaps she should ask him for his opinion, and his name was Jordan and not Dan. "It's your therapist; she says she wants to meet me." I handed him the phone and listened as to a one sided conversation about me for a few minutes. I wanted it done with so I told him to invite her for coffee tomorrow evening and walked out of the room.

CHAPTER 10

For the Love of Jillienne

I asked Virginia if she had heard what Jillienne said.

"I did Jordan; that is most gracious of her."

"Don't be too sure about that." I had mixed feelings regarding Jillienne meeting Virginia. I had the gut feeling that it wasn't going to go well.

"What do you mean? I'm scared to death to ask you how she is and where she has been…I mean it is really none of my business. Is she all right Jordan?"

"She's as good as a person who survived a terminal brain tumor can be."

"Oh my God! How in the world did she beat it? It has something to do with where she was doesn't it?"

"It does, but I am not at liberty to say anymore. It's up to her who she chooses to share her story with, but believe me it's a pretty gruesome tale. Anyhow, the important thing is that she's alive and that she came home, and that she still loves me as much as I love her. See you tomorrow okay."

I hung up the phone and went to find my wife. I told her that she could change her mind about meeting Virginia. She said she wanted to get it over with.

Jillienne put a pot of coffee on and cut up the pan of brownies that she had made from a mix. I had told her it wasn't necessary to serve a dessert, but she had gone ahead and baked anyhow. I eyed her discreetly trying to get a read on her mood as I licked the chocolate icing off the knife she passed me. She asked me if I knew that I was staring.

"Sorry, can't get enough of you."

"You're full of it Jordan Landon! I know very well what you are doing."

"Oh, and what is that?"

"You're wondering what kind of mood I'm in, and if I am going to be nice to Virginia."

"You got me, but just to be clear, I don't care one iota if you like her or not. I hope you didn't agree to this just because you think it's what I want?"

"And, I don't care one iota what you think or want!"

"Like hell you don't!" I pulled her down on my lap and kissed her hard.

She told me to wipe the lipstick off and go and answer the door. I had hope that it was going to be a pleasant visit.

Virginia barely acknowledged me. She asked where Jillienne was and brushed by me when I pointed to where Jillienne was sitting in the front room. She sat down on the sofa next to her.

"Jillienne, you have no idea what a pleasure it is to meet you." She said taking my wife's hands, and asked if she could give her a hug.

Jilly said she could if she wanted to and asked why she wanted to meet her so badly.

"Because my dear, I have come to know you through my sessions with your husband, and I along with him and your family have been praying for your safe return. I honestly have never known anyone like

Jordan before. His undying devotion to you has been an inspiration to me and restored my faith in love everlasting. You are just as beautiful as he described you. I would have known you anywhere even without seeing your photographs."

"I don't know how. I am but a shell of what I once was; I have no figure to speak of, and I have no hair. Jordan loved my hair." Jillienne said wistfully looking at me with her puppy dog eyes. "I am not the same person that left here two and a half years ago Miss Teal…or is it Mrs.?"

I was sitting on the coffee table, and reached out and squeezed Jilly's hands.

"It's just Virginia. You have the same face, the same dark eyes, and one day your hair will all grow back, you'll see Jillienne. Meanwhile, you just need to concentrate on healing, and that includes your emotional state of mind, and you have the perfect partner to assist you. I don't mind telling you that your husband is one of my favorite people, and if I had to choose anyone to help me over a hurdle, it would be him hands down, so you are already way ahead of the battle."

Virginia smiled at me a little too knowingly. I knew it spelled trouble.

Jillienne was quick to respond, but not before she let me know with her eyes that she was displeased. "So, I take it that you are an expert on the after effects of long term chemotherapy treatment? That is very reassuring as my doctors did not promise me any such results. But thank-you, I now have hope that I will have a full head of auburn hair very soon. Oh, but you probably don't know…I am not sure how much my husband has told you about my cancer and my prognosis, or about me even, but I may very well be on chemo drugs the rest of my life. I think that may negate the hair thing. May I ask if you usually take such an interest in all your patient's lives? I know that Jordan is a very unique person, but how is it that he is so special to you?"

Oh boy; we were in for some fireworks if Virginia's answer wasn't satisfactory.

"I am sorry Jillienne, I did not mean to overstep. You are right; I should not be making assumptions when I don't know the full story, and I won't again. To answer your question about Jordan, and why I feel such empathy towards him, I can't really explain; it's just one of those things. I knew from the minute that I met him that he was carrying the burden of guilt on his shoulders believing that he was the reason for your disappearance. Every session I got to know you and your life together a little bit more. I have to admit that I was envious. I contend with a lot of broken marriages and some very bitter people. I am not a marriage counselor though sometimes I feel like I am. My job is to try and heal the psyche, and to convince my clients that all is not lost, to help them deal with their aggressions, and hopefully find meaning to their lives again. Dan, sorry Jordan's story was different. His situation was out of the ordinary. Not to say that I haven't had clients whose partners had walked out on them before, but they always knew why, and usually knew where that person was. There was always trouble in those relationships while there appeared to be none in Jordan's and yours. According to him, he had the perfect marriage. Listening to his story, I had to agree with him. There had to be a reason or reasons other than that you had simply quit loving him to have left. I wanted desperately to discover that reason with him. Unfortunately, we didn't, but I like to think that I helped him free his mind from all the guilt and misgivings he was torturing himself with. I knew though that there would not be any closure for him if you never returned, so thank God you did."

I did not see how Jillienne could find any fault with what Virginia had said; after all, it was the truth. I was wrong again.

"I did not leave Jordan because I stopped loving him; I left because I did. I may very well have not returned if the unorthodox treatments I received did not work...alive, that is. I'm pretty sure my remains would have been sent home, with or without an explanation if I hadn't survived, but I did. Jordan can fill you in on the details, but there is not much to tell. I had an inoperable tumor, and I was offered an alternative, though not guaranteed cure. I chose to accept it despite the fact that no one, not even my husband, could know about it. If I had it to do all over again, I might chose death instead." Jillienne responded icily.

"Don't say that Honey." I pleaded. "You made the right decisions; we talked about this…"

"Yes we did, but that was before I knew all the facts."

"Facts, what facts are you talking about Hon?"

Jillienne turned away from me and faced Virginia. "I know you are familiar with my husband's association with Martina…don't look so shocked, he told me all about it the very first night. As it turned out, nothing happened between them at all. You're wondering how I know? She came calling the other day when Jordan wasn't home, and we had quite the conversation. Short version, she admitted the drugging, and she only made it look like they had sex. Good news, right? Jordan's come a long way since the wiles of Nell and Marlayna which I am sure he has told you about in great detail, and all the others before me. I sheltered him from the likes of other conniving women for thirty one years so he was totally unaware of their ploys of seduction. But, then I left, and he was vulnerable wasn't he Virginia?"

"Jillienne!" I loudly voiced my disapproval of her implications.

"Sorry Dear," she patted me on my knees, "I didn't mean to imply that you are naïve, but I think you are, just a bit." She winked at me. "He let his friendship go a little too far with Martina without realizing what she wanted from him don't you think Virginia? And, what is it exactly that you have been expecting from my husband?"

Virginia let out a low gasp. "I have no such intentions towards Jordan, Jillienne…what has given you such an idea?"

I was becoming more and more frustrated with my wife's line of questioning and insinuations. "I highly suggest that you refrain from this interrogation Jillienne. Virginia's only intentions were to help me with my suffering…"

She interrupted me. "Yes, my darling, I'm sure they were initially." She stood up and addressed Virginia again. "I will thank you for everything you did for Jordan over the past months, but I am home now, and I am pretty sure that I can fulfill all his needs. I may be wrong though, and maybe every sweet thing he has whispered to me has just been imaginary on my part. I'm pretty sure he is not that good at faking though. I gave up my claim to him when I walked out, so I guess he was fair game. Notice, I said *was*. I may not be willing to give him up so easily now, but then I guess that all depends on how serious you and he are. I will take my leave now and give you some privacy to discuss what comes next."

"Damn it Jillienne…what has gotten into you?" I reached out to grab her, but she dodged me and made her exit into the hallway without answering me. I heard the bedroom door close.

Virginia was visibly shocked by what Jillienne had insinuated. "That went terribly wrong Jordan; I'm so sorry. Who are these other women she mentioned? Oh Jordan…"

I stopped her from making anymore assumptions, and explained who they were without going into great detail, and that their presence in the here and now was all inconsequential. I was careful not to touch her in any way as I followed her to the front door. I did not close it just in case Jillienne was listening. Virginia apologised again saying she hoped she hadn't caused any new problems for me. I shrugged my shoulders and told her she had nothing to be sorry for and that it was nothing that I couldn't handle.

"You wanted to meet her, and now you have. I can assure you that she is much more charming than the version you just witnessed. I will not apologise for her outbursts as that is up to her to do so, but don't hold your breath. I told you that she wouldn't like you, and now you have seen for yourself. She's been through hell Virginia, and it is up to me to make her transition back to normalcy as smooth as possible.

I'm seeing a whole new side to her, and I can contribute it to the trauma that she went through and all without the people she loved. She's one remarkable woman to come through it as well as she has. I'm sure that all the drugs haven't helped either. She is still on some and smoking pot, I think for relaxation. I can't have her thinking that something is going on between us because we both know there isn't. She is still my one and only love, and I if I have to move heaven and earth to prove it to her I will. I'll say good-night now as I need to put her suspicions to rest once more."

"Dan…Jordan, I still don't know what to call you. She's emotionally wrought, and it will take time for her to heal. I hope she isn't using the cannabis as a crutch. I understand completely how hard it must be for her to believe that you stayed true to her. I did my best to assure her, but I feel it fell on deaf ears. I will not complicate things by trying to talk to her again."

"Its medicinal cannabis; and I can assure you it has no punch. If it gives her comfort, then so be it. Take care of yourself Virginia."

I closed one door and opened another. I found Jillienne standing by our bed wearing the birthday gown I had bought her the year she had left. She looked very pleased with herself.

Suddenly, my annoyance at her allegations took hold of me. "What the hell was that all about? What do I have to do or say to make you believe that there is nothing going on between her and me?"

"You can say it a thousand times over, but I saw the way you looked at each other."

"And, how was that exactly Jillienne?"

"A look that said you shared a secret, a secret that only lovers understand."

"You're imagining things. We don't share any secret and we certainly aren't lovers!"

"You protest a little too loudly. You called her didn't you? You told her to wear her long golden hair up and dress like a Lesbian didn't you because you didn't want me to see how beautiful she is? Even so I paled next to her. It must have pleasured her to see what an ugly duckling I am."

"A Lesbian, what the hell does that mean?"

"Just that she wasn't wearing a silk button up blouse that I am sure you have undid a hundred times, and a tight skirt that you have run your hands…"

"Stop it Jillienne! Stop this insanity right now!" I was yelling at her again, and I didn't like it.

"Then admit it; tell me how it is between you and her…tell me the truth for God's sake."

"What is it you want me to say Jillienne? You don't and won't believe the truth, so how about I tell you what you want to hear? I think about her all the time, and moreover, every time I have made love to you, I've pretended it was her lying with me. Is that what you want me to say…well, there I said it. I hope you are happy now, and take that bloody negligee off…red is not your colour anymore!" I stormed out of the room slamming the door behind me.

I turned and put my hand on the door knob, but changed my mind. We both needed to cool off. May as well check the doors and alarm in the basement like I compulsively did every night. It was dusk and some of the solar lights were flickering. Lionel was on his bench staring at me. I supposed that he heard me yelling. I decided to join him; I needed to vent before I had to face Jillienne again.

"Well Buddy Boy, I'm afraid I have really stepped in it this time. Instead of trying to pacify and put her fears to rest I aggravated your mistress instead. Funny, I say mistress as that is what she is accusing me of…having a mistress. Someday, maybe down the road I would have found someone to share the rest of my life with, but I would never love anyone the way I have her. I never put anything into motion because I hadn't let her go, and then she shows up out of the blue, and we rekindled our love and I was the happiest man on earth. But, her suspicions regarding my fidelity are becoming stronger every day. Just when I think I have convinced her of my faithfulness something happens, and she is right back into doubting me again. I have to find a way to banish those suspicions without losing my temper which was pretty much non-existent until she went away. Yeah, yeah I know you are very aware of that, and that's probably one of the reasons you ran away. I was on a rant and you were afraid I was going to lash out at you…sorry Buddy. She's challenging my patience, but I have to find a way to deal with her unpredictability because the Good Lord knows she means more to me than life itself. You're right Lionel; why I am telling you this when I should be telling her?" I gave him a scratch under his chin. "Thanks for listening; now let's hope she does."

I opened the bedroom door asking if I could come in. The room reeked of marijuana.

"It's your house so you can go anywhere you like. Sorry about the smell."

She was standing at the bedside stuffing things into a suitcase. She was fully dressed in the slacks and top that the girls had bought her. I walked around to the other side and asked her what she was doing. Her answer was typical.

"You are not very smart for a professor are you?"

"I will remind you that I never taught at a university. You look very nice." I said amiably.

She ignored the compliment. "Tit for tat. I'm taking the clothes you had the girls buy for me, and a few other things, plus all the money from the safe. You said I could have it, so I'm taking it. Sorry, but you are a little too inexperienced, and I don't want you spending it all recklessly on your concubines."

I was sure I saw a twinkle in her eye. I was becoming more amused by the minute.

"Thank-you for your consideration. Now, just where are you planning on going in the middle of the night?"

"It's not even nine yet. Don't worry; I'm not going to camp out at Hope's or Clay's. I won't be a bother to any of my family. You, I didn't mind, because after all you promised to look after me through thick and thin, in sickness or in health, come hell or high water, or something like that…whatever. Anyhow, I will take a hotel room for the night, and then I'm going home."

I scratched my head smiling. "Oh, so you are just leaving for the night, and then you're coming back here tomorrow?"

"This is not my home Jordan; I am going back to Shelton."

"This is your home Jilly, and you know it. Now let's dispense with the silliness, okay?"

She turned her back to me and walked over to her dresser. "Don't call me Jilly. I'm keeping some of the jewellery you bought me because I may need to hawk it, and my wedding rings…strictly for sentimental reasons. I'll contact Marlayna first thing when I get to Shelton and tell her that she has competition for your affections so she had better get a move on if she still wants you."

I had half her suitcase unpacked when she returned with an armful of jewels.

"What do you think you are doing?" She demanded grabbing her clothes out of my hands.

"You're not very smart yourself are you if you can't see what I'm doing?" I said cheekily.

"You have no say in this Jordan…"

I grabbed hold of her arm and in so doing the string of pearls that she had been holding broke and the little beads went dancing across the bed and floor.

Big tears rolled down her face. "Now look what you have done! Isn't it enough just to break my heart, you have to break my jewellery also?"

I threw the suitcase onto the floor and pulled her down on the bed with me. She fought me with all that she had cursing me with every breath. My laughing didn't help the situation any. After a few minutes she stopped beating on my chest and asked me politely to let her up. I kept a firm yet tender grip on her.

"I'm sorry; I'll buy you a new strand, half a dozen if you want. I haven't broken your heart, and I never will. I do have a say in your impulsive decisions whether you think I do or don't. You are my wife, the woman I love with all my heart and body; you are my soul-mate, my forever sweetheart, and my *only* mistress. You know this Jillienne, and yet you continue to challenge me with this incessant obsession of yours that I have been or want to be unfaithful. Why Jilly, why? Why can't you trust and believe me?"

She pulled herself free of me. "You can't replace what has been lost by buying new ones. We can't go back to where we were Jordan, and we can't fix what was once sacred to us. We were happy, and we trusted each other, but now we don't. That chain is broken, and so are we."

"We are not broken Jilly; we are just in a stage of adjustment. My love for you is stronger than ever. I will do whatever it takes to prove that to you."

"I know you think and feel that it is your duty to love me, but you just confessed to me not even an hour ago that you think about Virginia when you're with me. A woman can't live with those words echoing in her head. I almost believed that you weren't lovers yet, but then you said that. The desire is there and you can't deny it. I saw the way you looked at each other." She continued packing the suitcase even though it was lying on the floor. "You know I wish that you had acted on these feelings before I came back because maybe then it would be out of your system, or you would be in the full swing of a love affair and you wouldn't have to lie because it would be out in the open for all to see. Anyhow, I am going to make it easy for you and bow out because I can't be the other woman. We gave it a good run though didn't we? There are no regrets because for thirty one years you gave me a life most women can only dream about. Maybe if I had never got cancer…"

I picked up the suitcase and laid it back on the bed. "Nothing has changed because you got ill. I don't feel it is my duty to love you because I am still one hundred percent *in* love with you. You do go off the deep end with your insinuations now and then, but it's nothing that I can't deal with. You just have to give me the chance. I went too far when I said what I did, and I am mortified that you believed it. Have I ever cried out anyone's name but yours when we are making love? I have wept for you in the darkness for two and a half years, but you have put an end to my suffering so don't ever say that you are leaving me again; please don't break my heart again, please Jilly, please."

She wiped the tears from my eyes as hers slid silently down her face. "If I don't leave you then you will leave me because you will tire of my instability and my jealousy. I am the cause for our dissention, but I can't hang onto what we once had while your feelings for someone else go unchecked. You owe it to yourself to explore…"

"Stop it Jillienne! There is nothing to explore, there is no dissention, and I am never leaving you. I don't want you out of my sight for even a minute, and there is no way in hell that I am letting you walk out the door. I know that you are overly jealous of any woman who looks at me, and if the shoe was on the other foot and I thought another man was looking at you amorously, I would probably react much the same way as you did. If you thought you saw a look pass between Virginia and me, it was only one of compassion, and nothing else because there is nothing between us."

"I want to believe you, but there is something special between you and her isn't there? Can you honestly say that you didn't want her in your life as more than a friend?"

"I'm going to be completely honest with you. I did consider asking her out to dinner last week…dinner, but nothing more."

"Why didn't you? Were you afraid it would lead to something else?"

"I don't honestly know. I was lonesome and there wasn't going to be anymore dinners with Martina, so maybe I just wanted a new dining partner. Anyhow, I never acted on it. Do you want to know why…it's because you were in my head, and telling me not to. I think it was the same night that Delores told you that you needed to go home."

"But, you wanted to, and who is to say what would have happened."

"That's right, but nothing did. Besides, my three years weren't up yet."

"What does that mean?"

"Craig made me promise that I would wait three years for you, but if I ever felt that I couldn't wait that long then I was to come to him, and we'd talk first. I hadn't reached that point yet."

She started to say something about Craig, but changed her mind, and went back to doubting me. "I think you felt safe with Martina, but with Virginia, it would have led to something more, and it frightened you. If there is always going to be this longing and wondering, then go and do what you have to do, and satisfy your curiosity. I've made the decision to leave, but I will make it easy for the two of you. I will call her tomorrow and apologise and give her my blessings."

"That is such a bloody pile of crap! Does nothing ever register with you? Did you not hear a word I said?"

"Oh, do you mean like when you told me that day at the river so long ago that there could never, ever be anything between us, and now you're saying the same thing about you and her?"

"Yeah, and that's exactly what I am telling you now! Now listen, and listen with your heart because I am only going to say it once. **There will never, ever be anything between Virginia and me, never EVER!** You are my forever. There is no need for you to apologise because I am never, ever going to see her again. Got it? There is no need for me to add fuel to your imaginary thoughts so I will tell you that there is no reason for me to ever see or contact her again, okay?"

"But she's your friend, and your counsellor?"

"A friend that I no longer need as my best friend is right here, and I no longer have the need for her counselling do I?"

"You'll give her up for me?" She said tearfully.

"Sweetheart, I would give anything up for you, but I am not actually giving anything up because there was nothing there to give up. All I need is you."

"And, all I need is you. I feel like I may have won the battle, but not the war."

"There isn't going to be any war, and there wasn't even a battle, just the one in your head. It's over, and we are never having this discussion again."

"Did you ever kiss her Jordan?"

I took a deep breath. Nothing, not even the truth was ever going to satisfy her so what did I have to lose by confessing? "Once, I kissed her once. It was on the cheek after she told me about her fiancé's disappearance. It was merely a gesture of kinship; that is all. Are we done *now*?"

She nodded and said she thought so.

"Good, now let's go find you a nice warm coat and go for a ride down to Hidden Beach."

"Now…it's too late."

CHAPTER 11

The Final Chapter

Jordan said that it was never too late never too late because we had all the time in the world. He said he wanted to sit and neck with me in the backseat of the car like we used to do while listening to the surf crash and roll. I asked him if he was up to having a police officer shining his flashlight on us again thinking we are some horny teenagers. He said, "Oh yeah."

He dressed me in the long winter parka he had bought me three years ago and warm socks and rubber boots. I asked him why I had to dress up so much. He said that I'd see. We did not crawl into the back seat of the car when we pulled into Hidden Beach. Instead Jordan asked me if I would go for a walk with him. I said I would. He grabbed the blanket and flashlight he had brought and pulled my hat down over my ears. The path to the seashore was short but winding. A partial moon helped to light our way. When we reached the bottom he dropped the blanket off on a weathered log that had come in with the tide. We strolled along the shore hand in hand until we came to a rock bluff. We, along with the children had scaled those rocks many times in the past. I asked Jordan if he came down here often. He said that he hadn't since I'd been gone.

"I took that away from you too." I said sadly.

"It's not that I didn't try; I just couldn't come to one of our favorite spots without you. We are here now and that is all that counts."

"What about Oleander Park; do you go there?"

"I did once, but I couldn't stay. Let's go back okay?"

We retreated and sat down on the old log which was surprisingly dry. Jordan wrapped me in the blanket and asked me if I was cold. I answered that I wasn't. He found my left hand under the blanket and said that something was missing.

"Yes, my rings. You know they are too big and I am afraid that I will lose them."

"Well, until we get them resized I think that you need something in their place."

I asked him if he had brought a piece of seaweed that he wanted to wrap around my finger. He laughed and said that he had something else in mind. He reached into his pocket and brought out a little box which he opened. Inside was a ring whose stone looked like a diamond.

"What is this?" I asked apprehensively.

He took the ring out of the case and slid it on my finger. "Will you do me the honor of becoming my wife again Jilly?"

"You told me we were still married..."

"We are, but I want us to renew our vows. Yours are a little rusty you know. I do not remember there being any "through thick and thin or come hell or high water" in our vows; do you?"

"Maybe not, but if I agree to marry you again there will not be any of those old outdated vows in the ceremony. I will make up my own and they will come from my heart and not from some stuffy scribe who wrote them eons ago."

With a gleam in his eye he asked me if I was considering his proposal. I said that I was. I asked him when he had bought the ring.

"A year or so ago; does it matter…oh, I see where you are going with this. You want to know if I bought it intending to give it to someone else, don't you? You still aren't sure about me are you… never mind, I know what the answer is." He stood up. "Come on, let's go home."

"Jordan, I do trust you, but in all honesty, can you blame me for wondering?" I pleaded.

"I don't blame you for anything Jilly. Now in all honesty, do you really think I would give you a ring that I had bought for somebody else? God, I can't believe you could think that I would do that… here, you don't have to wear it…" he attempted to take the ring off my finger.

"Stop it Jordan! You are without a doubt the most honest and unpretentious man that I will ever know. I did not mean to accuse you of anything…I am sorry that everything I do or say is wrong. Please, let me wear your ring, please Jordan."

"You know, you hardly ever call me Jordy anymore… now look what I have done! I've made you cry and the tears are going to turn into icicles…"

He wiped my face with the sleeve of his jacket and said it was time to get me out of the cold. I was shivering, but it wasn't so much from the cold. "I call you Jordan because I have always loved your name, and just knowing that you didn't want to be called that while I was gone makes me believe that you weren't you while I was gone. I'll make a point of calling you Jordy from now on though. I love you and I don't know how I made it through all those months without you. Please don't be angry with me Jordy…please."

He put his arms around me. "I am so not angry with you; maybe with myself a little. You make me so happy that sometimes I forget that you don't know what went on in your absence, and I ramble on. You're right, the reason I asked to be called Dan was because I wasn't Jordan without you. I want to tell you about the ring…no, don't say it doesn't matter because it does. It was sometime after Cree and Faith became a couple. He had bought a necklace for her and asked me to pick it up for him as he hadn't had time to wait while it was being engraved. I was just browsing while the clerk went to find it, and I spotted this ring. I thought it looked just like the one that was on the bracelet that I had given you for your birthday, and so I bought it because I still had hope that someday you would come back to me."

Now I was really crying. I blubbered that if the proposal was still in play then I accepted and that I could hardly wait to renew our vows. I asked him when he wanted to do it.

"How about tomorrow?" He asked hopefully.

"Wouldn't we want the kids to come, and would we dare to upstage Faith's wedding?"

"It could just be us you know, and Padre Emilio."

"How about we go home and think about it?"

"There is always Valentine's Day."

"That day already is an anniversary, so I think not."

"You're right, and I don't want to wait that long anyhow."

"Well Darling, we are already married so it's not like our wedding night is going to be some big revelation."

He said the day would present itself and was I all right with that. I said I was most assuredly.

When we arrived home I went immediately into Jordan's office because I knew he always kept a calendar in there and I hadn't seen any others in the house anywhere. I found one on the wall. The first five days of September were all marked off with a big X while the last four had big red check marks. I took the calendar down and carried it to the kitchen where Jordan was sitting with two glasses of brandy. I asked him what it all meant.

"Simple; all the black X's are for the days you weren't here, and these four, should be five now, are red letter days because you are here." He flipped through the months. "See, they are all black just like the other two years. I don't ever want to use the black marker again Jilly."

"Oh Jordan…"

"It's okay Honey; it's over with now. Were you looking for a date for us to renew our nuptials?"

"Maybe, but now I am just sad."

"Don't be; we have many days of joy ahead starting with this weekend when all our kids will be home. I was thinking that we should cook a turkey and have an early Thanksgiving because we have much to be thankful for. Faith's wedding falls on the actual weekend and so we won't be doing it then. What do you think?"

"I think it's a wonderful idea. Do you think we will be able to find a turkey?"

"It just so happens that there are two in the freezer, so we are all set. We'll plan the rest of the meal tomorrow, but I want it to be very simple. No pie making or anything like that…whatever we need we can buy, okay?"

"Yes, I am not so sure my pie making skill is one I want to attempt right now. And what do we want to do about dinner with Cree tomorrow?"

"Cree's easy; he will eat anything because I am sure he lives on fast food or grubs when he is in the field, so steak and potatoes is a feast for him. Now, back to the calendar; do you think you will be up to a trip to Shelton next week? Our parents really need to see you, especially your mother. And, while we are there you can meet Marlayna and hopefully cross her off your list."

"I don't want or need to meet her Jordan." I said crossly.

"For my sake I think you do."

"Well then, you may as well take me to school so I can cross examine Nell too so that I can be done once and for all with all the other women in your life!"

Jordan threw his hands up in the air. "It was a joke Honey, just a joke!"

"I'm not laughing." I picked up my drink and stormed off to the bedroom.

I heard Jordan go thumping down the basement stairs. A few minutes later he was back holding a large turkey in his arms. He asked me what I thought he should do with it.

"Well, don't bring it in here as it is already cold enough."

He grinned and said he would be right back to warm me up. I changed into a nightgown and climbed into bed with the diary I had written in Arcadia.

"What have you got there Jilly?" Jordan asked returning to the bedroom.

I patted the bed beside me. "Come, and I will read to you the tale of a damsel in distress who fought for her life and her love in a land far, far, away."

Jordan didn't bother to undress. He positioned his head against the headboard as he lay down beside me on top of the bedspread. I opened my journal to the first page.

> *Well I am here though I do not know where "here" is. The clock on the wall says four o'clock. I do not know if that is afternoon or morning. I didn't bother to ask Gayle, but it is dark out so I guess it is morning. I knew we left Victoria at noon on February 13th so it is probably the 14th now. This is my first birthday in thirty years without Jordan. I miss him already.*
>
> *I vaguely recall flying over water before the sedative took effect. I was still very groggy when the plane landed. Two sturdy young men escorted us to another conveyance. I am pretty sure it was a train, but then it could have been a carriage or even a car. My head hurts too much to think. I was put into a wheelchair and taken to my room by an attendant. As soon as he left Gayle acquainted me with my room and helped me to undress. There was a pink nightgown at the head of the bed which she helped*

me slip into. Pink was not my colour; Jordan always said that it clashed with my hair.

Five minutes later I met Dr. Banner. He asked me how I was feeling after my long trip and wanted to know if I had any pain. I said that my head hurt. I believe that he gave me the same medications that I had been taking for the last four days at home which was administered through a hypodermic needle. I was glad that I didn't have to give myself the injections anymore. He said he would access me again in the morning.

Before Gayle left she said she would have a television set brought in for me. I told her I didn't need one. She asked if I would rather have a radio and I said only if I could get country music on it. She asked me if I liked Johnny Cash and I told her that I did, but Ferlin Husky was my favorite.

I'm alone now. I don't think I can stay here. The medication has taken effect. I think I can live on it for the rest of my life. I will tell them tomorrow that I have changed my mind and that I want to go home. If they refuse to send me back I will demand to call Jordan. I know he will come for me. I can't do this without him. I should have told him…screw the rules. You'll come for me won't you Jordan, you'll find me and take me home, you'll find me…oh God, what have I done?

I tried hard not to get emotional, but I failed, and sputtered the last few words. Jordan took the diary out of my hands and laid it on the floor and pulled me into his arms.

"That's enough for tonight, that's enough for tonight. Shush, shush, my sweet baby, shush I'm here, Daddy's here."

I fell asleep in his arms.

I found Jordan reading my journal the next morning. I poured myself a cup of coffee and sat down beside him at the kitchen table. "Did you find anything interesting in there?" I asked.

"Well, there is nothing but a bunch of X's for the next three weeks; reminds me of my calendar. What's this here about WD40?"

I giggled slightly. "That's my name for the drug that was supposedly going to rid me of the tumor. Those days that are blank are the first ones in a series of when I was in the medically induced blackouts; coma, I guess is the proper medical term."

"I kind of thought so. I'm glad your plan to leave there never panned out or you wouldn't be sitting here next to me now would you?"

"Probably not, but I might be sitting on the mantel in an urn above the fireplace in the den."

"That's not at all funny Jillienne!" He said mortified.

"Well, it's a fact. Actually, I have no idea how they would have sent my body home if I hadn't made it. Quit frowning will you."

"I see you are in a much better, though a rather gruesome mood then you were last night."

"I am, but I'm sure that I won't always be sunny. So what happened was that I woke up the next morning and felt all right. I got out of bed and walked over to the window. That is the last memory I have until three weeks later. Apparently they found me on the floor and I was rushed into the surgical ward immediately where I received my first dose of WD40. That isn't its real name of course. It has about four more letters and numbers in its name. I chose to shorten it when I was told that it was also being used on different cancers and also other afflictions at the clinic. I guess I sarcastically remarked that it was like WD40 and could fix anything, and soon everyone was referring to the concoction as WD40."

"That is just too funny Jilly; you still believing that WD40 can fix anything."

"It fixed me didn't it?"

"I can't argue with that."

He put the journal in a safe place as I didn't want anyone else reading it. We made out our grocery list. Jordan tried to talk me into going to the market with him, but I declined. I locked the door behind him after I warned him not to go flower shopping. I wanted to do something but didn't know what. I opened the fridge door and stood staring into it not knowing what I was looking for. I spotted a bag of apples in the crisper and pulled them out wondering what I could do with them. I decided that I could make an apple crisp for dessert and hoped that Cree would like it. Hopefully there would be enough left over for tomorrow when Rusty got home.

Cree won me over the minute he walked in the door. He'd left Faith outside unpacking the car. I was throwing a green salad together and had not heard them arrive. Jordan was in the den, otherwise known as his office. I looked up when I heard the door open.

"Finally," he said crossing the floor to where I was, "finally I get to meet the heart of the Landon family, and may I say that she is every bit as lovely as the reputation that precedes her!"

He bowed to me, and then kissed me gently on both my cheeks. "I am but a servant to you my dear lady."

Before I could utter a word Jordan bounded into the kitchen asking what all the commotion was about. "Oh, it's only you Cree. Don't believe a word he's saying Jilly because he thinks he can mesmerize all the women with his wit."

"Leave me to have some time alone to flirt with this audacious beauty before my fiancé interrupts will you Dad?"

I couldn't stop smiling.

"And, just where is my daughter?" Jordan asked looking out the window. "Dear God, you left her to unpack the car didn't you? You just couldn't wait to meet Jillienne could you…well, let me make it perfectly clear that I don't need another son-in-law who is obsessed with my wife."

Jordan grinned at me as he went out to help Faith. "I warned you didn't I?"

"What did my father-in-law to be warn you about?" Cree asked laughing.

"Only that you had a certain je ne sais quoi that would win me over."

"And, how did I do? Do you think I can give Craig a run for the money?" He retorted.

"Time will tell, time will tell."

I guessed Cree to be around five feet eight inches tall. He was powerfully built; muscular and robust. His complexion was that of a deeply tanned person which I expected was due to his indigenous ethnicity. His hair was black, long and curly. I was pretty sure that all he did to comb it was to run his fingers through it. His eyes were a dark coffee brown, bright and always seemed to be smiling. He struck me as someone who didn't have a care in the world. His love for Faith was evident in the way he looked at her, and talked to her. No one had mentioned that he had a faint Scottish accent. He had spent the first twelve years of his life in Peebles Scotland where his parents owned and operated a hotel. His full name was Cree Dakoda Chabot Maylard. He had told Faith before their engagement that he had inherited the "wanderlust" from his mother's semi-nomadic family so she had better be interested in travelling.

He was the complete opposite of Craig who was six feet two inches; he was slim and lanky, yet strong. He had straw blonde hair and hazel eyes. He was quick to smile, and good natured. There was always sadness in his eyes because of all the trauma and suffering from being an ER medic. I think I was more conscious of his emotional state then even Hope was, and I had added to it two and a half years ago when it had become necessary for me to leave home. Tomorrow I would see Craig and hopefully have some private moments with him.

Jordan asked me if I was nervous on the elevator up to Craig's office. I told him I wasn't because he was worried enough for the two of us. Of course he wanted to be with me for the whole exam, but Hope said she needed his help in setting up a bookcase and that I needed a few minutes alone with my new doctor.

Craig had barely shut the door before he breathed a sigh of relief. He enclosed me in his arms. We just swayed together for a few minutes. He kept saying over and over how much he had missed me and how he was so worried that I might never come home.

"Thank God that you made it Jill. I don't think I could have made it much longer."

"I can't imagine how you managed Craig. Seeing Hope and Jordan everyday must have been agonizing. Now that it is all over and done with, it might not have made any difference if they had of known. I just don't know. I am going to tell Jordan one day; you know that don't you?"

"I do, but Hope can never know."

"Hope will never know. For now, it's just you and me and our consciences."

"I guess we had better get to the reason you are here then. There's a gown waiting for you behind that screen. You slip into it and I will call Hope to come in to attend with the exam."

"She doesn't have to Craig. I'm perfectly safe with you." I said from behind the screen.

"I know Honey, but it's kind of the law."

"Well, screw the law; I want to talk to you more."

"Is something bothering you Jill? Let's weigh you first."

I got up on the scale. "I think I have gained two pounds! That's good isn't it, and yet I feel that I am gaining weight way too slowly. I've been off sugar and salt for over two years. I lived on liquids and "mushy" foods for a year or more at Arcadia. Gradually I was introduced to fresh fruit and vegetables; I think I ate carrots and bananas every day, and then rice and whole grains, dairy and yogurt.

I ate very little meat except for chicken and fish. Nothing was ever fried. Sometimes meals were very bland. I probably had eight small meals a day. Sometimes a meal only consisted of seeds or nuts and custards. When I left home in 2006, I weighed 143 pounds. In June of 2007 I weighed 77 pounds. When I went to live at the convent in May 2008, I weighed 87 pounds. By the end of the summer I was 93 pounds. Everything was metric over there, but the the technicians were kind enough to translate for me. I always hated metric."

Craig laughed. "I remember. Just be patient, the weight will come Jill. Your body and mind is still in a state of readjustment. Here, let's get you up on the exam table. Are you still following the cancer diet? I noticed you hardly ate anything last Sunday."

"I try to eat what's good for me and little meals, six or eight times a day. I stay away from processed, sugary and fatty foods, but I am also eating cheese cake, and peanut butter and honey sandwiches. Oh, and I have a little brandy ever night…is that okay?"

"It is; the weight will come back with time. I know you think you are a bag of bones, but you are not. Models would kill to look as good as you do. You are beautiful in every way, and don't you ever doubt it. Now let's get on with this exam before Jordan comes barrelling in."

Craig began his assessment by starting at my head and my neck and my shoulders. He gently manipulated and probed for any lumps or swelling. Next were my arms and then my feet. I had no discomfort at all. He said he would conduct the chest and lower abdomen examination when Hope and Jordan were present. He asked me what it was that I wanted to talk to him about.

"I think I am driving Jordan crazy. I have these periods where I lash out at him. I seem to have no control over my accusations and distrust at all."

"What are you accusing him of Jill?"

"Infidelity…he swears he wasn't unfaithful, but really Craig I was gone an awfully long time, and he's a very virile man…"

"Why don't you believe him?"

"Have you met Virginia?"

"Do you mean his therapist? No, I haven't, but need I remind you that your husband is the epitome of righteousness, and that having an inappropriate relationship with his therapist would be out of the question. What's led you to believe something is going on?"

"She came over to the house on Wednesday on the pretense that she wanted…no, needed to meet me. But I know it was just an excuse to see Jordan. It's not only her; you know about Martina don't you, and we are going to Shelton next week and he wants me to meet Marlayna."

"Martina is just a friend; I can guarantee you that there was nothing romantic about their relationship. I have never heard Jordan mention anyone by the name of Marlayna…who is she?"

"Jordan's once fiancé."

"What?"

We were interrupted by a knock on the door. Jordan asked how long he was going to keep me in captivity. Craig laughed and told him to come in and bring Hope with him promising me that anytime I felt insecure or doubtful I was to call him and we would talk. "You know your husband's love for you is genuine Jill. Your absence did not diminish his love one bit; there is no one else for him; past or present so quit inviting trouble."

Ten minutes later Craig put his stethoscope down and gave me a clean bill of health. He had already booked an appointment for me at the hospital for a variety of tests including a body scan, x-ray of my skull, and MRI. He said that once Dr. Ben had reviewed the results he would be consulting with me about future treatments.

"So I see you are playing along with Jillienne and not revealing the neurologists' real name. I guess that means that he will remain incognito, and I will not be able to attend her appointments with her?" Jordan said rather accusingly.

Craig looked at him curiously. "I'm not sure what you mean Jordan, but Ben Casey is his real name, and I am sure he will be more than happy that you accompany Jill to her appointments. Did I miss something here?"

"Oh, she told me that I cannot know the real names of her "undercover" physicians, and Dr. Ben was one of them, so I am a little confused…Jillienne, do you want to clarify?"

I smiled. "I am sorry if I confused you Jordan; some names are real and some aren't."

"Yeah that explains everything, but *nothing*! My wife has come home with a handful of mysterious stories, and her doctors names are ones that she took from the television screen. Dr. Ben I had assumed was for Dr. Ben Casey, and she had agreed. I suppose it won't be long before her favorite is revealed…a Dr. McIntyre. Any ideas on who that might be Craig?"

"Come along Darling," I coaxed, "Craig has other patients to see you know."

My life was as near to perfect as it could possibly get. There weren't any signs of cancer anywhere in my body. Jordan had promised that he wouldn't admonish Dr. Ben for the surreptitious conditions that I was forced to agree to for my chance of survival. They shook hands cordially upon meeting, and Dr. Ben remained professional right up to our leaving.

"I knew that you were in good hands Jillienne, but I did struggle with how the whole procedure was conducted. When I agreed to participate in this experimentation three years ago, I hoped that I would never have a patient who would meet the requirements as I wasn't on board with all the secrecy. It was an incredible coincidence that Gayle just happened to be here that day we found you unconscious in the elevator. She made my decision easier. You know about Gayle's role in Arcadia don't you Mr. Landon?"

Jordan said that he wasn't sure. I told him I would elaborate more at home.

"So," Dr. Ben continued, "you were my first, and so far, the only one I have sent to Arcadia. Believe me when I say that there was no hope for your survival if I hadn't made the difficult choice. Seeing you alive and thriving, I am rewarded that with the knowledge that someday, thanks to these revolutionary physicians, cancer may be eradicated. My only hope is that these experimental treatments will be offered to all soon, and not just in some foreign underground clinics." He reached for Jordan's hand. "I ask for your understanding Sir and look forward to our next visit. Look after this little lady as I can assure you that she is one in a million. Dr. Ross and I are going to take very good care of her."

Jordan thanked him saying that it was a long and hard two and a half years of anguish, but that his bravery in making the decision to have me admitted to Arcadia was one he would be forever grateful for. Dr. Ben walked us to the door and embraced me. I'm sure I saw a tear in his eye.

Jordan accompanied me to several physiotherapy and massage sessions. I don't think the therapists were accustomed to having an audience but Jordan insisted on observing. Once he was satisfied that he had learned enough he took over from them and I never had to leave home for another treatment. I was much happier to have my husband's hands helping to heal me, and that I didn't have to leave home twice a week.

I had found Jordan with my diary again one morning. I could see that he was distraught by what he was reading. I was pretty sure that I knew what had him so upset. I put my hand on his shoulder and read what I had written on December 24th, 2006. My writing was a little wobbly.

> *They say I am improving and that the treatments have shrunk my tumor by 7%...7% in ten months. I will be here forever. I feel no different. The pain is still excruciating at times. The only time I have any peace is when I have been sedated and I sleep for a few hours, or of course when I am in one of the medically induced*

comas. I feel nothing at all then and may as well be dead…I am wondering if I can will myself not to wake up My agony would be over then and so would my family's.

Before I go though, I need to tell them how much I love them. I agreed to this for you Jordy, but

"Why didn't you finish that sentence Jillienne? You were thinking of giving up weren't you?"

"Maybe…I don't know. It was Christmas, and I always loved Christmas…anyhow I'm here, so whatever was in my drugged and confused mind back then doesn't matter anymore. See, there is only scribble for days and days afterwards. You don't need to read anymore."

I took the journal from him and proceeded to tear out page after page. I crumpled them and threw them on the floor. Jordan protested. I told him he did not have to live my pain through my writing. I had done it, and once was enough!

I passed the book back to him minus a hundred pages. "Here… here is where I become hopeful and know that I have defeated that demon that took over my life. These pages are the start of me making my way home to you. Now what say, we gather up these depressing papers and your black calendars also and have a bonfire in the backyard?"

His answer was to pull me down on his lap and tell me he loved me.

My family was all whole again. I had voiced my strong disapproval to my sons in a private conversation regarding their abhorrent treatment of their father during my absence during our early Thanksgiving celebration. I did not ask them to forgive me for the way I had left because the telling of my nightmare was self-explanatory. They were both shamed and begged my forgiveness. I told them that I was not the one whom they should be apologising to. Jordan was Jordan and he told them that he loved them and that the only thing that mattered was that I was home. I wondered if he truly had forgiven their behaviour.

My husband's love for me had intensified. It was evident in everything he said or did. We did go to Shelton and I did meet Marlayna. I was not at all threatened by her or that she had once been engaged to my husband. She was just average looking and no great beauty as I had envisioned, but perhaps she was threatened by me. Maybe threatened is the wrong word. I believe she saw how devoted Jordan was to me and that she hadn't a snowballs chance in hell of ever turning his head.

As fate would have it, I also met Nell. Jordan and I had gone shopping for the new dishwasher. I had offered the *old* one to Hope, but she said she wouldn't touch it with a ten foot pole so we donated it to the Habitat Foundation. I am sure Jordan was amused by the way I treated the whole melee, but knew better to comment on my insistence that it had to go.

I was sitting on a bench in the appliance store when this lady sat down beside me. She was sporting a head of curly, fly away grayish white hair. She was dressed all in black in what I thought was an early Halloween costume. Three inch high laced-up boots, long black skirt, elbow length gloves, and a cape that looked like it had come from Dracula's closet completed her ensemble.. Her cheeks and lips were bright ruby red. It was the smile on her face that caused me to smile in return.

"You're Jillienne aren't you? I had not seen your husband for a great many years, but when I did in August, I saw a broken, devastated man. But, now look at him," she pointed to Jordan, "he is happiness personified! I am so happy for the two of you. Oh, silly me…I am the drama coach at Q.E. We have all been hoping that Jordan would bring you by for a visit." She took a glove off and introduced herself as Dell.

Apparently, she always dressed as though she was auditioning for a role in a horror movie at this time of year. She said laughing that it wasn't much different than the way she usually outfitted herself. "Big, bold, and black hides a lot of imperfections." I liked her immediately.

So, I had banished all my fears regarding Jordan's ladies, past and present, hadn't I? So why couldn't I let sleeping dogs lie? I was going to take heaven and turn it into a nightmare that there may be no coming back from. I was going to confess to Jordan.

It was October 9th, two days before Faith's and Cree's wedding. I put the macaroni and cheese casserole in the oven on low, covered the salad with saran and placed it in the refrigerator along with the rice pudding. The ham was cooked and resting on the counter. These were all Jordan's favorites. Maybe I should feed him first…

I found him in the den researching exotic locations on the computer. He still planned on whisking me off to some romantic island for our second honeymoon. After tonight, there probably wouldn't be any honeymoon less even a renewal of vows. I asked him if he would come for a walk with me.

"It's kind of late in the day Babe; what did you have in mind?"

"Could we go to Oleander Park?"

"Okay if that's where you want to go. We'd better get a move on because it is starting to cloud over. I'll get our jackets and an umbrella just in case. Maybe you should take your cane."

On the ride over Jordan told me to remind him to look up why the park was named for a poisonous plant. He said he had been going to a number of times but always forgot to do so.

"I thought you knew that it wasn't named for the plant, but for a man whose name was Ole Anders. He was some nineteenth century entrepreneur who funded several local parks, and so this one was named after him. Somehow the two names became incorporated into one so you see it has nothing to do with the plant at all. There are no oleander shrubs planted anywhere as it is true, the flowers, leaves, stems and twigs are all poisonous, not just to humans, but animals also."

"How is it that you know this and I don't?"

"Perhaps I learned it at the library, I really don't remember. You may be interested to know that the seeds and leaves are used to make medicines for heart conditions, asthma, epilepsy, leprosy, and malaria."

"Again, I ask you how is it that you know all this?"

"Because I looked it up on a computer at Arcadia because it was one of the plants that was used in conjunction with other plant fibers in my treatments."

"My God, they gave you poison?"

"Remember, I was already poisoned so no big deal."

"Damn it Jillienne, I hate it when you talk so nonchalantly about your ordeal!"

Luckily, our favorite bench was available. I told Jordan not to get too comfortable because he probably wouldn't be staying all that long. He passed me a bag of treats for the birds that he had brought from his stash in the basement, and asked me what I was talking about.

"I have something to tell you Jordan. It has been keeping me awake at nights. I am not eating, and I am sneaking off in the middle of the night to "smoke". It's all because I have kept something from you, but it stops **now**. I only ask that you hear me out and put no blame on Craig, and you must promise me that you will never tell Hope. Can you do that?"

"What could anything that you've kept hidden from me involve Hope and Craig…my God, he had an affair while they were separated didn't he?"

"No, it is nothing like that. It only involves Craig and me."

"What are you trying to say Jillienne?"

"First you have to promise me you will never tell Hope."

"I can't promise anything."

"Then you are just going to have to wonder for the rest of your life what your wife has been keeping from you because those are my conditions." I started to get up.

He put his hand on my arm. "Sit down Jillienne; I'm listening."

I looked directly into his eyes. "Craig knew."

"Craig knew what?"

"He knew about the tumor and that I was going to an underground clinic." I said calmly.

Jordan was furious, just as I knew he would be. "You chose to tell your son-in-law and not me, your husband…why Jillienne, why?" He stood up and stared sorrowfully down at me.

"I didn't choose to tell him Jordy; it was an accident."

He laughed rudely. "Oh, so the words just mistakenly fell out of your mouth?"

"I listened to your confession regarding Martina,; will you please allot me the same courtesy?"

"I suppose I have no choice."

"You do have the choice Jordan, you may listen or not, Craig had no such choice. It was the Friday before I left. I was on my fourth dose of the drug that was keeping me alive. I had administered it via a preloaded needle to my abdomen twice the night before. It was not an easy thing for me to do, but the alternative was that I would have to be hospitalized as I would not be able to function, much alone live without the injections which contained morphine plus a multitude of other drugs. Gayle had picked me up early that morning…yes, you heard right, she picked me up in the back alley so she wouldn't be noticed by the nosey neighbors. The concoction works best and has a longer affect when it is administered intravenously. I was resting comfortably in a recliner in Dr. Ben's private office when I heard the door open. I still had two hours left to go on the drip so I just thought it was the doctor or Gayle checking up on me. I recognized the voice calling out to Dr. Ben asking if he had forgotten their luncheon date. It was Craig. I couldn't do anything; I had no place to hide."

I took a deep breath. "Craig was in the midst of an apology when he realized it was me in the chair. He was dumbfounded. "Jill what in the hell are you doing here? Oh God, don't tell me, don't tell me…" Dr. Ben came in and saw Craig talking to me. He asked Craig if he knew me. Craig said, "She's my mother-in-law for Christ's sake! What the hell is going on here?"

Dr. Ben said this was an unfortunate incident and that it complicated matters drastically. He called Gayle in and together they explained what had happened to me, that the tumor was inoperable because of its proximity to my brain. I could continue with the drug protocol in the hospital, but it was not a cure, and my time was very limited, but there was one other option. Craig sat beside me holding my hand trying to make sense out of the opportunity for recovery that I was being offered. He objected strenuously when told that he could not divulge that information to anyone. He said that Jordan and I were not just his in-laws, but were his best friends. He said I was like a sister to him, and he could not, and would not keep the truth from Jordan. Dr. Ben told Craig that I had already made the decision to accept the proposal, and that Craig was bound by the Hippocratic Oath to keep my information confidential. He said that they would give us some privacy to discuss my options. He turned at the door and said, "She's already dead Craig; don't be the one to sign her death certificate. Let's give science a chance."

If I live to be a hundred I hope to never see such agony on another's face ever again as I saw on Craig's that day. I couldn't stand the distress that I was causing him and so I told him that he didn't have to worry because I had decided that I would go home. I would live the rest of my days with my family beside me because the cost to him would be too much if he had to keep the truth from you. We cried together for a few minutes. He got up and called Ben back in and said, "Let's get this bizarre show on the road." He stayed with me for the duration of my intravenous drip, and agreed to help me with the injections over the weekend as they were more effective if they were injected into my neck. That's it, you know the rest."

Jordan was standing. "That's it, you think that's it? He should have told me; you should have told me. For two and a half years Craig was in contact with your collaborator, this Gayle person, and he knew you were alive, but he didn't bother to inform me?"

"Gayle is my friend; there was no conspiracy. They were only in contact by e-mail every six months or so. You know why you couldn't know Jordan."

"That makes it all right then, is that what you are saying? You got to know that I was alive, but I was not allowed to know that you were…yeah, it all makes perfect sense; I wasn't trustworthy enough. I was only the husband, the man who loved you. I can't process any of this right now."

He turned and walked back up the path we had come on. He was angry and hurt, and he had every right to be so. I waited for twenty minutes thinking he would come back, but he didn't. I took my phone out of my pocket and called Craig. He asked me if I thought Jordan was coming back for me. I said I didn't think so. Just before I told him where I was and that I would wait for him, Jordan appeared. He asked if I was talking to Craig. I nodded as he took the phone from me.

"I think we need to talk Craig. Yes, half an hour at the house then. Of course I'm bringing Jillienne! Do you really think that I would leave her out here freezing on a park bench in the middle of nowhere…you really don't know me at all do you?" He passed the phone back to me. "Your confidant wants to make sure you're all right."

I told Craig that I would see him at the house. Jordan asked if I needed help getting up. I leaned on my cane and said that I didn't. He walked ahead of me. I followed at a sluggish pace. He looked back at me every now and then to see if I was still moving. I swear it took me half an hour to get to the car. Jordan opened the door for me, but he did not buckle up my seatbelt. I asked him what he was going to do. He looked at me pathetically and said that I would know when he knew. We never spoke another word all the way home. Hope's car was in the driveway.

I didn't even bother to shut the car door. I ran faster than I thought I was able to across the lawn and up the front steps and into the house. Jordan was yelling at me to slow down. Hope was coming down the stairs. Breathlessly I said that I hadn't thought she was coming over today.

"The girls had to check on their dresses one last time. Why are you breathing so hard Mom, and you're shivering…where have you been anyway? I'll put the kettle on and make you a nice cup of tea."

Jordan came in the back door. "We didn't think we would see you today Hope."

"What's so different about today? I come over every day don't I?"

I opened the oven door. "We haven't even had supper yet; do you want to stay?"

"No thanks, ours is in the oven also. We are going soon as Craig promised he'd be home by five thirty. So, where were you two?"

"Your mother wanted to go to Oleander Park." Jordan said simply.

"It's almost dark and Mom is…I wonder why Craig is here?" Hope said.

She went out to meet him in the front hallway and ask him why he had come over. Craig said that he had something to discuss with her father. My inability to keep silent was about to bring the house down. Trembling I suggested to Hope that we give the men some privacy and go see what the twins were up to. She said they were in Rusty's room attempting to play chess, and she wanted to hear what Craig and her dad were up to.

Jordan told Craig and me to sit down and have a cup of tea. I said I would rather stand. Hope poured the tea and handed me a cup. I set it on the counter.

"Well, let's see it then Craig; you did bring it didn't you?" Jordan asked.

I had no idea what he was referring to and Craig looked just as confused as I was.

Hope laughed. "No, he doesn't have it Daddy, I do. I can't believe that he won't take my word that there are no grammatical errors in his speech. I bow to the master."

She retrieved a piece of paper from her handbag and handed it to Jordan doing her little curtsy.

"That's enough of the smart stuff kid." Jordan ribbed.

Craig and I looked at each other apprehensively. It all became clear when Jordan put the paper down. "I can find no errors in this Craig. In fact I'm sure it will bring a few tears to Faith's and her mother's eyes...perhaps you should read it first Honey", he said smiling at me, "so you won't be so emotional at the wedding." He passed it to Hope who gave it to me. "As I said Craig, I find no fault with it just as I have never found any fault with anything you do. You've always had the best interests of this family at heart, and especially Jill's" He laughed a little; I guess because he never calls me Jill. "To be honest, I don't know how any of us made it through the last few years, but thanks to all your beliefs and love we did."

My husband got up and walked over to our son-in-law and shook his hand, and then embraced him. "I admire your scruples, and your devotion to this family. I am very proud to call you Son."

I was crying so hard that I could barely breathe. Hope's and Craig's eyes were wet also. Jordan took me in his arms after making a poor attempt at drying my tears.

"Let's be done with this okay? No more tears, no more tears; it's all good."

The twins came bounding down the stairs saying they were starving, and what treats did I have for them. Hope and Craig corralled them and said they were going home as dinner was waiting. Jordan and I walked them to the door. Craig hung back. He said there were no words to express how thankful he was for us and for Jordan's understanding. He said he loved us.

Jordan said that we loved him too, and called out just before Craig got in the car. "One last thing Craig, if Jillienne so much as gets a hangnail, I want to know about it…comprehend?"

Craig saluted him.

"I love you Jordy." I said still crying.

"I know you do. Now let's get you into bed so you can stop shivering. I'll turn the heating blanket on, and set you up to eat in bed."

"When did you decide Jordan?" I didn't have to say more because he knew what I was asking.

"I don't honestly know. I have to admit that I was incensed at first, but the outcome was worth more than my wrath. You are healed and that is all that matters. My love for you is greater than my wounded ego. But, what I said goes double for you…if you even sneeze, I want to know…are we clear on that?"

I said I was. He said, "Good, now we are done with all the secrecy, right?"

He tucked the covers around me. I smiled and waited until he got to the doorway. "There is just one thing Jordan…I think I know where Arcadia is."

He laughed heartily. "And, you think this is news to me? No, my lovely Valentine, I am well aware that you have more information in that pretty head of yours than even you are aware of."

I blew him a kiss and snuggled under the blankets. I would probably fall asleep before he got back with dinner. My conscience was clear. Visions of a land far away danced in my head.

THE END